THE SECRET
WEAPON
OF AFRICA

YAO FOLI MODEY
Assoc. Professor of History

Order this book online at www.trafford.com
or email orders@trafford.com

Most Trafford titles are also available at major online book retailers.

This book is a historical fiction. All the characters are fictional, any
resemblance to anybody dead or alive is purely coincidental.

Printed in the United States of America.

ISBN: 978-1-4907-4378-3 (sc)
ISBN: 978-1-4907-4377-6 (e)

Trafford rev. 08/12/2014

 www.trafford.com

North America & international
toll-free: 1 888 232 4444 (USA & Canada)
fax: 812 355 4082

To Da Grace Yawa
For being there for her children
And for her unconditional love

And to all my children
For your love and patience
Strength in the face of adversity
Rattled but never defeated.
I salute and adore you

The Darker Side of Africa

If the blue ocean can speak
And talk about Africa's past
If the old trees could reveal
What they'd seen in this land
The bloodshed, the death throes
The groans, the moans, the tears
Infants with crushed skulls screaming
Stomachs growling from hunger pain
The wailing of heart-broken mothers
The battle cries of brave soldiers
Warriors with no weapons in battle
Fighting for honor, not to win
Ready to die for the motherland
Fell like leaves and died like flies
The victims of heavy cannon fire
The latest fatalities of human greed
The usual casualties of racial hatred
What would they all say?

The gods saw their desperation
And refused to let the Africans perish
They had to defend their offspring
End the violence and starvation
So did they send in the mosquitoes?
To save the children from slavery
To stop the death of millions more
To bring back peace, dignity and pride
To return them to the African way of life

Professor Yao Foli Modey
Cape Coast Castle, Ghana

PROLOGUE

—◦◦◦❦◉❦◦◦◦—

I T WAS IN THE MIDDLE of the Harmattan season and the weather was hot and humid. The scorching rays of the sun had sucked the moisture out of every plant in the land and had turned the green leaves into dark yellow in color. Many of the leaves had fallen to the ground and had begun to decompose into dark loamy soil---rich fertile land, innocent and untouched.

And that was the way it was in ancient times. That was the way it was until the Oburoni slave traders arrived on the continent and changed everything, imposing their greed and guns on the inhabitants..

The dry, humid air left many people panting for breath and sweating profusely. The women complained bitterly, the children suppressed their discomfort, but the men simply ignored the weather, because they had bigger problems on their mind. They'd been thinking about the death and the devastation that the Oburoni intruders, these uninvited aliens, had unleashed on the land.

The goal of the men was to get rid of these uninvited guests in their land and return to the good old days of peace and progress.

The griot, the aged, bald headed man, sucked into his tobacco pipe greedily, exhaled loudly and then started to narrate the history of the ancient land to a group of anxious youths who sat in a large circle at his feet. They listened and doted on every word from his kola-nut-stained mouth as he spoke his words of wisdom. He told them, in graphic detail, how their ancestors had once been very prosperous. But that was before the arrival of the Oburoni---the Europeans slave traders to the continent. He told them that their ancestors had been at the forefront of human civilization. But the Oburonis invasion of their land ended their progress. These aliens began to destroy everything their ancestors had worked to build. "They hated the way they looted our gold, stole the youths and reduced the land to a mere shadow of its former self," he told them. "The enemy left the Africans fighting hard just to see another day the same ways these "alien locusts" were determined to raid, loot and destroy everything in their path."

He continued to spit his anger on the Oburoni invaders every night and did so for nearly a month, until the full moon waned. He never ran out of stories about how their ancestors had been at peace with nature and how they had plenty of food to eat before the arrival of these Oburoni locusts. They came from Europe and they arrived from America.

He loved to tell them about how these invaders came into the continent uninvited, but lied that they just stumbled upon this ancient land of gold. He also narrated how their unwanted guests hid their plot to enslave their people at the back of their minds, to surface soon afterwards, not long later.

"Would the continent have proceeded on its upward march, if these white locusts had not invaded our land?" Continue on its upward material success in the world? Would the inhabitants be spared the never-ending inferiority complex they'd pinned on them? The griot asked the children loudly, but did not expect any answers from them.

"Yes, definitely yes," the children shouted anyway.

"You are right. There would have been less starvation, less disease and more respect for the inhabitants of this unhappy continent today," he told them, answering his own questions.

"Yes, there would have been more food, more security, more pride, more dancing and more happiness," the children replied, gleefully, to the griot's delight.

The griot often paused in the middle, cleared his throat and then gave the children some more details about how these uninvited guests introduced the notorious slave trade among the African people, planted an evil religion among them and imposed tremendous suffering on our ancestors. He resented the nightmare these uninvited visitors had created in the land, an ordeal that lasted so many centuries---uncountable years, in the minds of these children.

During these marathon sessions, the griot often fed the children roasted peanuts and corn on the cob, as he told them these sensational stories about the ancient kings, queens and elders in their past, people who had been the founders of democracy at their royal courts, and a beacon of hope for people around the world. He also told them about how their forebears had been the first in many areas of life, including government, philosophy and many other areas of human activity.

The griot paused and felt the silence among the children. He noticed the disappointment on their youthful faces and the resentment inside them anytime he spoke about how the "white locusts" came from beyond the blue ocean, forced their way into the land with their cannons and rifles and proceeded to destroy their way of life.

With so many exciting tales about the past, the children simply looked on with amazement as this aged storyteller, who had memorized the history of this ancient continent, filled their ears with many titillating and exciting, but sometimes disturbing stories about their past, pouring out tons of raw facts about their history. He sometimes worked them into emotional frenzy with facts that spanned many centuries, facts he'd committed to memory in songs, adages and proverbs.

Did some of these children feel any guilt and remorse for the painful truths he'd revealed to them? Did they feel it was the fault of their ancestors for letting the aliens inside their land? What did they think about the role their ancestors played in the infamous slave trade? Some certainly felt ashamed about how some of their own cooperated with the enemy, but most of them felt nothing but pride in the way their ancestors, with their impotent guns, fought against these intruders.

"These were the days when men were men and women were women," he often told these anxious youths. "Though the men fought for honor and the women held the families together the best way they could, they still saw everything collapsed as the Oburoni enemy used their big guns, their cannons and their rifles to mow down our ancestors like elephant grasses."

"If our ancestors had no good guns, how did they fight against these heavily armed invaders?" Kofi Bako, the son of the war captain, asked the griot, staring directly into his face. "I wouldn't want to be in their shoes back then, because they were like sitting antelopes waiting for the greedy enemy to kill them."

"It is alright to ask questions, but you must stop staring directly into the face of an adult person whenever you speak to one. Who failed to teach you this custom, is it your father or mother?" The griot asked him, speaking harshly, trying to put him on the right path. "But you know not to do this from today."

The griot proceeded to tell them some more stories about how, in spite of the danger lurking all over the land, the men still went to their farms hunting. He also narrated how some of these brave and hardworking men and women were abducted, never to return home to their children. How the women went to the riverside to wash clothes, fetch drinking water, or visited their farms, or went to funerals in the neighboring villages, but were abducted and never to return home to their children.

"Why should these uninvited visitors be so cruel to our ancestors? What was worse, the Harmattan or the Oburoni slave traders?" one of the youths asked the griot, making the griot very happy because the youth seemed to understand the ugly past and how these aliens were very unfair to our ancestors.

The king stopped by on his way to his palace. He sat on a huge mahogany stool next to the burning hearth as he sipped the frothy palm wine from a big, brown calabash. Then he paused to share his words of wisdom in between several big gulps of palm wine.

"You are the future of our land," he told the children. "You are the yam heads that we have planted each year and would continue to do so for generations to come. Just as no farmer allows his yam heads to die, we would never watch our children die."

"Why did these "white locusts" do all these evil things to our people without the king asking them to leave?" Dompo, the son of the town crier, also known as the gong-gong beater, asked innocently, his eyes teary. "Who asked them to come to our land? Who invited them? And we want to know who let them into the land in the very beginning?"

"Some matters are so painful that we can only talk about them after we have given sacrifices to the gods and poured libation to the ancestors," the griot intervened, staring at the king and shaking his head.

There was an obvious puzzled look on their face. The children seemed to understand the pain, but they wondered why it had to happen.

"King Zendo Batuka, like the thousands of kings who had ruled the kingdom before him, could not end the heavy blanket of fog the Harmattan weather had unleashed on the land," the griot told the youths candidly. "He could also not save the land from the Oburoni traders who'd brought many big guns and a lot of bloodshed in their trail. But our leaders never lost hope, they knew that the ancestors would one day hear their cry and rid the land of these unwanted invaders, and let the ocean swallow these greedy human pests."

"During the worst years, the traders forcibly removed over a million youths each year. In the process, they'd left behind rivers of blood, streams of tears and mountains of agony," the griot told the youths. "We had nowhere to hide from the greed in their hearts and the devastation they brought in their trails trying to satisfy their greed for wealth."

"So sad that our ancestors were unable to defeat the Oburoni traders in their own land," the young man said, quite innocently. "Where were our gods? Was it because their gods were more powerful than our gods?"

"In fact, it was all because they had better guns than our ancestors. And anytime they fired their big guns, they mowed down hundreds of our people, spilling blood on the green grasses and killing our ancestors in cold blood. Indeed, there was blood all over the forests, the valleys, the hills and inside the rivers. In fact, anybody who refused to participate in the notorious enterprise of greed that they'd imposed on our ancestors, these evil traders quickly gunned down."

"In all how many people did they kill?" the youth asked.

"They killed enough to create "the wall of shame," sitting next to the king's palace. This is a constant reminder of the deep sorrow and grief inside our hearts," the griot said and then let out a deep sigh as he shook his bottom on his ebony stool, pondering and meditating briefly. "The enemy killed the king's grandfather and a few years later, they gunned down his beloved father. He father was a proud and stubborn king; he died on the battlefield while still fighting on his feet."

"They killed both his grandfather and father," Mankrado repeated, trying to control his own anger. "The loss could drive anyone insane, or force that person to go on a journey of blind rage in order to get even with the enemy."

Well, even with all the tragedy, it was when they stole the king's nephew, the heir to the throne that he lost all respect for them. It was then that he crossed the River of Vengeance and decided to wipe them out of our land at all costs."

"This loss definitely drove him insane," he told the children bluntly. "He couldn't eat, concentrate or think about anything else. He was like a lion possessed, enraged. He was ready to tear apart any Oburoni that came his way."

"Well, it was then that I swore on my father's grave to send all these Oburoni invaders into early graves," Mankrado the war captain said. "We had to save the youths from being hauled out of the continent in droves as if they were cows, huddled inside their many boats of shame."

The mood in the land was grim and gloomy, just like the dark clouds of Harmattan drifted over the land, spiraling to the other side of the mountain. Inside the gloomy weather our ancestors received the threats of these invaders to burn down our villages and towns. All the king could do was to try his best to slow them down.

The war captain pointed his rusty gun toward the empty blue sky and mumbled some words. "It is not whether Dente would send his messengers to force these invaders to pay for the crimes they'd committed in our land, it is when he would send them," he assured his soldiers and the youth. "None of these slave traders would escape the wrath of the ancestors when that time came."

Zotor, the high priest, who was trying to overcome his own despair, went into the Shrine of Dente, the most sacred of all places and then "placed himself in medicine" for seven days. He had to cleanse his spirit so he could reach the gods to help his people, and save the continent from total destruction---disappearing from the face of the earth.

During the seventh night, however, as he slept in the eerie dark shrine, a shiny light entered the cave from nowhere. It was the surest sign that the ancestors had agreed to intervene on behalf of the people. He also had a puzzling dream in which the king's grandfather and father appeared together before him in an angry mood. They told him to tell the war captain to face the Oburoni soldiers with courage. But, most importantly, they also gave him a secret weapon to use to defeat the enemy.

When he finally emerged from the shrine, he became a new person again; he was refreshed and extremely happy. His eyes were bright; he was beaming with joy; in fact, he was quite a jubilant priest. He'd been sanctified and he was grateful for what the ancestors gave him. For all that, he poured libation to the gods. He gave them lots of "akpeteshie" moonshine, and placed generous sacrifices on the altar---seven rams, seven he-goats and seven roosters. He wanted to calm down the anger of the gods to help them to defeat the Oburoni enemy.

"We have been waiting a very long time for this day, for this very moment of destiny. It looks like the beginning of our freedom and a time to go back to our old ways, the way things were before the "white locusts" landed," the high priest told the king and the elders. "This secret weapon would definitely drive these invaders away, and help us retake our land. We would recover our self-rule and go back to our old ways of life."

The king made the elders "eat fire" and then he told them about what the ancestors had given them. He knew that this was a breakthrough and he was happy for the precious gift that the gods had made available to them, though they had it in the land all along.

"What took them so long, anyway?" the queen mother asked in a loud irritating tone, she was trying to question the wisdom of these ancestors. The queen mother was always asking questions. She always asked questions when the king asked her to do something. "Why did the gods leave us at the mercy of these shameless invaders and did so for so long? Did they fall asleep, or maybe these gods went hunting?"

These were taboo questions coming out of the mouth of the queen mother.

"As Dente's former wife, you know better not to speak evil of the gods, especially about Dente," Zotor the high priest warned her. "You already know the consequences, if you insult or double-cross these gods one more time."

In spite of the king's hopefulness, his critics, led by his own brother Batuka, undermined him for not driving away the intruders as he'd promised in his oath when the kingmakers placed him on the golden stool. These critics talked about him like a rooster behind his back.

They even secretly plotted to remove him from the golden stool and put their person on it.

The king remembered the saying that the palm branch does not open its mouth without cause, so once he'd mentioned the secret weapon, he knew he had to use it to drive the enemy out of the land sooner or later.

"We have traveled that bushy path before," Elder Landonu said. He'd heard him promised to rid the land of these aliens several times before. So he didn't want to believe the king until he'd actually done what he said he would do.

"Well, unlike the Oburoni enemy, we are not fighting out of greed, we are fighting for the soul of our land, for the future of our children's children---in fact, we are fighting for our birthright and for honor," the king declared before a large audience at the grand durbar. He got such a huge round of applause from almost everyone present at the gathering that he felt very much connected to his subjects. "We must save this land for the next generation, because the ancestors would never forgive us if we allow these Oburoni traders to continue to haul our children away in droves, to continue to take them by the boatloads to the land of no return."

"Well, we need to stop them in their tracks, and punish them for their crimes against our land," Zotor the high priest added. "Don't worry; the gods will put a curse on their trail."

"I know they can't survive the secret weapon," the war captain told the elders. "Their big cannons would no longer matter, nor the newest rifles they'd brought from their homes. As soon as they begin to die slow and painful deaths, they would flee like cowards and return home quickly."

"The best part of it is that they have no armor against this secret weapon," the king told the elders. "They don't have any defense against the devastating effects of this weapon."

"Just count the number of trees we have planted for the millions who had departed this land, for the dead and for those forced out of their own land," the high priest said, pointing toward the rows of trees inside the mahogany grove. "The number is so large that we have lost count of all the dearly departed souls, but the Oburoni losses would be swifter and filled with much more drama."

"Don't worry; it is just a matter of time before the gods send death to the camp of the invaders. They would shift the burden of dying from our people to the enemy. There would be no more tragic losses and no more rivers of blood running in our villages and forests. Instead, these "little soldiers" would send the traders to the Coconut Grove, to their final resting places. They would be buried unsung, laid to rest huddled in mass graves, hurriedly, and without any ceremony or fanfare whatsoever."

"They ought to know that the price of greed is death," the high priest added, speaking in his usual nasal voice. "We would put this on their tombstones and ask the gods to put curses on them and on their children for many generations to come."

Meanwhile, the king waited like a restless leopard for the heavy rains to end. He wanted the dry Harmattan season to return so he could use the secret weapon, so he could unleash his "sansabonsam" little soldiers of vengeance on these unwanted and uninvited aliens.

"Soon, there would be no place for these aliens with itching feet to hide. The castles would become places of grave danger; there would be no more safe hiding places for these Europeans. They died because of the avid greed in their hearts," Mankrado said when the high priest finished talking about what to put on the tombstones of these Oburoni traders. "Soon the past would begin to defeat the present. Our gods would attack and destroy them. The gods would no longer sit by and watch them satisfy the greed they'd brought to our land."

The king had been breathing easier now that he'd got this new weapon. He also drank more of the frothy palm wine as he waited for the moon to wane and the rains to cease. Though he was a kind-hearted man, he wanted to bring about the era of vengeance that they'd expected in the land for so long. After the darkest and longest of storms, he wanted to bring some sunshine, a brighter future by bringing back the good days of old, the time when they were in harmony with nature.

Like a farmer with new seedlings, the king knew that there would soon be a new day in the land. From the Upper to Lower Guinea, from the coast to the hinterland, inside the forests, on the savannah grasslands and along the meandering rivers, this long, ugly storm would come to an end and the sun would rise again, bringing happiness to many villages, towns and kingdom again. The youths would dance once again in the evenings, and the children would play ampe and hide and seek freely.

Would the gods really end the wicked trade and force these intruders to flee the land or risk dying ghastly and awful deaths?

They king rose up, walked to the balcony like a lion king, proud and regal as he looked into the dark, cloudy sky and said: "The sun would shine again in this land. The ancestors have decided to make this land that they called the African Slave Coast "the Oburoni man's nightmare."

"They would lose the sap of life they'd brought with them and die in their own filthy vomit," Abrewa, the oldest lady, told the gathering. "The curse they'd brought into our land, hauling away our people like cattle, killing those that could not be enslaved, would come to a screeching halt."

"Well, as the saying goes, if you do evil, you will definitely die an evil death." Elder Goro, one of the elders, a warrior who had once killed seven slave raiders in one encounter, told the old lady. "So why do we blame the gods?"

"What of your missionary friends who use their words of religion as a front for their bloody activities? Your friends that dabble in the slave trade, but mix this evil with their holy task of converting souls?" Zotor asked the king.

"Well, we would have no mercy on them when the time of atonement comes. Just like the other greedy traders, they'd brought nothing but bloodshed and chaos into our land while indulging themselves doing it," the king replied. "The odds of the secret weapon skipping them weren't great."

"It is not all of them that do that," the queen mother said, sighing heavily as she tried to explain the problem. "It is rather unfortunate, because just as a few bad palm nuts in the pot can spoil the taste of the soup, so a few of these missionaries have given all the missionaries a bad name."

"That is why they must all die," the high priest said, reminding her of the saying, "the stranger can never outdo the host in his own land" so these invaders would finally meet their end one day. On that day, they would confront their creator and explain their thirst for blood and pay for their crimes."

The children continued to huddle together in a big circle around the camp fire to listen to the griot's tales of wisdom. But after they'd heard about the bloodshed, many of them shuddered in fear. Some of them hesitated to go anywhere near the woods. They were worried about the future, and about the safety of their parents, their siblings, themselves and especially about their mothers.

"Maybe this is just another vain promise from the king," the young flute blower said, frustrated as he cleaned the bamboo flute with some coconut oil. "This oil smells like raw kernel oil, but it is better than the alligator oil, which had a choking smell."

"Remember the saying that the white ant is able to devour everything except stones," the high priest mocked the enemy in his powerful voice. "In the past, our ancestors extended their hands of hospitality to these traders and look at how they'd abused them. Look at how they'd taken over our land, degraded and disrespected us in every possible way. And for this, they must die and be buried without honor."

The queen mother was a fun-loving woman and radiated her inside and outside beauty everywhere she went. Except for one particular missionary, she did not have any love lust for these Oburoni aliens. In fact, she had several layers of frown on her forehead, worried and anxious about what these "unwanted locusts" had done to her fatherland.

"What did we get from these aliens in return for our hospitality?" the queen mother asked. "We got nothing in return, except thanklessness, bloodshed and cruelty all over the land."

"Even their religion is worthless. How can you baptize someone with water and fire and then ship him away into slavery?" Abrewa, the oldest lady on the king's council asked, mocking the missionaries. "Their religion is a disgrace and not a proper faith, if not so, they would not be worshiping their god in a chapel that sits directly on top of a slave dungeon."

"Don't forget the bloody wars and the rivers of bloodshed. How could human beings be so cruel to others?" Mankrado remarked. "It did not take our ancestors long to find out that these are very greedy people, heartless, every one of them,"

The booming sounds of the cannons, the big guns that reverberated inside the hinterland echoed all the way to the meeting ground. The king shook his head and wondered how many more years his people would continue to suffer this kind of horror. He wondered how many more years would these Oburoni traders continue to deny his people the dignity and fairness they deserve in their own land. Above all, he wanted to know how long they would continue to deny them the simple joys of life—freedom to go to their farms to get foodstuff to feed their children, freedom to visit their relatives in the neighboring villages without the enemy pouncing on them from behind the tall elephant grasses like lions, then enslaving them. He yearned for the return of the good old days, when they would be truly free to play the drums, sing and see the young women dancing in the square in the evenings again.

Just as the gods had fought on behalf of the animals that cannot protect and defend themselves, the king hoped that one day the gods of the land would rise up and rid the land of these uninvited guests, and bring back a new day---return to the days of old.

ONE

I NTO THE SILENCE OF THE rain forests, on the green grasses, the uninvited aliens repeatedly fired their deadly cannons. You could hear these booming sounds echoed inside the forests and ricocheting against the green grasslands from dawn until the dying rays of the tropical sun drifted into the deep dark void.

The next morning, for the seventh time, the cannons had sent the youths running into their hiding places. You could see the fear in their eyes as the loud booms sent chills down their spine. How would the children feel safe with all the mangled bodies of victims scattered everywhere with blood still oozing from some of them? There were dozens of skulls of infants, which had been bashed and scattered all over. Several of them were still lying in pools of blood. What about the victims that were too injured to walk, or too shaken to even talk.

Meanwhile, the ocean breeze, which was pregnant with evil, and incensed with the suds of anger, continued to gather strength. But the angry ocean could not stop the evil plots of greed that the enemy had brought into the continent. It continued to witness these traders shipping millions of people out of the continent into places unknown to the ancestors.

Greedy eyes, seething with their hearts craving for wealth, these traders would impose their will and needs on the rulers. They heard them talking to the chiefs and queens with sugar in their mouths to convince them to sell the flesh and blood of their people to them.

From ancient times, the people had lots of gold and diamonds. The gold had been buried inside the bosom of mother earth since the beginning of time, and the diamonds buried in shallow riverbeds in many places. Everywhere, scattered across the vast grasslands, the ravenous hawks circled and swooped down to snatch these precious items.

Their favorite catches were the chicks---the youths of the land.

The people were at peace with nature and they were hardworking and happy. There were a few skirmishes and some wars among them, but the inhabitants fought these wars with their eyes on tomorrow, with some level of caution. The bitter racial hatred that the Oburoni aliens brought with them, the tremendous contempt they showed for the inhabitants in their wars, the various groups did not have in their souls.

But when the greedy locusts descended on the continent and claimed that they'd stumbled upon it, the inhabitants lost the peace and balance in their lives. They became prisoners in their own land.

These aliens brought their guns, rum and trinkets. But, above all, the fierce greed they brought to the land, no amount of bloodshed or tears from the victims could ever quench that. The inhabitants hated them from the very beginning because this vicious passion, the look of contempt in their eyes. They immediately wanted them out of their land.

But they bribed some of the leaders with gifts of trinkets, calico broadcloth and rum. The millions of guns they brought each year and sold or exchanged for slaves created tremendous power struggle, destabilizing several kings, chiefs and queens everywhere in the land.

Many of the rulers got duped or coaxed and the enemy easily defeated them.

When these visitors looted their gold and continued to abduct their youths, the rulers started what to them was the mother of all battles. But without the new weapons for these conflicts, every encounter was a serious challenge for the African leaders. Though the Asafo soldiers fought every battle as if it was a fight to death, the soldiers were defeated and many of them bled and died freely. But these soldiers refused to give up, because every day was a day for honor, for glory and the chance to join the ancestors. Though many were killed in cold blood, mowed down with cannons, the asafo soldiers regarded these wars as fights for honor.

For the king, these were fights for self-preservation against the fierce greed of the enemy. It was pristine innocence in the land against the shameless greed of the enemy. It was an insensitive and heartless group of alien locusts devouring everything in their path, unleashing violence and chaos in their trail, evil passions that overwhelmed the Africans in their own land.

It was amazing how many of these brave soldiers were willing to die for their motherland, but they did not die because of lack of courage. It was because they did not have the guns to fight the enemy. The king failed to provide them with these weapons and did not have the resources to do so.

But luckily, once a while they prevailed against the enemy in a few of these battles. The war captain led his troops back to the kingdom, after they'd gathered inside the mahogany grove to nurse the injured and bury their dead, tucked inside the bosom of mother earth, a land that was tired of receiving the bodies of youths too young and too innocent to die. Can you imagine their only crime was being born in a land that had become a hunting ground for these uninvited aliens?

A week later, the king's soldiers, the inner circle of brave warriors, put their fear aside once again to confront the enemy. They would return from the battle field that day without many of their fellow warriors, victims mowed down in cold blood like the green grasses in the savanna.

But these soldiers never resigned; they continued to fight the enemy. They knew that the enemy had much deadlier weapons, but given the choice between fighting for honor and running back home to their wives in shame, they accepted the challenge to fight and die for honor.

"We ambushed and defeated these evil traders the next day, a misty, hazy morning that was pregnant with all sorts of misfortune. But later that day, the enemy returned and turned their big guns on us, mowing down our soldiers in the thousands," the young warrior reported. "They used a deadlier force to pay us back for the few losses they'd suffered earlier that morning."

There were many wounded enemies still lurking in the forests, roaming the grasslands like hungry leopards looking for the chance to kill our Asafo soldiers. They wanted all the innocent victims they could round up, so they could haul them to the land of no return on the other side of the blue ocean. These traders were very angry, so they freely vented their anger on thousands of innocent people.

In spite of their losses, King Zendo was still unwavering in his decision not to sell his conscience, not to exchange prisoners of war for guns. His mind was made up, fixed and inflexible. He had drawn a line in the sand on the white sandy beach on the shore. Not even the voices from the past could change his mind to trade his war prisoners for guns, to follow this vicious cycle of more guns breeding more violence.

He did not want to go down in history as the first king of the kingdom to sell out to the Oburoni enemy. So he withstood the pressure from the governor. He kept the faith. He kept the slave trading routes closed.

But for some kind-hearted missionaries, feeling sorry for this noble but stubborn king, gave him some weapons through the backdoor. These were men of character who wanted no slaves in return for these guns. They just wanted to give the king and his soldiers a fighting chance, to help them in the war against their own countrymen and women. It was like feeding lobster to lobster.

Though King Zendo really didn't want these good Oburoni people to help him, but one Captain Wyndham, who had shown him the pureness of his heart, who hated the slave traders with passion, the kingdom would have disappeared from the face of the earth. The war captain and the queen mother worked with the captain and got some of these weapons behind the king's back to use in their wars. But whatever weapons she got through the backdoor were too little and too late.

After another battle, the king waited in his palace for the latest casualties. Earlier that day, his sense of helplessness mounted with every cannon shot that he heard from the nearby woods. And every shot that ricocheted against the innocent shoreline was like a knife that pierced his angry heart. That day the number of the dead, the wounded and those who'd been taken away in chains as captives was staggering.

The brutality of the enemy did not amaze the king, so he vowed to wipe these unwanted aliens off the land one way or the other. In fact, he swore before the gods and the ancestors to drive them into the gaping mouth of the Atlantic Ocean, to send them back home where they came from, beyond the mighty ocean.

"How did the latest battle go?" the king asked the war captain pointedly. "How many soldiers did you lose in the latest battle and how many stepped into their shoes to replace them. How many were willing to take up arms to fight for their birthright and defend the motherland?"

"The Oburoni killed one thousand soldiers in cold blood and wounded another one thousand during this latest assault," the war captain reported to the king, rubbing his eyes angrily and gnashing his teeth like a leopard. "We buried the dead and we sent the wounded to the nurses. But I must tell you with pride that another one thousand soldiers stepped forward and took the place of these fallen heroes, replacing the dead."

The king stood up in anger and stumped his feet on the floor. "This is a fight for our motherland, a fight for honor. And so I am not surprised that though one thousand died in this battle, another one thousand stepped up to take their place. We fight for our destiny; remember we are in this fight to the last person."

That weekend, the king's guerrilla forces ambushed and killed fifty more slave raiders. They surprised them from behind, approaching from behind the tall elephant grasses and hacked them to death. The king lost only seven soldiers in that encounter and another half a dozen seriously wounded.

He didn't want to spare the lives of any of the enemy, but he loved the idea that the soldiers captured and brought the fourteen enemy traders to his palace. He would use these captives to bargain with the governor for more firearms, if he wanted to do so. He was not blood thirsty, so he asked the high priest not to sacrifice these captives to Dente, not to give their blood to the god of gods, but to secure them in the "secret shrine of woes."

Although Dente, the chief deity and all the other gods of the land, deserved praise from the people for the help they'd given them in the latest rounds of war, the king refused to reward them with any human blood. In the past, the people gave them some unique sacrifices--- seven virgins each year, several captives from war and the blood of those who violated any of the king's wives. But the rulers realized a clear unfairness to women in this practice, because it caused the young virgins to destroy their virginity before they were ready for marriage.

The king became much more confident in his role after he'd fought the invaders in three wars. He felt the presence of the ancestors and their willingness to help him more than ever before. But he gave the gods burnt sacrifices of ram, roosters and cows, and libations of rum and gin. Though he had no virgins for them, he thanked them because they'd made a big difference in the conflict.

The high priest lifted the seven bottles of Kantamanto drinks one after the other and pointed them toward the sky, showing them to the gods as he opened them, one after the other, and gave them to the gods in the libation. More than that, he poured one bottle of Kantamanto gin completely into the angry ocean---asking the gods to hear the cry of his people for help. He told them that their fate rested in the hands of the ancestors.

And so the high priest, with several talismans around his neck, signaled the executioners to slaughter the rams, the roosters, the cows, and smear the blood on the feet of these gods. In ancient times, these gods used to refuse sacrifices that did not include human blood. But for nearly a century, the leaders had decided never to give the gods the blood of the innocent virgins in the land. Instead, they'd given them the blood of cows, rams, and roosters; they forced them to quench their thirst with "akpeteshie" moonshine or Kantamanto gin.

The high priest went on his knees, threw seven cowry shells on the floor and read the mark on the ground. "Let us see what the gods have in store for us," he told the elders, after a quick sigh. His broken knee gave way and it took the help of the war captain and Elder Landonu to get him off the ground and place him back in his chair.

"Old age and family troubles have caught up with me," he told them laughing. "It was only yesterday when I could run like a leopard and kneel for hours or jump and even reach the moon, but look at how yesterday has swallowed today."

"Come on, it is not that bad; you are still a young man," Zotor told him jokingly. "But I hope I don't become this weak in the future when I reach your age."

"Are you asking an alligator why its mouth is so long? You are a youth, but you would certainly grow and reach my age some day," he told him sarcastically, with everyone laughing at his expense.

According to the Oracle of Zendo, the king's rise to power in the land was not by accident. It was the ancestors that had placed him on the stool and blessed him. They'd also given him the nickname "the Black Lion" because he would be the king to defeat the heavily armed Europeans, the Oburoni intruders that were so thirsty for blood. He would use his intelligence, creativity and courage to defeat them.

The son of the war captain fired a gun into the air as he remembered the heroic acts of several past Bakano kings. He toasted King Zendo with palm-wine for his efforts to preserve the golden stool for the next generation, to save this treasure for his children and grandchildren. He also remembered the heroic fights of King Gizenga and King Batazinga, especially their courageous stand not to open the trade routes for the slave traders. He remembered how they defied the threats of the governor to keep these vital arteries of the iniquitous trade closed.

"I should have listened to Queen Mother Mambo," the king admitted, his solemn voice causing urgency among the women. He pointed his right hand toward the shrine of Dente and spoke loudly in his baritone voice. "The gods have the power to destroy the enemy with thunder and lightening, but they are still waiting for the right time. We must give to them generous sacrifices and libation so they could help us drive away these "unwanted locusts" that came with itching feet, from faraway lands, from beyond the angry ocean."

"Sometimes, many heads are better than one," Abrewa, the oldest lady in the kingdom, suggested to the king. "The queen mother is always patient when the cannons are banging the shoreline with fury, and she is also of sharp mind, so you must listen to what she has to say to you, sometimes, if not always. Don't let her beauty and bubbling honey personality disarm you. You are the king, the final decision maker, but you must sometimes listen to her advice."

"Well, the evil curse that these Oburoni traders had brought into our land had destroyed our progress, and we are at the verge of going into slavery," the king told her, pointing toward the Cape Coast Castle as the symbol of what he meant, venting his anger generously. "This castle, standing like a devil's house against the blue sky, is a big eyesore against the skyline and an awful curse on our people."

"Well, I hate the way they'd looted our gold, destroyed everything of value that our ancestors had built in this land, accomplishments that spanned over one hundred million years, really uncountable years. But look at all the confusion they'd brought into our land, everywhere you look, they had reduced everything into shambles," Abrewa said.

"From the good old days, and during the lives of our recent ancestors, our shoreline had been pure, free and full of happy, progressive people, but these traders had stopped even fishing, drumming, dancing, farming and all the simple things our ancestors used to do. They'd even tried to destroy most of our traditions as well," Elder Landonu told the elders, scratching his head looking for what to do.

For the king, this tragedy was even much more personal.

Almost every night, the king saw in his dreams the ghosts of his father and grandfather roaming the fields, angry and restless. After all these years, he was surprised to see they had anger on their faces as they yelled and chastised him in the dream. They told him that the Oburoni traders did not come from the gods or from the ancestors; therefore, he must use everything he had to destroy them. He must never spare their lives, or let them have their way in the land, his forebears told him. He was glad when they told him to use the secret weapon to drive these aliens out of the land. That actually made him intoxicated with joy when he heard about this weapon.

After stealing millions of their youths, the enemy also planted a deadly religion in the midst of the inhabitants. The king hated the way they'd been playing a deadly mind game with the leaders, his elders and with the general population, all the inhabitants. The Oburoni forced many of them to choose between their traditional gods and the new alien Oburoni religion. While many of the people saw no reason to leave their traditional religion, some flirted with it, realized the contradictions and quickly abandoned the new religion because it was hypocritical.

There was the fifty-year old priest of xebioso, who had converted to the religion of the Oburoni traders. His name was Xebioxogana, the chief priest of the god of lightening. He had been a priest in the shrine of this god for more than twenty years, serving this deity to the best of his abilities. In the good days, it was his job to decide whom the god of thunder should punish with thunderbolt, or who should drink poisoned honey for their crimes.

He used to respect the traditions and honored the ancestors, but he fell for the sugar-coated tongues of these aliens. He wanted a taste of the enemy's baptism of fire. So he became a member of a religion which asked the converts to make room somewhere up in the sky for a better life after death, but then they saw how the missionaries were busy helping themselves to their gold and hauling away their youths, sending them into slavery for money on earth.

He realized these weaknesses after he'd left his work as the head priest at the Shrine of Xebioso and joined this new Oburoni religion. But what drove him most to the new alien religion were the Holy Communion they had once a month and the new sweet hymns they sang at worship each Sunday morning.

Nevertheless, though he converted to the new religion, it did not mend the gaping hole and pain he always felt in his heart. He was still searching for something much deeper than church hymns, holy communions with bread and wine each month. He was yearning for inner peace and serenity in his life; instead, he ended up with a new storm that preached love of one's neighbor but visited all sorts of horrible sins on his people.

The king gave him a piece of land to return to the shrine, but Xebioxogana refused the king's present and still stayed away. The king filled the vacancy by appointing, Dukure, a new priest to the god, to take his place. Dukure, still very angry with the former priest for betraying the god, secretly placed two different plants beneath a stone next to his house and during a storm; they triggered a loud thunderbolt that killed seven of his fourteen children in a bloody vengeance.

So, the former priest quickly gave up his new religion and with lots of regrets and sorrow, quickly returned to Xebioso to the laughter of his colleagues. The high priest told them that this should serve as a strong warning to the people to stop disrespecting the ancestors. For those who run away to this new alien religion whenever they had the least disagreement with the priests or the king, they must expect vengeance from these gods. "If you disrespect the gods, they will punish you and destroy your family," the new priest warned the inhabitants, speaking in an urgent tone. "Our gods are not dead; they are just patient and wise. But if you insult, violate or disrespect them, they would teach you a lesson that you would never forget."

Following the death of Xebioso's children, the king asked the soldiers to weed out the alien traders and end their outrageous religion. The missionaries could operate outside Bakano, they could find converts in the villages in the forest areas, but they could no longer convert the people who lived along the coast. He gave them the places the people found it harder to abandon the ancestors and follow this new abomination.

As for the king, he clung to the traditions. Although he'd rejected the more bizarre practices such as human sacrifice and smearing the blood of virgins on the gods, he loved the ways of the gods. He'd always believed that the solution to the alien problem rested in the hands of the ancestors and the gods, and not in what the Asafo soldiers could do. The problem was, whenever they needed these gods most, they went to sleep on them. They turned deaf ears to their call for help.

In the African way of life, the king knew that the gods were alive in the land. Their world was made up of a trinity---the dead, the living and the unborn. He knew that these gods were protecting them from this world from the world of the ancestors. He asked these gods to send confusion into the enemy camp and plant a deadly disease among these invaders. He also asked them to weaken their soldiers, so the king's Asafo soldiers could defeat them.

Zotor, the high priest, had given the enemy the nickname---the "white locusts," after they'd destroyed half the crops they'd planted that year. "You have turned our land into a land of sorrow; our homes into abodes of hunger and our civilization into houses of chaos. They have become a mere shadow of their former selves."

"They'd prevented men from being men, women from being women and our children from doing what children normally do, and for this, every one of them must die," the king said. This quest for vengeance dominated his mind like a heavy load, but he had no regrets for his evil wishes for all these Oburoni aliens. Once a while, however, his thoughts went to the likes of Captain Wyndham, the kind-hearted missionary who refused to look down on them, always looked up to see the good in them, lifted their souls up and was always ready to lend a hand.

"Well, just remember to help the good ones that had helped us in our times of war," the queen mother dragged her stool toward the high priest, covered her face with her palms feeling very sorry for these good Oburoni missionaries.

"Well, as the saying goes, when you do evil to someone you would also die an evil death. So the gods had decreed that these invaders would meet their end after this rainy season. But until that time, we must continue to fight them from behind the tall elephant grasses, from the top of the hills and from the thickest of brushes in the grassland."

"It is annoying how they'd lied about the trade in gold and then they suddenly started stealing our youths, using them as "black cargo," and hauling them away in chains to the land of no return like cows and sheep," Abrewa told the elders. "We are people too, just like them,"

"Why they found the slave trade much more profitable than the gold trade, why they'd risked the wrath of the ancestors on their heads and switched to this horrible trade, we would never fully understand," Mankrado, the war captain, told the elders as he swayed the palm branch in the air to express his disgust for the enemy.

"According to the African way of life, no crime against the gods can go unanswered. So these aliens will definitely answer to the gods for hauling away millions of Mama Africa's children to work for them. The gods won't forget how they'd killed several infants and aged people that they found unsuitable to be slaves. The gods would demand they account for all the bloodshed," Zotor said angrily. "Even the gold they'd looted from the king, they must answer for, so they better think again."

The king got up from the golden stool and walked elegantly to the balcony. When he looked down below, he saw a sea of heads; he saw hundreds of people waiting to listen to his words of wisdom. These were the returnees, people who defected, but had second thoughts about the alien ways and returned to Dente, to their heritage. He readmitted these people, victims of the sweet tongued Oburoni missionaries. They'd already apologized to the gods and to the priests. They'd all forgiven them their treason and shifty behavior.

Xebioxogana the head priest of Xebioso had traveled the shameful road of desertion. He'd sold out his conscience to the enemy. But the ancestors couldn't let him stay away from his father's traditions forever. So when the god gave him a sign, he quickly returned to his father's house, to his inner beliefs. But his move was too late to save his children from the anger of the god of lightening. But through his actions, the entire kingdom, his entire family of brothers and sisters, had seen what Xebioso's anger could do and how it could destroy an entire household.

The high priest accepted the rams and roosters that these deserters or returnees brought to the shrine to quiet down the angry gods of the land. They blessed them and they hurriedly feasted on these animals with joy and used the Kantamanto gin to quench their thirst.

King Zendo was a tall, robust man who became king at twenty-seven. But the young king was wiser than his age. He had an imposing body. He was tall, dark and handsome. He shaved his bald head religiously and rubbed coconut oil on top of it to keep it shining, but his bushy eyebrows and hairy body, which left him looking like a black lion scared some of the women. He wore his royal kente regalia proudly, but unlike the other bald king, who was in love with his own voice; he did not allow the pomp and fame of the office to go to his head.

So he remained humble. He was not like the foolish leader who was too big to greet his subjects and marched away from them with contempt to avoid exchanging greetings with them. The crown fit his bald head perfectly, and he walked with pride but he'd also never lost sight of the heavy burdens he'd inherited from his own father.

As Bakano tradition required, the king had to wear tons of gold jewelry at durbars and state functions---necklaces, bracelets and rings on all his fingers. He must impress his subjects with his wealth and silence his critics and rivals with his pomp. The large gold staff he carried in his right hand was a symbol of his power. It assured his subjects that he'd become the undisputed lion in the forest, the one charged to stop the enemy in their deadly tracks of horror. The king was never disrespected in the land, because he would remember this when your case arrives at his palace.

"You are now the biggest whale in the ocean," Zotor told the king. So the king went to the beach and waded knee-deep into the ocean like a stranded whale, raised the golden staff into the sky to show that the ancestors had asked him to drive the "Oburoni locusts" out of the land, to push them into the bottom of the Atlantic Ocean. "If they look for mercy from me, they would find none."

Though he did not crave it, he finally got the mantle of leadership, what he and others had been waiting on for centuries to save the motherland. He accepted his role and took an oath before his subjects and the elders to do whatever the gods wanted him to do.

"This is the most difficult task for me as your new king, and this would demand a lot of sacrifice from everybody," he told them in a pleasant but firm voice as he took the oath of office, swearing an oath before hundreds of chiefs, thousands of queen mothers and promising several millions of his subjects to deliver them from the enemy.

"You don't have to tell us about where you want to lead us, we know that from your long family history---you are the new leader and you would light a bamboo fire blaze under these wearisome Oburoni aliens, who had taken our hospitality for a weakness, and had thanked us with their anal parts," Nana Osei Okotor told the new king. "Let them know that our hospitality comes from our traditions, of being kind to helpless strangers, of giving water and food to total strangers. And to us, this has never been a weakness."

The king nodded repeatedly to make them feel his gratitude and his sense of responsibility as the servants wiped the sweat off his face, rearranged the gold jewelry on his chest and hands, and straightened the crown on top of his bald head. The women eyed and made faces at him, but he remained unaffected and solemn, considering the heavy burden of tasks on his shoulders. "The honor you have given me today,

I would use to free our youths from bondage, freeing them from the evil hands of these traders. I'll make sure our women are not only safe, but also able to fetch foodstuff from the farms to feed their children and are ready to give birth to new ones," the king said.

These tasks brought spontaneous fear in him, but he did not show it.

Each village chief marched and brought him gifts of gold nuggets, presenting him with some beautiful young females to serve inside his court, which made the king to light his face with smiles of gratitude. These were presentations to assure the new leader of their undivided devotion and loyalty to him and to the kingdom.

"If you want to swear your allegiance to the new king, this is the time for you to do so," Mankrado told the sub-chiefs as he cleared the arena of the drummers, the dancers and the clowns. He was too humble to do the first dance before the king did his. It was rude to dance better than the king at that moment. So, he slightly tapped his feet, jumped in the air with the black mpaboa sandals for a minute and gave way to the king. He didn't want to out stage the king, but inside his soul, he badly wanted to do his unique war dance, to sway his body to the sweet rhythm of the pulsating Adowa music and prove his wife wrong that he couldn't dance very well.

"It is important the king knows where we all stand," the sub-chief from Prampram told the other chiefs. "He needs to know where we stand, whether we would stand with him against the Oburoni or speak with other voices."

"Mbo! mbo!" Chief Motchere of Abum said. "I present these seven big gold nuggets, seven male servants and seven of the most beautiful women in Abum to your majesty. We assure you that whenever you call on us, whether in the night or during the day, we would never hesitate to answer your call. And whether it is for war or for peace, you can always count on us. And if we ever break this promise to you, let the god of thunder strike us down."

The king thanked the one hundred or more chiefs and the millions of subjects for coming to the durbar and for their tributes to the kingdom. He told them that he valued their allegiance and their kind gestures.

After all the talks about war, there was still joy in the air, but the horn blowers blew their horns and fontomfrom drummers played their war drums for the warriors, who took their turns to do their masculine war dances. During the war dance, the women sat down quietly. They knew the rules for this dance. This was a dance for only the male warriors. According to this ancient tradition, the men who had been to war and had killed before went first, followed by warriors who had been to war but had never killed any enemy. Then the men, who had never been to war before were forced to sit quietly among the women and watched the other men display their valor. If any woman tried to join in, the men quickly pushed her away or wrestled her to the ground and took her to secret shrine for debriefing. They made her know quickly that there were clear lines between male and female roles.

But when the drummers filled the air with pulsating borborbor and Adowa music, it was the turn of the women. Many of these voluptuous women jumped up, sang and wriggled their hips creating sizzling vibrations. Some swayed their hips as if the wind was blowing them from side to side as they continued to dance their hearts out. And the men played the drums with intensity; their eyes attentively fixed on these vibrating behinds. Some of these succulent looking women caused many of these veteran warriors to forget about the Oburoni enemy temporarily, especially the recent bloody losses in the last battle.

And there was no shortage of moonshine and palm wine at this event. According to the war captain, "Even when you carry gunpowder in your hand, you can still smoke your pipe, so the warriors must make merry." Except the reserves, all the men got drunk like bees and made merry as if they had no tomorrow. The king made sure that one battalion was sober and ready to go to war in case the enemy decided to surprise them once again during this festival. The enemy did the same thing a decade ago, when they caught them off guard, with many of their men in festive mood, drunk and completely unprepared for war. He remembered how the Oburonis took advantage of that situation and mercilessly butchered their warriors leaving thousands of orphans and hundreds of widows looking for new husbands.

The soldiers loved the festival because it gave them a temporary relief from the deafening sounds of the cannon guns and from all the anxiety they felt from the slave raids, which never ended in the kingdom and all across the continent. It also gave them the chance to meet with family members from far and near and friends. Everyone was glad that they'd survived another year. They were glad to still be alive in a kingdom that was an eternal war-zone that you could not safely go to farm, or even go to the riverside to safely draw water.

Six months after this durbar, the inhabitants prepared for the next big celebration----the Oyster festival. New kente cloths were woven, gold jewelry were designed, new shoes were made, and new "batakaris" for warriors were also crafted. Also, sheds were erected and new crowns for royalty were made for the momentous occasion.

The high priest made sure that the seven day fast, which was a tradition that preceded the event, a ritual intended to prepare everybody spiritually for the occasion, went on without any tragic death, or anybody violating the king's decree to remain spiritually fit. Unlike in the past, no one violated the peace that year and the high priest did not have to take anyone to the king for the proverbial punishment of seven rams and seven bottles of Kantamanto whiskey. Though the people were glad, it displeased the priesthood. They did not have a lot to feast on that year.

"The moment you have all been waiting for has arrived," the queen mother motioned to the ladies who were blocking the entrance to the arena to move away. "Clear the floor; it is time for the king to do the opening dance of the festival. This is the time to reach into the past and remember the ancestors."

The king, with his spiritual protector closely behind him, got up to do the opening dance. He was wearing his full regalia and his wife wiped the sweat from his forehead with a piece of white calico cloth, which caused the women and children to roar with laughter.

The durbar ground was filled with joy and merry making. There was music and there were clowns playing around. There were dancers showing off their skills.

"He looks so royal and so handsome," Abrewa said about the king as she looked at him with her aged but flirtatious eyes. "He is more handsome than his father."

"I love the way he walks with dignity and speaks with authority," the queen mother added. "I wish he was my husband and not just my king. I guess in my dreams."

"Stop dreaming about what you can never have," Abrewa mocked her. "As a former wife of Dente you know very well that you can't get married to any of these men around here, especially not to the king."

The elders burst into an uncontrollable laugh as Abrewa shook her head at the queen mother's remarks. They knew the old lady was right and the queen mother was simply daydreaming. Every one of them knew her predicament when it came to the gods and her personal life. How could they forget Mama Nornyi who violated the custom and drowned in a river, a tragic death from the gods?

"We must let some of these ancient traditions that put women in inferior positions die out with time," she told the elders bluntly. "Why should a nice-looking woman like me, with plenty of love to give, become a "gbolo woman" because I was forced to marry a god, a victim of the priests because of an ancient belief?"

"This is part of the wisdom we have inherited from the ages. We cannot throw it away and say our ancestors were wrong," the old lady told her.

The women enjoyed watching the king do the opening dance. He stood proudly like a tall ebony tree, towering over everybody as he did the opening dance for the special occasion. Some people just watched him silently; others were filled with admiration and loved the fact that he was the person placed on the golden stool to get rid of these evil traders. Some onlookers shed silent tears as they remembered their loved ones, some of the losses during the year, especially those who died or were forcibly taken in chains and did not have the fortune to be present, those unfortunate warriors that the greed of the Oburoni traders had swallowed.

The high priest raised a small broom in the air and recited some incantations to make sure no spectator got hurt. He warded off the evil spirits making sure these spirits did not overpower any one. These evil spirits love to attack their victims during such big gatherings. They love to possess and even kill some of them.

The king rode in his colorful palanquin. Twelve men carried him shoulder high, balancing it on their shoulders showing off their tight muscles. The king's face showed nothing but pride as he looked at the pomp and glory, the colorful audience and the sea of colorful royal umbrellas that adorned the inside of the arena. The audience shouted loudly every time he made fresh moves with his torso, or swayed from side to side like a mahogany tree responding to the wind with a golden sword in his hand, greeting the people at short intervals.

The oldest woman, Abrewa, told the audience in a shrill voice that the king danced like a "proud black lion." She shouted repeatedly just as she used to do years ago when the king's father danced before a similar audience as the ruler of the kingdom. "This king dances like no other king before him ever did. He moves himself proudly like a lion-king, a leader who presides over his surroundings and struck fear in his subjects."

In the end, just before the king descended from the dais and sat down, he raised his right hand toward the blue sky, and reaching above his head, pointed the sword as high as he could and swore another oath of vengeance against the Oburoni enemy. The setting sun radiated a rich colorful rainbow out of the expensive, unique kente outfit he wore. Though royal, he also looked more like an old warrior that had seen many battles. He was sweating when he finally sat down, but he showed off his solid black "mpaboa" sandals, which had strings of gold nuggets and rows of glittering diamond ornaments that hurt the eyes, and also struck awe and respect into the hearts and souls of his subjects, targeting his critics.

Then the "brafuo" and many of the king's personal body guards formed a circle around the king to protect him from any evil-minded subject present at the function. They blew their horns loudly to announce the king's readiness to receive his subordinate chiefs, paramount chiefs, divisional chiefs, queen mothers, clan leaders and all notable elders.

It was time to for the Parade of Homage and Gifts of the year to begin.

As soon as the king sat down, his subordinate chiefs took turns in doing their dances, marching and dancing around the arena as they made their way toward the king's dais. He knew all these chiefs personally, he also knew how wealthy each one was, but, most importantly, he knew those that had fought the Oburoni locusts the hardest that year. But he smiled and accepted whatever tribute each leader brought with him, large or small. But he paid more attention to the leaders that the "Oburoni locusts" raided and tormented that year. To show his sympathy and honor, he got up from his golden stool to greet these chiefs cordially. He embraced them heartily and extended his special sympathies to them and to their people.

The parade of queen mothers was the next show of shows. It was also a highly competitive affair and an important event. As these queens paraded around the durbar grounds with their groups, they stopped briefly in front of the dais for the ladies who had accompanied them to display their best dance moves for the king and the elders. The newly-initiated girls, with beautiful, firm bodies, eligible single women, were paraded before the king and the elders. The king watched more attentively as these girls did their intricate adowa dance moves, swaying their hips, vibrating their behinds, tempting would be suitors, just in case any of the eligible bachelors wanted any of these young women who had just finished the annual initiation rites for a wife. Those that caught the king's eyes or the eyes of any other royalty at the durbar---the divisional or sub chiefs at the durbar---became extremely excited.

The ordinary citizens followed their chiefs and did their own dances. The warriors got in line to march before the others followed. The fontomfrom drums filled the durbar ground and the warriors, who were the only people who could dance to these war drumbeats, made their brave, manly dance moves as the women looked on silently without even moving their bodies to the beat. Any woman caught dancing to this beat was taken to task and must pay a heavy fine. So, the women sat still and watched these gallant warriors displayed in detail what they did, or how they killed their attackers on the battlefield.

The women laughed when the men who had never been to war marched. The women, who had contempt for these men, regarded them as either invalids or total cowards. And their wives were also treated with very little or no respect. Where they were when the Oburonis attacked them from the forests, or came to their villages with their guns aimed at their homes, or started shooting and killing children and women? The king needed every warrior to step into the path of danger to defend the kingdom.

When it was the turn of the women to sing their latest songs, followed by other songs that were thousands of years old, the queen mother took control. She made the women dancers from different villages, clad in matching clothes, sing their songs and do their happy dances. And some of them behaved as if the music had captured and possessed their souls, as they danced in unison like a school of doves.

As the Ewe say, "Even if you are carrying gunpowder on top of your head, you can still smoke your pipe." So, these women, who normally sang sad dirges and mourned the dead, decided to put their misery aside for that day to sing happy songs and to do some happy dances. It was such a dramatic sight to see these women, heavily buried in grief and sorrow all year, out of their dark adinkra mourning clothes during the festival singing, dancing and looking their best.

But Ayeko, the assistant to the queen mother, a strong individual with a mind of her own, refused to let go of her sorrows. She still wore her adinkra mourning clothing and refused to join the other women in the happy dance. "How could we be doing happy dances when the Oburoni enemy has not yet been defeated? As I speak these evil traders are still forcing our youths out of the land and hauling them away in their boats of shame," she asked these jubilant women who'd been doing the happy dances.

"Well, she has a point. We have to worry about the fact that we have no weapons left for our soldiers to fight the enemy, and so why are we dancing as if everything is alright?" the queen mother also asked bluntly. "Why should the king be enjoying this day, dancing his heart out like a hero who had already defeated the enemy? Where are his victories? How many Oburonis has he killed?"

"These evil traders had been here years before we were even born so don't get too worried about their presence. Take heart, and sometimes you must try to enjoy life. We will prevail against them one day," Abrewa, the old lady, told Ayeko and then she asked the queen mother to comfort her. "Don't let them drive you into an early grave before your time of death arrives."

"The king should have canceled the festival this year, because there had been too much bloodshed," Ayeko said. She had some support from a few of the elders, as her eyes darted from Zotor, the high priest, to Mankrado. In a sense, she was right. The festival came shortly after another bloody raid into the kingdom. It was the bloodiest of many raids that year. That tragedy was gut-wrenching and it had left many dark clouds on the horizon. It had also forced every man to sleep with his gun leaning against his bed, in case these slave raiders returned to the kingdom in the middle of the night to do some more destruction.

The war captain asked armed guards, whom the war captain had hidden in the bushes, to defend the land while the inhabitants slept. The king, a warrior himself, a distinguished veteran who had fought in seven wars before he sat on the golden stool, wore a red cloth around his neck expressing his grief for the fallen men and women. He removed this red cloth and waved it in the air to the sub-chiefs of those kingdoms that the slave raiders had recently attacked and destroyed.

The griot, the traditional storyteller, always ended the addresses at these gatherings on notes of optimism. "Just as the gods do wipe flies off all the animals without tails, so will the ancestors dry our tears, protect our children and rid the land of these "human pests."

Then the griot proceeded to sing the praises of members of some prominent families, people who had defended the kingdom gallantly, and those who had lost their lives. He started with the king first, praising the long line of kings and queens that had ruled the land. He devoted five minutes to the exploits of the king's grandfather and father. Then he serenaded all the brave warriors and all the deserving ladies, the devoted mothers, those who had the moral authority to keep life going in the land. He never forgot to mention the "sacred forests," and he praised the virgins in the land in his songs. His stories with no beginnings and no ends delighted the adults and titillated the youth. And on that special occasion as the dancers, the drummers, the singers and the on-lookers were enjoying the festival, having the best of times, he seized the opportunity to instill pride into the hearts and souls of all present, pride that had been missing because the Oburoni had dehumanized and depersonalized their souls.

"The Bakano kingdom would never come to an end. It would continue to move forward with the help of the ancestors," he assured the people. Many of them did not listen, but they simply contented their hearts with the many gourds of palm wine the palm wine tapers brought in to mark the festival, to make the event a joyful occasion.

The war captain hadn't any kind words for the cowards, draft dodgers and those men who'd run away from battle, hid themselves in the forests only to return home when the battle ended. He told the people that they were cowards who refused to fight for honor, and chose to return to their wives in shame rather than seek honor.

"I have no respect for cowards and deserters," Mankrado declared in his baritone voice with the women cheering and jeering some of the men. The women giggled and shook their heads. "Next time around we would execute all these deserters and cowards in the public place."

The obrafuo proceeded to serve the one-day old sweet wine to the women and gave the same drink to those men who had never been to war. But the palm wine tapers, however, reserved the "strong intoxicating drink" for the pleasure of the warriors and the war captains.

The year before the king got the secret weapon, the Oburoni traders had been particularly blood thirsty and brutal. Everything seemed to have gone against the king in the conflict with the alien intruders. One of the chiefs had betrayed the whereabouts of their soldiers and had given their war plans to the enemy. So the Oburonis had been able to easily defeat the kings' soldiers, even when they ambushed the enemy.

One day the war captain heard the attackers had raided the neighboring villages and had taken many prisoners of war. So he went after the raiders and freed some of these captives before they could reach the dungeons on the Atlantic Slave Coast. The rescuers believed that it was Dente who had sent a pack of lions after the traders, who'd delayed the caravan's journey to the Slave Coast, thereby enabling the rescuers to get to them. On that fateful rainy morning, these brave warriors managed to rescue many, if not all of the victims by surprising the traders in the middle of the night.

The chief brafuo executed the slave raiders before he brought the victims back to the king, entering the kingdom with war songs and joyful fontomfrom dances. Everyone was sentimental, intoxicated with joy. The war captain wanted to execute the ring leader of the African traitors, but the king ordered him to spare his life and gave him a future date with destiny.

As for the victims, they were visibly overjoyed that they'd got a second chance at life. You could see the relief on their faces when the asafo soldiers broke the iron bracelets off their hands and untied the shackles and wooden restraints around their necks. Many of them went directly for their dreams, for the utmost desire of their hearts---to drink water from the Volta River once again.

"Who says our gods are dead?" the high priest asked loudly, celebrating the success. "Let that person who says that they are dead stand up and step forward." He paused for a few seconds, but nobody came forward.

"No, our gods are very much alive," Abrewa declared in her weak voice. "They have been there for us since the beginning of time. And they would never leave us, or desert our children in the future."

One of the victims broke the silence and made a loud sound of joy. "I am so happy that I have the chance to drink water from the Volta River again," Voko said in an expressive voice. There was a visible sign of relief on his face. "I am one of the luckiest people alive today, because it is unheard of for anyone to escape from these evil traders and return home to his family."

"Don't thank us, but rather thank the gods for hearing your cry and sending the soldiers to rescue you," Zotor the high priest told him.

As the saying goes, the palm branch does not open its mouth without cause. He believed, therefore, that just the way they'd stumbled upon the land; they would meet their end in the same way. "I believe that they'd conceived this deliberate plot to enslave our people, and, as Captain Wyndham told me, this is because they need the African people to do labor for them on their sugar and tobacco farms."

"Well, he told me that his people were weak and had lazy work habits," the queen mother joked.

The reality was that in the forest, the one with the bigger guns controlled the actions of everyone else, and so with their cannon, the Oburonis reigned supreme on the continent. They controlled the actions of the kings and queens, though some of them refused and opposed them every step of the way.

"Whatever brought these aliens to our land; it is very obvious to everyone that they'd destroyed the peace and quiet that prevailed in the land for millions of years," the king told the audience. "The saddest part is that they'd made our once lively civilization in the world a mere silhouette of its former self."

The king once again stood on the shoreline that high noon gazing at the deep blue sky questioning the fate that the gods had pinned on his people. The waves were silent and the breeze was plentiful as he stood there like a mahogany tree, beaten, but looking undefeated and told the gods to get rid of the uninvited alien locusts once and for all. Though he was a seasoned soldier---well prepared for his role as king---getting rid of the Oburoni traders had proven extremely difficult for his forces. With next to no weapons, his soldiers had been the underdogs in every clash and could not drive the enemy into the ocean as he'd promised.

"Definitely, we have to continue to go after them," he told the war captain. "It didn't matter if we died in our effort to get rid of them. Even if we died, we would have died with pride, knowing that we were fighting for the soul of our beloved motherland."

The war captain smiled and rubbed his face with his rough palms. "I am completely behind you in these war efforts." He then ate "fire" publicly before the king and the elders to prove his commitment and loyalty to the cause. "We must sacrifice our lives to the very last soul," he told the king as he tried to stop the bleeding from the cut he made on his right index finger, "this should be everybody's goal in our never-ending struggle against these evil locusts."

"I have already sworn on my grandfather's grave to stop the greedy enemy from doing further harm to the kingdom," the king declared. "Unless I fall on the battlefield as my father and grandfather did, I will not disappoint you, or the ancestors."

"These Oburoni people are worse than the locusts," Mankrado joked. "The locusts come every seven years, but this enemy had overstayed their visit. They'd looted, terrorized and brutalized us from generation to generation. Now let us see how many of them would be willing to put their lives on the line in order to get the slave cargo they craved so badly."

King Zendo tried everything he and his generals knew to end the nightmare, to drive these pests out of the land, to push them into the gaping mouth of the Atlantic Ocean, but nothing he tried seemed to work. It wasn't because he was a coward, but because he didn't have the latest cannon, the Danish rifles and enough gunpowder to wage this bloody and never-ending war.

Before he was born, the king's forbears tried everything within their power to end the horrible nightmare that the "Oburoni locusts" had imposed on them, and forced on the motherland. He also heard about these Oburoni locusts capturing some of the women, raping many of them and then turning some of them into sex slaves in the castle.

The griots, the storytellers, told the people not to worry because as the Ibo saying goes, "when someone is holding you down, he is also holding himself down as well." He knew that the invaders, if they had any conscience at all, had a heavy burden of guilt in their hearts. But he assured the public that these aliens would hear from the god of thunder and the god of lightening. He knew that Dente, the god of all the gods and the ruler of the land, would punish them for what they'd done to his people.

"When the time comes, the gods would not have any mercy on them, they would be unforgiving when they visit their anger on them," he declared.

Meanwhile, there was widespread starvation in the land. Insecure roads to the farms, with slave traders lurking on the pathways to these farms, crisscrossing the hunting grounds in the forests and bushes, led to shortage of food in many homes. Many mothers hurt in their hearts when they had to watch their children complain of hunger pain. They hated to see their children grew thinner and thinner until they'd started looking like skeletons---a nightmare especially when most of them had been hard-working mothers---whose children had become walking zombies because of hunger and starvation.

The women could not go to their farms because the slave raiders were hiding on the outskirts of the village or town ready to enslave them. Though there were rows of yams in their barns, the roads leading to the farms were risky and often ended in the slave traders catching several of these brave mothers and hauling them away as slaves.

But this visible danger did not stop Kaniwa, the mother of Mankrado, whose son would later on become the war captain. She finally, got tired of looking into the hungry faces of his seven children. And anytime she heard her children's stomachs growling with hunger pain, she became extremely disturbed. Angry and helpless, she would pace the floor back and forth like a caged leopard muttering juju chants. Whenever she thought about all the yams she and her husband had inside their barns, she would lose her patience and curse the Oburoni locusts.

"I have to go and get some yams from the barn in the farm," she told her children. "At this point, I don't care what happens to me. I just hate to watch you press your stomachs against the bed at night so you could lessen your hunger pain. I can't take this sight any longer. Maybe I prefer death to watching my children starve so miserably while we have plenty of food in the barn in the farm."

"Let us hope that the sun might shine brighter tomorrow morning," Abrewa told her, urging her to continue to be cautious and not to take any foolish chances that she would regret later.

"I just have to do something different, to take a chance," she assured herself. "I might get away with it. Perhaps the slave traders might be somewhere else. Maybe the hunters might protect me if I come under attack. But if they catch me I would submit to whatever they want from me---but I refuse to sit idle and watch my children starve to death---I can not sit idle and watch that happen any more."

"Forget about the yams and just cook some kontombre leaves for the children," the husband insisted. "Your life is more valuable to them than the best of yams from our barns. Don't play into the hands of the enemy; because I am not going with you, as bad as it sounds to you, you are on your own when they catch you."

"Well, you should stay behind and take care of them in case they abduct me and I never return home, my warrior husband," she told the husband with scorn.

"A warrior knows when to fight and when not to fight," he told her sternly. "Take a good look at your children before you leave them, because you are an antelope walking into the den of the lion. You don't stand a chance."

Her spirit of adventure, her daring attitude, but most importantly the bigness of her heart steered her actions. She took her husband's gun, strapped it to her waist and went to the farm anyway, and she went over her husband's objections. In her mind, she went to the farm to fetch some yams to feed her children, but to the slave traders, she just walked directly into a deadly trap. She never made it to the farm. Though she'd put up a gallant fight, she was quickly overpowered, shackled and marched to the slave dungeons on the Atlantic Coast.

Was she playing the role of a good mother or did she make a deadly date with fate?

"The worst nightmare had hit my family, the locusts had attacked my family," Kani, her husband, told the gathering passionately. "All she wanted was some yams to feed her children. What a shame that mothers cannot even go to their farms to get foodstuff to feed their children without these greedy traders seizing and separating them from their children forever. How can we continue to live like this in our own land?"

"Why should we live in such great fear?" Abrewa asked and hated that she felt so helpless. "Why do we live like caged animals in our own land?"

"The enemy usually lay in ambush on the farm for these brave women to pass; sometimes, they are accompanied by their husbands. Then like hawks the Oburoni traders emerged from behind the bushes swooping and snatching their victims quickly with the speed of lightening," Voko said in disgust, "Why are they so heartless and so thirsty for blood and money?"

"These mothers face several horrible dilemmas with every passing day----risk the trip to the farm to get some food for their children, or watch these children starve to death---and many usually chose to risk their lives to save their children from starvation rather than sit down idly and watch them grow so lean that they looked like ghost-like skeletons."

The pain and suffering of the African people had taken a deadly toll on the entire land. When Agbaka, the drummer and town crier, wanted to check his traps on the outskirts of his village, he fell into the slave trader's dragnet. This was something he'd done every morning for the last twenty years. But on that fateful morning, unknown to him, the slave traders were lurking in the woods, waiting like lions, hidden not far from his house.

What happened that morning shocked his wife, who had sensed the danger and warned him not to venture out that morning? But he defied his wife and went out, because of what his wife called his sweet throat, his love of big chunks of meat at every meal, so he refused to listen to his wife. So, he took his powerless gun and went to the outskirts of the village to check his traps, but he got the greatest surprise of his life. He did not get very far when fifteen heavily-armed men pointed their rifles at him and after a brief hectic struggle; they chained and marched him away to the Slave Coast.

The search party later concluded that Agbaka struggled with the attackers and fought like a true soldier. He shot and killed two of his attackers, but in the end, the old warrior was no match for the thirteen heavily armed slave traders. When it was all over, Agbaka took the life of a few of the traders, but he'd lost his freedom, and he made his children fatherless. His wife had to remarry or play both roles for her children.

His hunting clothes, which he'd dyed deep brown a month earlier, and memories of how angrily and hurriedly he left for the woods that fateful morning remained with his wife and the children. She remembered she tried to stop him from venturing out that morning, but he used his big arms to push her out of the way, so he could go into the woods, And being a very muscular warrior, he pushed her easily out of the way, even to the ground, hurting her knee before he rushed away. But all she could do as a wife was to cry out and plead with his husband to stay with his children on that cold and fateful Harmattan morning. "You don't have to leap into the jaws of danger or dash into the forest anytime we have problems at home. What did I do this time around to make you run into the woods?"

"It is your big mouth, I hate the way you run your mouth," he repeated angrily. "A wife must stop talking and listen to the husband just for once."

"You know if anything happens to you I can't raise these children by myself. Please don't go into the woods. Whatever made you angry this morning, I would make sure that won't happen again. I will keep quiet from now onwards, if that is what it will take to keep you from leaping into the jaws of these Oburoni lions."

This exchange played in her mind for months. But it was too late. She remembered how he slammed the door angrily; still complaining about her like he always did as he disappeared into the nearby woods, still boiling with anger. And so his wife's behavior sent him into the forest looking for inner peace---he found danger and lost his freedom.

They just had their last fight in their long bittersweet marriage.

Though he'd always bragged about how he knew the land better than the "Oburoni locusts" and how they could never abduct him, he was paralyzed with fear when the reality knocked at his door. He found himself staring down the barrels of a dozen Danish rifles. He didn't want to be shot, so he had to give in. He didn't believe a warrior who had given several sacrifices to the ancestors, and poured libation on the ground to the gods, could be so easily captured and taken away in chains from his wife, children and from his motherland.

His wife's lasting memories of him were his big muscles, the sounds of his wooden sandals hitting the ground and him leaving. She also remembered his big brown hunting bag, which had a hole on one side. She remembered his deep voice saying, "If I don't go to the woods, do you want our children to eat stones? I will be back very soon."

But the vultures circled the forests and feasted on the corpses of the fallen youths, brave mothers, devoted fathers, whose corpses were scattered in the valleys, on the hills and along the shoreline. The members of the search party buried many of these victims, but the horrible scenes of death overwhelmed the younger members. Many of them broke down in tears, especially when they found broken guns or sandals or rings that once belonged to the victims, items that had been intentionally left for the search party. Some members of the party nearly took their own lives; the horror was too much for them.

It rained in torrents drenching the remains of the deceased; this was such a gloomy and horrible sight. The putrid smell of decaying corpses did not make matters any easier. Some of these men fought as hard as they could, but they were subdued, and gunned down in cold blood.

The death of the victims sent the village into deep mourning, a very sad period for the inhabitants; some of the bereaved never really recovered. The women cried because their world had been turned upside down. The men fired guns into the air to remember their friends and the village heroes that they had lost in the struggle to defend the motherland.

The news of Agbaka's disappearance hit the village like a thunderbolt. Many people took his loss very hard. Apart from his jovial demeanor, he was the best drummer the kingdom ever had. He was like the human storage of all the traditions in the land. He knew all the songs, sounds and drumbeats. He could also play "gabada," "borborbor" "komkomba," "Odoom" and the most sacred of all, the "adabatram" war drums, the drumbeat that only men who had killed and prevailed in battle against their enemies were allowed to dance to.

The saddest part of it all was that he'd just started teaching his son, who'd turned twelve, some drumming skills when he disappeared. But with the master-teacher gone, the teaching of this young man would never be completed. Some of these skills would not live on. They would be lost forever. It was sad that the next generation would never get to use these skills or pass them on to their children.

He was a stocky man and partially blind in his left eye. His hands were huge and his arms were very strong, perhaps this came from several years of drumming and farming the land. His legs were big and he had the biggest calf in the kingdom. Many of the people remembered the way he carried himself, the unique way he bent his neck sideways whenever he got excited on the drums. He usually nodded his head, jumped up to the rhythm and beat the drums louder. They remembered how he modulated the beat and made the rhythm rose and fell like a cascade of ocean waves. He kept the women twisting, turning and vibrating their behinds as if they were in Harmattan heat. He was a man who'd endeared himself to everyone in the village. The women could never forget his theatrics, how he stopped the drum briefly, and when they started to go to their seats, then Agbaka would resume playing the beat, playing it even louder, and with a much more dramatic and enticing rhythm than before. Then the women usually glanced at one another's faces and then they would all spring back up to their feet, get back to the dancing floor together, laughing, giggling and dancing at the same time.

He was such a great human being and a lovely character.

His sudden and untimely departure had left a gaping hole in the cultural quilt of this ancient kingdom. The drums would never be the same again and the atmosphere would also never be as dramatic as when he was on the drums. They would miss his warmth and vivacious personality.

Such was the story of many of the men and women who had ventured into the woods outside their villages and towns. They never returned to their homes and they never saw their families again. They'd been seized, shackled hauled away, crushed under the wheels of history. They'd also been swallowed into the nothingness of irreverent time. They'd become the latest victims among the millions of victims that came to only belong to the ages.

These were people who'd tried to earn a living, to work on their farms or to get some food to feed their children, but because of the greed of a bunch of predatory aliens, they'd become the latest victims of the Oburoni onslaught on this pristine land---in a struggle between vice and innocence---vice prevailed.

Millions of women cried for the return of their children and many wives mourned the seizure of their husbands, but the tears never stopped the enemy from this sinful trade. They could never understand why the gods had allowed this misfortune to befall them. Their children simply learned that their fathers went hunting and the slave traders caught them. So they would never see them again.

This was because the greed in the hearts of the Oburoni slave traders was so huge that it knew no boundaries, and it had no sympathy and no humane feelings for the African victims. These traders wanted the opportunity to make money, the market to sell the Africans for the blood money.

Maybe it was the way the gods had ignored them, or because of the many lives that had been lost, the future looked very bleak for everybody in the kingdom and for the entire continent. Why should these Oburoni missionaries preach love of one's neighbor and then turn around and snatch children who were still suckling breast milk, from the bosom of their mothers and hauled them away as slaves? Why should they crush the brains of little children, splattering their blood all over the land because these innocent infants wanted to suckle milk from their mother's breast?

"Why these god fearing people took the lives of infants to satisfy their greed still amazes me?" The queen mother asked a million times. "Why did they have any mercy or compassion in their hearts?"

Would the gods make these Oburoni traders answer for their crimes against the people and the land some day? Would they finally know as a group what it meant to die in large numbers?

Several mothers and wives, including Agbaka's widow, wiped their bitter tears of sorrow for their loved ones with black calico cloth. For some of them, the tears blinded their eyes more than even the scorching rays of the tropical sun. And for seven months the drums and the flutes continued to air their sad notes, to fill the sad void with their sorrowful beats and grief-stricken notes. The women continued to sing these sad dirges, but these tears did not stop the slave traders from raiding their villages and seizing more youths, starting the ritual of mourning all over again.

"Oh, how could people be so cruel to their fellow human beings on this big earth that we all share?" Mambo, the queen mother, asked. "We live on the same earth, we have the same blood and we breathe the same air, but why should these Oburonis people look down on us and treat us as if we are less than human beings?"

"They think they are better than us, so they treat us any kind of way that they want," the priest told the gathering. "I hope the angry ocean, at this very hour and the gods of the land, "Hogbetsotso" the gods of the Ewe people, the Manche, the gods of the Ga people at Homowo, and the gods of thunder would stop the bloodshed, would seek vengeance on our behalf. The gods would see that these traders meet their Day of Doom soon," the high priest said at the top of his scratchy, whisky voice.

As an African proverb says, "Though a dog can gnaw at bones, it cannot gnaw at rod iron." He knew that the time would come when these uninvited guests would run out of luck, when they could no longer escape the anger of the gods. But until then, the dark clouds of vengeance would continue to gather on the horizon ready to avenge the forty million that had been taken away and the forty million that had been gunned down in cold blood.

"Well, all the talks the "white locusts" did about the kindness of their God and loving one's neighbor as oneself turned out to be nothing more than sugar coated hypocrisy," the king looked at a chapel and laughed briefly. "Obviously, they brought no love to the land and he saw not a shred of love of one's neighbor in what they did either. What they'd brought to the land is raw greed, the single most important passion behind every move they made in our land."

"You are right," Mankrado told the king. "The desire to get rich quickly from the blood money, the urge to return home wealthy have driven these traders to do ruthless and wicked things, unimaginable of any human being. They take many risks; go on dangerous adventures, some of which had turned deadly for them. But they are yet to face the mother of dangers---death itself."

"Watch how the greed in their heart would bring about their downfall. We know they didn't come to the continent to die, but their ruthlessness, their pride and their greed would soon come together like a waterfall and send them downhill into early graves," Mankrado told the elders. "We would bury them inside the Coconut Grove, the burial ground for the unwanted, and the resting place for these greedy alien invaders. They would taste of death in the most horrible manner---it would be slow, lonely and painful."

"They deserve to have the Coconut Grove as their final resting place," Ayeko declared, getting up from her small stool. "They would know how painful death is when they start to die unloved, unsung and unappreciated."

"Of course, many of them declared that they made the trip for the sake of adventure, but once they'd found out how much blood money they could make from the slave trade, they forgot about the adventure part," Mankrado explained, repeating what Captain Wyndham had already told him. "The glittering color of gold and the tons of money they could make from selling other human beings had been so tempting that it got the best of them involved in this enterprise of shame."

At the height of the trade, Governor Geberg, the most humane of all the governors that ever served in the land, lost his life to the deadly malaria disease. He was a lanky man with a kind heart. He'd dedicated himself to making the Gold Coast a better place for all. The other Oburonis decided to give him a royal burial. And so instead of him being laid to rest in an unmarked grave in the Coconut Grove, he was laid to rest in the courtyard of the Cape Coast castle, which was an ideal location, very breezy and honorable. It was a spot directly overlooking the Atlantic Ocean, a fitting graveyard for this kind-hearted man. He rests there even today, basking in the sunshine and soaking in the gentle breeze of the mighty ocean. He'd been in the full glare of the governors that followed him, those who either supported or opposed his idea of living and letting the Africans live.

The fallen governor had tried to turn his people's hearts away from the slave trade back to the gold trade, but he failed. From this comfortable resting place, he could hear the banging of the Atlantic Ocean against the shoreline. He could also hear the high-pitched voices of the white seagulls and black crows fighting for food. But, though much more disturbing, he could also hear the gut-wrenching pleas of the thousands of slaves from the filthy dungeons below, from the long spacious warehouse directly beneath the courtyard on which sat the governor's grave.

This governor loved the inhabitants very much. Though he could not stop the notorious trade, he told his wife that whenever he died, she should bury him in the heartland of Africa so he could continue to fight against the slave trade and carry on his dreams of peace. His goodwill, however, collided sharply with the greed in the hearts of his countrymen and women. And so the poor governor lost his crusade, and also lost his life trying to achieve this grand, compassionate goal.

Governor Geberg was so loved by so many people that when he died, beside the Oburoni traders and missionaries from all across the Guinea Coast, the kings and their people from many kingdoms came to the Cape Coast Castle to mourn his loss. Several of the missionaries along the Slave Coast who attended the funeral wept openly. Though the king hated every Oburoni, he'd put his anger aside and came to the castle for the governor's funeral. He even brought gifts and insisted that the governor be buried with the gold nuggets and the unique kente cloth he'd brought as a special symbol of love from the people of the land to the fallen governor.

"Good and kind-hearted people like this governor, men and women with such big hearts, were rare anywhere. So, the pain and suffering for his loss would last many more centuries after his death," the king said at the governor's funeral.

"These aliens had brought disunity among our leaders; they had planted seeds of division among us," the queen mother said, gesturing with her hands wildly. "They use the guns and rum they'd brought to buy the silence of many subordinate chiefs. They'd lured other leaders with dreams of elevation in ranks from sub-chiefs to paramount chiefs or to divisional leaders. These had been done to get them to sell their conscience to them."

"Oh well, finally," Mankrado, the war captain, said grinning. He looked at the Shrine of Dente and swore. "The gods are ready to wipe them off our land, and that time would soon come." Their end is near----no king has ever been this close to driving them off the land before---to send them into their graves," Abrewa, the old lady said, laughing. "I am just lucky to be alive to witness this moment of vengeance."

"These "little soldiers of fortune," ironically speaking, could bring their end about without much bloodshed," Mankrado declared. "Even with their big cannons, the Oburonis would be at the mercy of our "little soldiers." They would buzz into their ears, bite and infect them with the disease, injecting them with the silent malaria parasites."

These "Oburoni locusts" would eventually meet their fate in the most surprising manner. Maybe their ruthlessness would meet the misery of the inhabitants and the latter would win.

"Each slave trader is living on borrowed time from now onwards. When a woman gets pregnant, she would certainly deliver the baby one day. So the time for the gods to deliver on their promise is near," the king told the elders.

Still, he would rather use the asafo soldiers to defeat the enemy, if he had the weapons. But the air was filled with expectation. They would soon watch these Oburoni locusts meet their fate.

"Since they'd sown evil, they must certainly reap evil," Abrewa told the king and the elders, as she bit into a big chunk of yam from a black earthenware pot. "The servants at the castle would bury them without any tears, drums or mourning. I can't wait for them to meet their maker and pay for their crimes against our people."

Two

THE KING KNEW THE NEW governor would not be like the one that just died, kind, considerate and respectful of everybody. And so the elders chuckled when they heard that the new governor that replaced the dead one had arrived. His first actions left no doubt in anybody's mind that he was going to look down on the king, and on the African people. He condemned the gods of the land---the very center of their being---the spirit of their life. "Your gods are useless and you must throw them away. Every leader, king or chief must break into pieces the idols they worship as gods," the governor demanded from every leader.

"Leave this fool alone, the gods would soon teach him a lesson he would never forget," the queen mother said as she arranged her gold bracelets around her arms in seven neat rows and sent an evil curse in the governor's direction. Then she broke into a loud laughter, coughing uncontrollably in between. "There is no doubt in my mind that these Oburonis locusts are hypocrites; they practice none of the things they teach their converts to follow."

"Well, they are very passionate about slaves and blood money," Zotor told the elders. "They don't care how they get the slaves, fair or foul."

The governor even made bolder demands of these leaders.

"He told us to forget about Dente, the god of gods, and leave our youths unprotected," the king revealed to the people. "He also asked us to stop pouring libation to the gods and end sacrifices to the ancestors."

"When he asked us to stop honoring our ancestors, he'd lost his mind completely, because he'd made a pact with the devil. How can we forget about our ancestors? How does he know they have nothing to do with our present and future lives? This is completely wrong, from what we know from the ages," the high priest said, playing with a huge amulet around his neck and balancing seven talismans on his broad chest.

The worst was when the governor asked the king to release all the Oburoni prisoners he'd kept in his basement for seven years. Still, as annoying as this demand was, it was still not as ridiculous as the next one. When he asked the king to allow him to sit on the golden stool, making himself the king of the land, at that time he'd crossed all boundaries of reason. He also violated the royal authority of the leaders in the kingdom. By that he'd also committed the ultimate treason against the kingdom and so the king must pay back his outrageous demands with the same disrespect. He must meet his foolishness with a curse and fire.

The inhabitants fought back anytime the governor brought up these silly ideas. They also vowed to retaliate against him if he tried to kill the king or tried to seize the golden stool. The king blocked the trade routes and shut down the wicked trade completely because the governor tried to send his forces to crush his soldiers.

A week after the king's declarations, the governor rode through the land with a platoon of soldiers and arrogantly tried to force the king and the elders to do his biddings. The king refused to release all the Oburoni prisoners that he'd kept in his basement for years, and when the governor called a garrison from the Cape Coast Castle and tried to seize the golden stool and the ivory crown of the queen mother, the king got his soldiers together and declared war on the Oburoni enemy.

The governor ordered his soldiers to invade the king's palace and empty the royal treasure, looting tons of golden ornaments and valuables, torching the king's palace. All these made the king extremely angry. Fortunately for the king, however, three days before the governor's arrival, the stool father, who was the supreme kingmaker in the kingdom, hid the golden stool inside the nearby forest, denying the governor the opportunity to sit on the golden stool, preventing him from claiming the symbol of supreme power in the land. The Obruafuo executioners hated the governor's ridiculous demands and recalled when they'd executed two chiefs who tried to steal the golden stool.

As the saying goes, "two kings could not rule in one kingdom," so he made sure the governor did not sit on the golden stool. He closed the trade routes for the rest of the governor's tenure in the land. That led to the trade through the land quickly drying out, leaving the governor frustrated, restless and angry. His sponsors reacted callously to his indiscreet foolhardiness.

Meanwhile, the king assembled a coalition of forces to confront the governor's forces. Soldiers of all ages turned up ready to fight for their motherland. Whether they had the weapons capable of winning a war against a trained Oburoni enemy or not, that was another matter. Some of them just wanted to go to war. Others wanted to fight for honor, even if it meant the very last one of them losing his life. They knew they would have died fighting for honor---defending their motherland.

The king loved the solidarity from most of his subordinate chiefs— so loyal, so devoted and so patriotic---they were the foot soldiers in the struggle against these shameless aliens. But since he did not have the weapons to defeat the enemy, a few of the chiefs sold out to the enemy by doing what he vowed not to do---exchanging prisoners of war for guns.

The king admired how Goro Kwame, a platoon leader, who joined the coalition with twenty of his children ready to fight for their birthright, showed his love for the motherland. His oldest son was forty and the youngest was fifteen, and he also had his seven brothers and twenty cousins willing to fight the enemy. Goro Kwame, a war veteran himself, knew the war uniforms of soldiers and the sweet-sounding drums usually enticed young warriors to join the military, but when the war actually began, with blood flowing everywhere, bullets flying in all directions, the excitement quickly turned into regrets and second thoughts. So he was secretly hoping that the governor wouldn't bring another war to the land. He wasn't ready to lose an entire generation of relatives, and he definitely didn't want to see any of his children abducted and taken as a prisoner during the war.

The king breathed a sigh of relief when the governor decided to back down on some of his offensive demands. The governor did not want to irritate his home government or double cross the Royal Trading Company, the sponsors of the slave trade because he owed his position as governor and owed even his very life to them. If the trade slowed down to a complete halt, he would have to lose everything too. And so, he had no choice but to call off this war.

The king thanked Captain Wyndham for the advice he gave him; it turned out to be a reliable advice. Any time he closed the trade routes for long periods of time, the governor shook in his boots. He'd always backed down from going to war every time he closed the trade routes.

"If these young men could not whisper sweet words into the years of these young women in the village square, how were they going to have children to fill the shoes of our fallen heroes?" the queen mother asked. "How is the next generation going to survive?"

"We just have to arrange their marriages, pair them together because we need them to have these children," Abrewa said. "When we were growing up, we used to enjoy a lot of fun. But they'd denied our children even the simplest of pleasures."

"I remember how the young men and women used to dance into the night and ended up in their lover's arms until dawn the next day," the queen mother told her. "But all these have come to a stop, sad to say, because of the alien invaders."

In their anger, the youth formed armed guards to frustrate the Oburoni enemy, to ambush and kill them from behind the elephant grasses. They set traps to catch them and some of them even dug holes to trap them.

Zotor, the high priest, who took the sad state of the kingdom and the insecurity of the people to heart, went to the ancestors for help. For seven days, he slept at the shrine to plead for help from the gods. He sacrificed roosters and rams to appease them.

When he told him that the verdict of the gods finally favored them, the king smiled broadly, chewed his kola nuts and spat the bitter yellow juice happily---it was the beginning of the era of the final vengeance---jubilation time for them, and death to the enemy.

"The gods had heard the cries of their children; they'd seen our desperation and had felt our pain," Zotor told the king and the elders. "They have finally decided to help us defeat these unwanted aliens, to send them back to where they'd come from, bringing an end to this wicked trade in the land, killing off these stubborn locusts."

And so they waited anxiously for the secret vengeance to come to pass.

As for the queen mother, who was filled with the sap of life and the spirit of the ancestors, the whole thing was like a wild dream to her. It was marvelous that the ancestors had finally decided to come to their aid---something the king and the elders had always dreamed of. Though she grew up in the royal family, had served several gods, the queen mother still did not fully believe that these gods would free them from the enemy.

Meanwhile, King Zendo sent Captain Wyndham to calm down the governor's anger, to ask him not to start another bloody war over the trade routes. He was just bidding for time to get his secret weapon into action.

The secret weapon, the king's "little soldiers," remained shrouded in mystery, though the plot was almost ready to unfold. The young men stayed busy digging the dark clay, and the old women worked around the clock molding the clay pots. Another group of women fired these pots to make them stronger so they could hold water and the weapons of vengeance. Then fifteen-year-old girls carried the finished pots on top of their heads to the lagoon for the soldiers to cultivate them with the secret weapon.

When Batuka, the king's brother, the biggest arch-rival of the king, showed up at the lagoon with his friends, the Asafo soldiers quickly sent them away. The war captain simply asked a young man to insult them, and once they responded and a fight broke out, the soldiers quickly separated the fighters and escorted these unwanted traitors out of the project site and asked them never to return. This project was a race against time; and it was promising, if only they could keep it from the ears of the Oburoni governor.

"This is the best chance we have ever had," Mankrado told the workers. "Let us not stab ourselves once more in the back. You must never mention the contents of the pots and what they were intended for to any of these rum-drinking slave raiders. You know they would go to the governor and quickly betray us."

"We can't let them disrupt this plot. We cannot allow Batuka and his supporters to continue to take their differences with King Zendo on the whole kingdom," Mankrado assured the soldiers, scratching his head repeatedly. "We must send these traitors to the fifth river landing if we caught them. Since their friends have no conscience, they would be glad to buy and ship them out to the land beyond the blue ocean. When it comes to blood money, these Oburonis did not have a shred of conscience."

"You are not telling a lie," a young soldier remarked. "These Oburonis would buy their own mothers if it would bring them some blood money. Have you forgotten what they did to Bruku, the half-breed son of Mr. McSwain? He was seized and shipped off as a slave." Bruku had exchanged some slaves for guns, but when he stole the Oburoni trader's gunpowder behind his back, the trader seized, shackled and shipped him off into slavery for double-crossing him."

Don Pedro had also sold some of his "kosinor" female companions as slaves, after he had assured them that he would treat them fairly and kindly. He had about seven of them scattered along the coast. These were very beautiful middle-aged women who had once been married to Dente, the god of gods for the mandatory seven year period.

"Who wants to marry a "Kosinor" lady anyway?" Fakpi asked. "These unique women come with a lot of baggage."

"Well, the Oburonis don't mind, so they take some of these women as concubines and loved to make love to them," Bata told him.

The king did not mind that the Oburonis took advantage of these women, but he made some of them his spies. He asked them to get weapons from their friends for his soldiers and they must also report any intelligence they'd picked up from the castle to the queen mother and to the elders. Since these were some well-disciplined women, the Oburoni traders enjoyed their companionship and they did all they could to help them.

Don Pedro seized three of these Kosinor women, and forced them into the Liberty Express, shipping them out of the land. She told them they were to go on a secret romantic get together. These women just wanted to travel to an exotic place and did not want to go into slavery. But little did they know that Don Pedro was actually selling them into slavery.

It was too late when they found out what he was really doing.

"You have lied to us," Azinor told him angrily, scratching his face with her nails, leaving sharp marks on his face. Though she showed him her protruding stomach; because, she was carrying his baby, it did not make any difference to him. "You know I am carrying your baby, so why did you lie to me? Why did you sell us?"

"I knew you were pregnant, and I didn't want to leave you at the castle while I travel to do business," Don Pedro told her without feeling any remorse for what he'd done to her. "Sorry, we had to secure you in the slave cabin because my colleagues don't trust you on this boat. They think you could free your country men and women in the night and turn them against us."

"Well, that is their problem. But didn't I tell you that I want my children to be born free, never to become slaves?"

The king had declared Don Pedro the most wanted trader in the land and he'd placed seven pots of gold on his head for what he'd done to these women, for desecrating the shrine of Dente and for his notoriety as the leading slave trader in the land. "Bring him in dead or alive and collect pots of gold as ransom money," the king told the asafo soldiers.

"Tell Don Pedro that if he doesn't return Dente's three Kosinor women he'd taken from us, this god would strike him down," Zotor, the high priest told Captain Wyndham to give him that message.

But when he found him six months later, Don Pedro did not have the women to deliver to the king and the elders. He sent them off to the land of no return. He'd sold his lovers, women who had placed their trusts in him.

The high priest was angry with him---in fact, he was furious. Whatever excuses Don Pedro had for stealing these sacred women, though he made up many excuses, the high priest asked Xebioso, the god of thunder, to strike him down for desecrating Dente.

The people expected the god of thunder to destroy him instantly, but he surprisingly lived for a few more years. Why he still lived and did not die immediately remained a mystery to the people. But from that time onwards, they knew that he was living on borrowed time.

"Don Pedro said that he'd shipped the three women out of the land on the Eastern Trading Company vessel, and there was no way he could bring them back to the Gold Coast," Captain Wyndham told the high priest. "There was no chance of him ever bringing these women back home."

Upon hearing this, the high priest got very angry. "If a pregnant woman slips and falls, the baby in the womb is the first to scream. So tell this man that he'd stolen Dente's former wives and if Dente does not kill him soon, Xebioso, the god of thunder will finish him off. He will soon hear a loud thunderbolt."

"Two kings do not rule in one kingdom," the king mused. "So, either the governor stops his foolish demands or I die defending the golden stool, which contains the spirit of my people."

"Everyone must treat the weapon as the kind of secret one carries into the grave," Zotor, the priest, sternly warned everybody. "This is our only chance to become free in our own land once again."

No one, not even the king's wives, were allowed to break this code of secrecy. Even the gods did not allow the king or queen mother to divulge the secret weapon to the few friends they'd among the missionaries, regardless of how many guns and ammunition they'd supplied them in the past. No one could talk about it, not even the queen mother could reveal it to her dear missionary male friend.

The king barred the queen mother---the diplomatic genius---from visiting her friends at the castle for security reasons. But being a strong lady, she went on the offensive against her detractors and even against the king. She was lucky the king only gave her a stern warning to comply with the decree or face the consequences. Even though she'd done so much to help the kingdom and she'd brought tons of weapons into the kingdom, the king never like her pigheaded temperament. He threatened to banish her from the kingdom for seven years if she leaked the information to the enemy.

The queen mother's pride was hurt. She did not believe what had happened. So she went before the elders to plead her case. She felt she deserved better treatment than the distrust she'd received from the king.

"It is wise to stop you from going to the castle just as I have asked of everybody else. We don't want to impose the death sentence on you or banish you from the kingdom later, in case you give in to the temptation to give away this piece of information," the king told her in a solemn tone. "This is to save you from more drastic punishment down the road."

"I have never betrayed anybody, nor have I ever revealed any state secret to any of my friends," she told the king in a passionate voice, looking serious and speaking from her heart. She was without her usual smiles. "In spite of the gossips and suspicions, I have always put the kingdom above my personal interests, so I deserve more respect than what you have all given me."

"You know the saying that "small wounds are better than bigger ones, which always develop later on," the king told her. "And so I advise you to accept my decision, because in the long run, this is better for your own good."

Though it hurt her deeply to hear the king that she'd served faithfully for more than ten years, threatened to banish her from a land she loved so dearly, she knew this was not the time to test the king's patience or question his resolve.

Some of the women viewed her as morally weak and someone who had slept with the enemy. And the men saw her as a suspect, a potential traitor, and a danger to the state. "It didn't matter how well you'd served in the past, the times demanded extra vigilance from everyone," Elder Landonu told her.

Why her sweet tongue and magical charisma could not lift the aura of suspicion off her baffled the elders. She had to remind the king more than three times about the weapons she'd brought for the soldiers to use to fight the enemy.

"You have been very ungrateful and unfair to me," she told Zotor and seven elders. She was obviously frustrated. "But for all the guns I'd brought into the kingdom, tell me how could we have survived? Where would the kingdom be today?"

"Sit down and have a drink with us," the war captain told her in a pleasant voice. "Why do you think we have forgotten so soon about all the guns you brought into the kingdom? Do you know how many times we'd sung your praises?"

"Many women are saying that I am a common prostitute who slept with the enemy, so everyone is treating me like a traitor," she told him playing with the beads around her arm. "I am none of these. I am a proud queen mother with excellent skills to get things done."

"We still remember your good deeds, but when it comes to matters of war and peace, the king is the only one who makes these decisions."

"Then, next time tell him to go and get his own weapons for the troops," she told the war captain angrily, looking even prettier as she angrily brushed aside the calabash of sweet palm-wine the young virgin girl had brought to her. "What sort of queen mother am I if I can not keep this top secret from the enemy?"

"It is because you have love relations with that captain of yours," Zotor replied sharply. "Your heart might control you better than your head."

"It didn't matter what sort of relationship I have with these Oburoni traders, you ought to trust that I know not to do that against my fatherland," she said.

"Many people have misunderstood you, so we have to apologize to you," Mankrado told her, nodding his head repeatedly.

"Well, the future will tell if what the others are thinking about me is right or not."

"You sound very discouraged and angry," he pointed out to her.

"Yes, I am. Maybe the state has no more use for my services and that is why everyone is treating me like a traitor," she told him. "Remember the saying that yesterday's porridge is left for the dog, so when the next battle arrives, don't come to me. You must go and get your own weapons."

"Oh well, here comes the dark clouds of trouble again," Mankrado told her. "The enemy has begun to sow clouds of confusion among us."

"Well, this war is within days, judging from the king's angry war of words with the governor," she told him. "How would you feel if you were in my shoes?"

The king saw the two talking and knew what it was all about. So he came to make peace with his old ally.

"Mankrado, can you explain to our lovely queen mother why this weapon is such a sensitive matter," the king asked of the war captain. "Make sure she understands that we appreciate all she'd done for the kingdom in the past. But this is a new direction we are heading now, so she must work with us until we have seen what this weapon can do."

"It better be successful, because if it doesn't I am no longer risking my life to save the kingdom," she declared boldly. She had swallowed her pride and decided to resign to her fate. "They will certainly put the chains on all of us and drag us into "aboyome, to the land of no return."

The king grimaced and gnashed his teeth angrily. "Just wait on us for a while, maybe for a month or two. I know what you are feeling inside, but you must be patient. Everything would fall in place very soon and we shall all drink and make merry later on."

The queen mother, however, in spite of her anger, asked the women to stand firmly behind the soldiers, to keep the weapon a top secret, though many of them were still mourning the abduction of their loved ones. Many were also suffering from the devastation the enemy had left behind---the tragedies in their families---lost of sons, daughters, husbands and mothers, all over the kingdom. "We must find the strength to overcome our sorrows and continue to live our daily lives," she told them after she'd gathered the women who had recently lost their youths or their husbands to the enemy and encouraged them to continue to hold on until the gods avenge the death of their loved ones.

"Our recent victories show that the gods have heard our cry. Dente has finally decided to shed the blood of the enemy instead of the blood of our children," the king said. "I can see the rising sun in the blue sky."

"I have never personally experienced this pain of loss," the queen mother told Abrewa frankly. "Because I never had any children of my own, but I have seen the tears on the faces and the raw pain many of these women felt."

"Well, you were once married to Dente, the god of all the gods, so we know that you could not have any children except for this god. And then no man would give you any after you got out of the shrine," Ayeko said. "So do not continue to worry about being childless, not unless you slept and got one with an Oburoni."

"No matter how beautiful a woman is, she would always lack something if she died without having children of her own. You can borrow another woman's child, but that would never fill the void of motherhood in your life, which is certainly the sacred role of every woman," she said with her emotions running very high.

"Well, you still have time to have children," she told her.

"Well, I better hurry up, because I don't want the soldiers to bury me with "nyakpekpe, the forbidden fruit next to me in my coffin."

"Hold your tears. We know your story already," Abrewa told her. "I think you are better off than those of us who have had many children and have to watch the Oburoni enemy snatched and hauled them away in the millions into captivity."

"Well, I blame Dente for denying me the sacred experience of motherhood, for stealing this joy from me. Maybe that is why I work so hard to protect the future of other people's children," she explained fervently to the women. "That is why I use my charms to get the guns to stop the youth from ending up in slavery."

"Well, whatever pushes you to do what you do; we admire you for it; you have done such a great job. You don't hear it very often, but many of us sing your praises behind your back, because we appreciate how much you've done to help us, especially your efforts to save our children."

"Some of these women have refused to remove their mourning clothes. They've kept them on for several funerals. They don't remove them anymore, because we go to funerals almost every day," the queen mother told Mankrado, who had arrived with some rumor about the plot leaking out.

"Why are they so deeply buried in grief?" he asked her.

"In fact, they go to the riverside in their mourning clothes, they cook in them, they eat in them and some even sleep in them. They say they know the next funeral is just a few hours away."

"I regret to have lived so long to see all these losses, to feel all these sorrow and to see all the bloodshed in the land," Abrewa told them.

"Oh well, what else can we do?" Zotor mumbled. "There'd been too much sorrow and pain in the land because the Oburoni had turned our land upside down looking for blood money."

"How I wish I had died early like my friends did. They died in their sixties like most of their friends. It would have spared me the pain and suffering, all the foul smell of death, and the devastation that the Oburoni had left behind everywhere in the kingdom."

"There is so much sadness in this land?" Mankrado mumbled.

"You know long life is not supposed to be a punishment, but rather a blessing from the gods," Abrewa told him. Cold tears continued to streak down her cheeks in torrents as she looked into the depressing eyes of the other mothers. "If we drive them out of our land, the joy of motherhood will return to them just as plants return to life in the rainy season."

"That is taking it to extremes, don't you think so?" the queen mother asked her jokingly. "Though the times are rough, we cannot stay buried in our grief forever. Life must continue, whether we like it or not. Those who'd been trying to harm themselves must know that no one should prefer death to life, not even when the Oburonis are swallowing our children like pythons."

"How can we be happy when tomorrow is not promised to us? Our fate is always in the balance, with the enemy in control of our lives every minute of the day?" Ayeko asked her. She started to chew her bare gums repeatedly, expressing her disgust and anxiety over the future.

"Well, we have a brand new sun, a brand new day. We are all happy that we have lived to witness this day," she tried to comfort her. "Don't you think that is reason enough for you to smile and be happy that you are still alive and not dead or enslaved?"

"This is easy for you to say, because you have never been a wife who had lost a husband or a mother who had lost a daughter or a son to the slave traders," she told her sharply, gnashing her gums. "The losses that some of these women suffered, the hurt these mothers felt had been so deep that words could never fully express the depth of their sorrows. For as long as they live, it is true nothing can ever soothe their pain."

Mankrado paused briefly before he spoke to her again. He admired her strength of character and her services to the kingdom. "You have got so used to your friend's honey in the castle that we were afraid you might sell us out for love." He laughed jokingly. "Maybe you simply put up a front, but you actually don't love him very much."

"Here you are. You are carrying one of the weapons I'd brought into the kingdom," she told him. Mankrado fastened this Danish rifle around his shoulders as he inspected the nozzle of the gun and nodded his head thrice. And they both laughed for a brief moment.

"We are testing your patience. What could we do without your help, without all the weapons you brought to our soldiers?"

"Some of the women are jealous of me because of my looks, but many are jealous because I am their queen mother and they are naturally jealous of me because of my position," she revealed to him. "Do I have to stop working for the king as his spy in the castle, and stop getting these weapons because of what these women say about me and the way they treat me?"

"Don't be so sensitive?" he told her bluntly. "You are the most dependable source of weapons we've had for decades. Without you, we might all have ended up in the land of no return as slaves years ago. So think twice before your anger gets the best of you. Remember the ancestors are watching us."

"Coming from you, I take it as a compliment," she said smiling broadly. "I have decided to continue to save the children for as long as I can."

The stage was set for the drama of vengeance to unfold.

The king---the hero king who had brought high expectations to everyone at the time he was installed, but had begun to turn into a disappointment for many people---a weak monarch---a concern for many of his supporters had started to turn things around. The recent turn of affairs----the intervention of the ancestors made him extremely happy.

"Who would blame him for drinking gourds of palm wine, or for eating double portions of grass cuter meat, or for spending a lot of time with his wives celebrating his good fortune, basking in the good news?" Mankrado asked.

Kaniwa, the king's special wife, whose shoulders many of the women who had lost their children usually cried on, was happy for her husband. She remembered the moments of secret plots to unseat her husband, and so her cheeks were filled with uncontrolled tears of joy for him. Her husband had finally got the helping hand that he needed----the ancestors and the gods---had decided to crush the Oburoni invaders once and for all.

The women started singing and dancing around the palace. They'd started singing her husband's praises and they did so for many days. Though many mothers were still grieving, they found some time to celebrate the good news. They drank and poured libation on the ground, though women were not even allowed or encouraged to pour drinks as libation to the gods. They were so happy that they had to thank the gods their own way.

Many of the women also decided to get pregnant again. Obviously, they were no longer afraid of losing their sons and daughters to the slave traders when they became youths, from thirteen to thirty-five years of age.

"Who wants to feel that pain again?" Kaniwa asked.

"Death to the looters, and we wish sickness on the abductors. I hope they know that they would soon end up in shallow graves inside the Coconut Grove---their final resting place," Abrewa murmured to the elders.

"We would have to burn the bodies of some of these traders for the harm they'd caused us," Zotor threatened. "If we don't burn their bodies, they might return to torment our children again."

"Well, for all the horrible things these greedy locusts had done to us, the gods would stand behind us if we burn their bodies," Abrewa repeated a dozen times on behalf of the women.

The war captain asked the women to make more of the herbal mixture, the antidote to the disease. Then he reminded everybody once again that it was another top secret in the kingdom. The elders knew that the secret weapon would only work against the enemy if they denied them the antidote against the disease. So the soldiers prepared these herbal mixtures in a large quantity and sent it to every household in small pots. The king asked the heads of these households to hide them in their inner rooms and told them that their lives depended on it.

Meanwhile, the children continued to starve; the women could still not go to the riverside to wash their clothes or to fetch drinking water without armed guards. The men could also not go hunting without the fear of being caught, chained and sold. They had very little peace of mind in the kingdom.

Nobody thought more people would die and many more marks would go up the wall of shame when King Zendo became king, but many more marks went up on this infamous Wall of Sorrow. The elders also had to plant more trees for the dearly departed victims more than ever before.

"Why did the gods allow this to happen?" Voko another elder took a deep breath as he pondered over what had happened to his motherland.

"We suffer these losses year after year," the queen mother said, almost choking with grief. "It was after the planting and harvesting season that the griot puts more marks on the wall of shame, the last ritual for those who'd departed the land, for our relatives and friends. This wall had the names of all the youths who had been lost or murdered in cold blood. The griot would continue to put these marks on these walls until the king drives these "Oburoni locusts" out of our motherland. That is the least we can do to keep their memory alive."

Batuka became a disgraced man in the land. He never came to terms with the kingmakers putting his brother on the golden stool as the new king instead of him. He also resented the fact that they'd bypassed him for his own blood brother. But his fate had been sealed even before his quest for power began twenty-five years ago.

But as one of the elders told him, "sitting on a golden stool does not make you a great king, and so if you want to be a great king, you must create your own ripples, you must work for your own achievements. You could not live off what your father did as king, how he'd brought several paramount chiefs into the kingdom and had expanded the kingdom to areas where it took days to reach the boundaries. You must drive these unwanted locusts out of our land."

So King Zendo knew that he would have to rid the land of the enemy to earn the respect of his subjects. And he could not do so by merely sitting on the stool and judging disputes among his subjects. He must show some progress starting from where his father and grandfather left off.

The king, therefore, waited anxiously for the rainy season to come to an end, for the right moment to start his drive for greatness. He didn't care any longer about how powerful or how devastating the Oburoni cannons and rifles were. He knew that his people were no longer alone in the fight for the soul of this land. The ancestors and the gods have decided to lift them up and lend a helping hand.

He, therefore, accompanied the war captain for the final visit to the lagoon to make sure that his "little soldiers" were ready for action. After he'd seen hundreds of rows of the "black pots" of vengeance, he was very pleased and had broad smiles on his face. He nodded repeatedly and greeted all the Asafo soldiers and thanked them sincerely for their hard work, but most importantly, he warned them to continue to keep the plot a top secret.

Meanwhile, the crows and seagulls continued to circle the shores, crisscrossing the weapons zone from dawn to dusk. And the waves continued to break on the shoreline next to the lagoon as the king and the elders anxiously waited, bidding for time. The bats came out at night and fought over fruits leftover after the harvest in the banana grove, but none of the Oburonis knew that anything was brewing in those black pots. They had no idea what was buzzing on the far side of the old dirty lagoon, or what was waiting to end their wicked dreams.

"We can never be very sure," the king told the elders. "We need the women to fill more pots just in case we have to help our neighbors and other kingdoms in the land. We don't want to run out of ammunition in the middle of this new battle. It would be wise to keep the pressure on these greedy locusts and keep them slapping their ears as the secret soldiers, buzzed and attacked them, biting their defenseless bodies in the darkness."

The king's demeanor was gleeful when the rains finally ceased. He let out a deep sigh of relief when the moon waned, leaving a pitch dark night, the ideal weather for the soldiers to go out on the offensive against these traders. "I know the loud thunder blast, which came from nowhere and shook the land, was certainly another signal from the ancestors," the king said as he pondered if this was the final signal for the battle for the soul of this unhappy continent.

"I am sure the enemy has just run out of time," Mankrado walked restlessly toward the lagoon.

The king and his soldiers entered the lagoon to do battle against the once powerful enemy, to save the continent from the hordes of unwanted locusts that looted and desecrated the land.

For the first time, instead of the Oburoni cannons blasting against the shoreline, it was the god of thunder that was roaring loudly. And the king rose to his feet, held his staff high on top of his head against the angry waves of the Atlantic Ocean and shouted in a loud baritone voice.

"Let the ancestors open the floodgates of evil for the enemy to die and disappear into emptiness. Do not spare a single enemy soul. Let these "Oburoni locusts" get a taste of their own wickedness," the king shouted in the darkness.

"The moment of justice, the moment of atonement that we had waited for all these years, has finally arrived," Zotor said to the elders softly.

"The traders have two choices. They either flee our land or die slow painful deaths."

"No number of cannons could save them now," Mankrado told the elders sounding very confident that the end of the enemy had come.

Then the old lady said quietly to the elders, "The enemy arrived at night and so they must die at night." She knew the weapon would work well against the "unwanted locusts" perhaps even better than they'd planned. They couldn't wait for everything to return to the way they were before the storm from beyond the blue ocean arrived in the land. .

She brought an old quilt from the attic and spread it on the mahogany table. She showed the queen mother and the rest of the elders the number of generations that had lost innocent lives to the slave traders. And then she began to sow another patch into the quilt, telling the story of another generation. The quilt said more about the tragic history of the land more than the griot could ever do.

From the banks of the lagoon, the soldiers continued to sing their war songs and the women simply hummed the refrain. The old lady had a broad smile on her face because she knew nothing in this world stays the same, and no condition is permanent.

THREE

T HE KING FELT A SECRET joy in his heart as he saw the enemy set a camp in the swamps, and many of them waded in the mud firing their cannon from these marshes. But he told the soldiers not chase them, or ambush them, but let the snakes and crocodiles inside the muddy trenches deal with them.

The high priest thought maybe the gods had sent them into this part of the land for a reason. But he was now convinced that the ancestors were punishing the enemy the same way they did the inhabitants for years.

"It is so marshy and so muddy," Mankrado tried to wade into the muddy marshes, but retreated quickly. "This terrain is not only infested with vermin and serpents, it is also impassable."

"The best part of it is that these Oburoni traders have no idea that they have entered a snake-infested land," the linguist joked hilariously. "Wait till a cobra bites one of them then they will quickly retreat to the castle immediately, scared, confused, and shaking in their boots."

"I can't wait for them to get a taste of their own lesson. Though they are as stubborn as the white hippos, they will soon learn that hippos are also sometimes vulnerable," Mankrado noted, pointing toward some snake skins in the field nearby.

"Well, if the cobras do not bite them, the pythons that had been resting peacefully under the thick brushes, might swallow them up---or wrap around their bodies and squeeze the sap of life out of them. After that nobody would tell them then to leave this sacred ground immediately."

"The greed in them is so powerful that even the, marshes, the flood or the cobras would not slow them down," the high priest teased. "They act as if they are possessed. They are still trying to find different ways to continue the dirty trade they'd brought from home into our land."

There was fear inside many of them in the marshes.

"Our soldiers cannot go after them inside these marshes. So let the gods deal directly with them, forcing them into the path of the pythons, or sending the cobras after them. Even the hard nosed crocodiles might snap their jaws on their feet to get justice for the millions of victims."

Some of the youths the war captain hid under these tall grasses were only fifteen. They were hidden; panting for breath, sweating profusely, and many were wondering what was in store for them in their first encounter. What took place later on stupefied many of them? The fear of being in their first combat overwhelmed some of them and some had to fight the tears because soldiers do not cry, they retaliate. Two of these youths suffered heart attacks, but the rest held their breath as they lay perfectly still for the slave raiders to make their way passed their hiding places.

Muga, one of the youths who was in battle for the first time, passed out on the ground when the invaders came within ten feet of his hideout. The captain had to hold him down with his powerful arms, covering his mouth with both hands very tightly to make sure that he did not give away their hideout place. When the last of the enemy passed, he splashed the gourd of water he carried around his neck into Muga's face and brought him back to life. And then he glared at him like a wounded lion, forcing the youth to keep his silence.

"Sorry, my legs started shaking and I passed out and could not remember anything," Muga told Mankrado, still badly shaken.

"War is not for the faint-hearted. It is brutal and it is for the strong-minded," the captain told Muga, disappointed in him, but he was still supportive of him. "I'd this same fainting spell in my very first battle. But the next battle is always better, trust me."

That day the encounter with the enemy was a very bloody one. The asafo soldiers surprised the enemy. They were fortunate to have the upper hand as they sprang from their hiding places to attack them with deadly precision for a change. They shed the blood of dozens of the enemy and a few of the slave raiders and traitors. The Asafo soldiers killed seventeen raiders and captured another seven before the sun rose that morning.

After the battle, the soldiers buried their dead and scalped their victims with anger. But one of the raiders, who had gotten away from battle, returned and shot at them narrowly, missing Mankrado, the war captain. But Muga, the youthful-first-time warrior, became an instant hero when he shot and killed the Oburoni shooter who wanted to kill Mankrado. They'd lost three men in the fight and six of them had been critically wounded that morning.

After they'd buried the dead, the squad marched the seven captives to the palace to experience the king's brand of justice. The women and children came out to boo these captives, shouting insults at them. Some of the women asked the Obruafuo to decapitate the captives immediately; others, however, wanted the high priest to take them to the shrine of Dente and sacrifice them to the gods.

But it was hard to prevent the women from taking matters into their hands. Some of the women wrapped their undergarments around the faces and necks to desecrate the manhood of the enemy, the best humiliation in the land for men.

But Captain Wyndham suggested to the king to keep the captives and exchange them for weapons later. But, surprisingly, the king, knowing what he knew at the time, refused his suggestion without a second thought. He had something much more effective for the raiders, something much deadlier than any weapon they'd ever used in battle before.

Abrewa, the old lady, described how the Oburoni had forced out of the motherland "uncountable millions" of youths, creating a horrible bloodbath everywhere. "They'd reduced the kingdom into a land of burning houses, rivers of blood, crushed infant skulls, starving families and desperate men and women trying hard to still continue to earn a livelihood amid this chaos and insecurity," she observed.

The land had not known peace for years, so King Zendo's reign had left many of his subjects with nothing but horrible and bitter memories. He'd ruled his subordinate paramount and divisional chiefs, more than one thousand chiefs, sub-chiefs and queen mothers with intricate diplomacy, though he sometimes used iron fist or intrigue. In fact, he learned that the harder his soldiers tried to push these undesirable pests out of the kingdom, the more determined they worked to stay.

When everything else failed and they started to lose ground in the trade, these Oburoni locusts encouraged the king's subordinate chiefs to break away from the grand coalition and betray the king. They divided and conquered the inhabitants, and this was the master plan that they'd brought and used to subdue the leaders.

The secret weapon, which looked promising in the fight against the traders, brought back into his fold some of the king's supporters. He got the attention of some of these deserters when he told them that the weapon was revealed to him in a dream, an experience so real that it was the most puzzling dream he'd ever had. This weapon was a special gift from xebioso, the lightning god, which was not handed to him, but was wrapped and left at the foot of Mountain Afadjato, where Zotor picked it up and later gave it to the king as a gift.

As the saying goes, "The king was looking for the chance to run, and then suddenly someone told him that his mother-in law's goat had jumped the fence." Abrewa teased the king about his excessive palm-wine drinking and his excessive endearment to his wives. "He has been drinking like a camel, dancing for long hours in jubilation, celebrating what looked like an end to more than three hundred years of chaos, bloodshed and horror in the land."

"Will this weapon really defeat the enemy?" the queen mother asked the war captain shaking her head in disbelief. "Why not? We have had these insects in the land since the beginning of time. Why do we think that now is the time for the gods to use them to drive away the enemy?"

The king wasn't the strongest of kings they've ever had. They'd wanted a king who could drive the evil traders away while they hurled their cannons at his forces and burned down his kingdom. But King

Zendo, at first, turned out to be much more patient, very deliberate and extremely cautious in his encounters. But this new game changing weapon stunned his critics and energized his supporters.

"The bite of these "little soldiers" is so deadly that the enemy had no chance of recovery once they get this disease," the king explained to the elders, wrapping some of the tree bark inside some calico broadcloth. "It is like giving them the death sentence. And for many of them, this disease was their greatest fear. It was the same, the way we fear their cannon balls."

"What if they still refused to leave our shores after they'd started dying?" Elder Landonu asked softly, moving his eyebrows repeatedly. "They are so addicted to taking our youths, and like bloodshed so much that many might still refuse to leave."

"That is not true," the king said sharply, he was half joking and half serious. "We know many, if not most of them, love the blood money. This money was like honey to their soul, but they seem to love life more, so they would flee the land hurriedly when they see their friends starting to die like flies and did so in large numbers."

"What if they come up with a cure for the disease?" Elder Landonu asked, skeptical, though deep down him he was convinced that the king had what he needed to get rid of the enemy forever.

"Well the enemy might not value our lives," the king pondered. "But as soon as the disease sends many of them into comas, they would take off running like squirrels, and several of them would depart our motherland and go back to their homes like cowards."

"Do you think their gods would come to their rescue?" Abrewa asked jokingly. "Not when they are stealing, wounding and killing children in their own land in their name."

"Though the love to kill us like flies, they value their own lives," the queen mother told the king in a sarcastic voice, still angry about how the elders had recently snubbed and distrusted her. "Indeed, the fear to die in our land is more than anything else to them. They all want to return home some day to enjoy their fortune."

"Well, let them go and explain their greed and brutality to our people to their maker, I mean all the evil things they'd done against their fellow human beings," the king said in a bitter tone. "For years they'd committed crimes against us that go beyond human decency everywhere."

"Captain Wyndham said that the slave traders wanted to return home rich and live off the money they'd made from selling our people," the queen mother revealed to the king and the elders. "He also told me that the blood money often make them so wealthy back home that it brought them immediate honor."

"And so we do all the bleeding and dying for them to get honor and prestige back home," the king added, irritated. "They have no idea how much pain they inflict on us. From now onwards, they would get nothing from our land but slow and painful death."

The king asked the servants to add more wood to the fire to ward off the insects and warm up their bodies because the chilly Harmattan weather made many people shivering, and so everybody was looking forward to the hot, blazing afternoon sun. "I can't wait for the slow death of Governor Gerb, the one who killed my father in cold blood. I hope to be there when the servants bury him without honor, inside a shallow grave in the Coconut Grove."

"Why does the king stay so drunk these days? Is it because he is worried about the future of his kingdom or what?" Elder Landonu asked in a voice filled with frustration. He had his mahogany pipe stuck between his upper and lower teeth. The women shouted when he sent hales of thick smoke into the dark evening sky. When the aroma of the tobacco and the humid air collided, the smell was like burning leaves----the legendary "bibitama fragrance."

The king became completely defiant. He refused to do whatever the Oburonis asked him to do. Against the governor's threats, he executed seven Oburoni prisoners who tried to escape from his basement.

"Any one who does evil must die an evil death," the king reminded the elders when they were talking about how in their zeal for vengeance some innocent missionaries were also going to die. Except Captain Wyndham, the king did not care much for these double-tongued missionaries. He became suspicious of the missionaries because some of them supported their countrymen who were abducting his subjects. If he could separate the genuine missionaries from the "human lifters," he would save some of them. "The problem was that many of the

Oburonis were missionaries and slave traders at the same time, so how do we separate the two groups, punishing the blood-thirsty ones and saving the good ones?"

"Even if we kill some innocent missionaries, they would have died for all the innocent people their countrymen have killed over the years in our land," Zotor the priest declared. "They've killed more innocent people on our side than we would ever do to them."

"Oh, well, it is just that some of the missionaries tried to stop their people from slaughtering the innocent infants and aged fathers and mothers." The queen mother pleaded.

Mankrado reminded every gun-carrying adult to fight the enemy harder and not to worry about the missionaries. "In war, innocent people die. So let it be with these missionaries, if they die, that is an act of war and their fate had been sealed as well. They have themselves to blame, if they refuse to leave our land as the high priest had advised them to do months ago."

"Well, they should know that nothing in this life is permanent, and if they don't know that fact by now, they would soon find that out the hard way," Abrewa joked. "How many more people are they going to steal and haul away in the name of this evil trade before they finally give it up?"

For months, the soldiers continued to cultivate "the pots of death," and they hid them on the far side of the lagoon, ironically, placed next to the notorious Coconut Grove. Then, as soon as the rains ceased and the dry Harmattan winds started to soothe the land, squeezing the moisture out of the soil, the king welcomed the green leaves turning brown.

It was then that he gave the signal for the mother of all plots to begin to unfold. He ordered the drama of vengeance to wipe out the enemy to start to unfold. This time the victims would be the Oburoni traders and not the African people. The king knew that he would finally end the mass exodus of millions of youths out of the land.

He knew that slave ships such as the "Liberty Express," "the West Pacific Trading Company," the "Queen Isabella" "the Sun Never Sets On the Empire," would be grounded. So many Oburoni traders would have lost their lives that there would be no sailors left to haul any more "black cargoes" out of the continent. The alien sailors would either have died or become too scared to venture into the malaria infested land----inside the land that the missionaries later called "the white man's grave,"

On the banks of the lagoon waited the pots of vengeance?

The king was about to entrench his name in the annals of history. He would become a legend whose name would be on the tongues of every child and on the minds of every man and woman. Every griot in the land, far and near, would talk about his greatness as the king of kings for many years to come.

Mankrado, the war captain, pointed toward the ancestors. He remembered how he'd lost his mother years ago when the poor woman went to the farm to fetch some foodstuff and the Oburoni traders suddenly emerged from nowhere, abducted and shipped her away into slavery. He also remembered clearly what he felt, how angry and sad and helpless he felt. He remembered how he fainted when he heard the tragic news from his uncle and how his father had to pour water into his face to revive and get him back on his feet. His other siblings especially his sister, whose whole world had been turned upside down for the rest of her life, was devastated that fateful morning.

"My life had never been the same since that fateful day," he sighed.

Dodo, Mankrado's mother, was a voodoo priestess and the leading medicine woman in the kingdom. She was of help to many ailing women, especially to those who had female problems and could not have children. Her clients came from far and near and she used herbs to help those women who had difficulty in conceiving babies to have one. She also delivered babies and had cut hundreds of umbilical cords each year. She loved to tell the story about how she got the special gift of herbs from her grandmother, a talented herbalist who'd healed people for more than three decades. The disappearance of this woman from the kingdom with six other women that afternoon left a gaping void in the cultural quilt of the kingdom. It was as if a heavy black drape of darkness had descended on the kingdom, spreading deep sorrow and pain in all the corners.

The women sang dirges for seven days and seven nights for her, and they only stopped when the queen mother pleaded with them to do so. Some of them were filled with so much agony that they walked like zombies for days, making their way from one end of the village to the other senseless, too drenched in grief to think.

"These Oburonis are like chameleons. They talk about loving one's neighbors while the others penetrate our virgin lands abducting our youths, and breaking the hearts of mothers and killing our husbands," the old lady complained. "They have forced our women to mourn for weeks, months and even years, forcing on them songs of sorrow and agony for many bereaved families."

"Well, they'd struck another horrible blow at the heart of the kingdom again. They'd burned down our houses again, the one I have just finished building barely a year ago," the linguist told Mankrado and the queen mother. "But look at what they've done to my house. It took me years to build this house, but they'd burned it down within an hour, leaving behind only smoldering ashes, soot and filth."

"By Dente's mercy," Elder Landonu said sadly. "These traders are heartless and treat us like animals, but they would soon see the vengeance of the gods."

"Well, don't worry. Though the storm clouds have taken years to gather, the rain would finally come down in torrents, creating fear and agony in their camp. The gods have decided to tighten the yoke around their neck. They would hang themselves, and they would die without getting the riches they crave," Mankrado told his soldiers, speaking to them like a prophet of doom.

"As the saying goes, the bird with the longer bill eats faraway insects, so these evil traders would taste of death in the moment of judgment," Abotsi, a tall platoon leader with big arms and a very thick neck, told his soldiers. "We must make sure that they lose their lives here and never to return home with the blood money they'd made from trading in our flesh and blood. And if they look at our children with evil eyes again, let them die lonely and miserable deaths at the hands of the mosquitoes."

"They must never forget the saying that to despise one's equal is to despise oneself, and by killing our people they have invited death on their own heads," the linguist said, looking at the angry ocean. "For abducting and enslaving the heir to the throne, they would die."

Manchi inhaled deeply. He knew within a matter of days, their soldiers would catch the enemy unprepared. The enemy would hear so many buzzing sounds in their ears that they would begin to slap themselves in the frenzy to drive these insects away. But the insects would be tough; they would bite, infect and weaken them. The malaria parasites would invade their brains and other parts of their bodies, because they have no immunity against the disease. They would wonder why they have come down with this dreaded disease in the dry season. They would never suspect that the African people, the victims they had labeled as inferior in brain power but superior in physical power, had figured out a plot too sophisticated for their "superior" brains. They would have bred and released these mosquitoes their way.

The deadly disease would destroy their wonderful world.

What secrets the dry weather had withheld from them would soon come to light for them to see. They would get a taste of the wrath of the ancestors and hear the roar of the angry gods of Africa.

When a long rainbow appeared on the horizon, the queen mother felt that nature wanted to stop the impending storm, or wanted to keep the suspense a little longer. And so it brought a puzzling look on everybody's face. "Is this rainbow good or evil omen for what the king and the elders are about to do?" the queen mother asked probingly. "Is the plot dead or still alive?"

The elders saw more strange omens unfolding before their eyes. They heard the cock in broad daylight, a definite taboo in the land. And when seven rats came out in broad daylight, running through the town square, and they heard the owls hooting in the daytime, the elders became even more convinced that the future was pregnant with death and desperation to the enemy.

A few critics asked the king to call off the plot altogether, but he quickly overruled them. He did not want to lose the only chance he had to kill off the enemy once and for all.

"If a thief steals from you, the dispute must soon be settled," the king demanded.

"Well, the rainy season officially ended," Zotor the high priest announced at the shrine, sending joy into every heart. The women shouted in jubilation and the children clapped their hands during their "ampe" games. For the farmers, it was time to tend to their crops without watching their backs.

The inhabitants watched the Oburoni traders in the evening came out of their three month hibernation to enjoy themselves in the courtyard, drinking rum and eating their favorite bush meat, seated in their lazy chairs and hammocks, with the servants fanning them for hours. Others strolled along the pristine sandy beach dragging their fishing poles along with them fishing and relaxing. Even the missionaries came out in the courtyard bare-chested and their wives wore shorts that exposed their thighs as they sat in their mahogany chairs drinking rum, singing hymns and dancing their hearts out.

The servants knew the traders had finally made the final fatal mistake they'd been expecting from them when they came out half-naked. It was like a gift from the gods to them. The mosquitoes caught so many of them completely off guard, unprepared for these insects in the warm weather.

Whether the warm weather was for them to escape their sorrows, to drink away their guilt or to end their sleepless nights of hibernation, the gods would have to decide their fate that year. Seriously speaking, many of them saw the warm weather as a time to put their homesickness on hold, to suspend their dreams of wealth briefly and to divert themselves by going on adventures, fishing for sharks, octopus, or hunting for leopards in the grassland nearby, or looking for lions in the nearby forests five miles away. It was the best time for leisure, they thought until the king outsmarted them.

In fact, these impressive-looking castles, which were more like palaces rather than strongholds with dungeons that were holding cells for slaves below, angered the inhabitants especially the king. To the African people, these castles were nothing but houses of torture, hallowed tunnels of suffering, and a maze of underground death traps. More than that, they wanted to make these castles places of horror where death was lurking in the hallways and in the infirmary.

So, under the moonless sky, the king's "secret soldiers" went to work on the enemy, unleashing their rage with pitiless retribution. If the cannons forced the king and his elders to run for their lives, these mosquitoes, the king's "secret weapons," caught these traders unprepared and shocked them with the dreaded disease.

These aliens had left themselves vulnerable and the king exploited this weakness. Some of them got so drunk that they slept outdoors in the courtyard. Others could not make it back to their bedrooms upstairs, so the little soldiers feasted on their drunken bodies and infected them with generous doses of the malaria disease. The servants, secretly enjoying the enemy's predicament, shook their heads in dismay, marveling at their foolishness. They enjoyed the fact that as brilliant as they thought they were, they did not see through the king's deadly plot. Only time would tell how many of them had been infected.

On the other hand, the king sat back on his golden stool, clad in his finest royal regalia as he watched his secret plot unfold. He smiled and sat proudly at the head of his dinner table as the enemy began to feel the wrath of these little soldiers. The insects swarmed in the thousands and roamed the courtyard in platoon formations like soldiers of fortune. They flew, buzzed, bit and silently infected the enemy as these traders unsuspectingly continued to gulp down rum and whiskey or ate their favorite bush meat khebab happily. The only signs they noticed were the red bite marks, rashes and severe itches on their bodies.

But somehow a few kind-hearted inhabitants tried to help some of these aliens, especially the kind-hearted missionaries to beat the disease. But their hatred for everything African, their predisposition to label everything from Africa as being inferior, stood between them and their future. It was impossible for these African servants to convince them to drink the local herbal mixture, the cure for the disease. They refused the only known remedy at the time for the malaria disease and so their foolish pride got in the way. They chose death over life because of their foolish pride.

Why did they refuse to drink the mixture that could save their lives? The servants believed that the gods had hardened their hearts to refuse the mixture, leaving them open for the hot claws of death.

The traders were on the receiving end of the horrible nightmare. Their eyes became yellow, several of them were sweating like fish, and their hearts were palpitating like those of race horses.

"Is this the justice from the gods we have been waiting for? Why these "white locusts" have reduced our land into a place of sorrow and pain, only the gods would know," the king told the audience. "They'd turned everything in our land upside down, shattering our way of life, starving our children by imposing this horrible trade on us."

When the king learned that Don Pedro had come down with the disease, he jumped like a bird flying in the sky. He hugged his dear friends and shook hands with the elders because that was what he wanted more than anything else.

"The cobra is finally in trouble," the king joked, teasing him.

The news also sent the soldiers into frantic jubilation. "The greed, the bloodshed, the brutality and the heartbreaks have collided with the efforts of the soldiers to end the notorious trade," Elder Landonu said. Then he tried to put it into perspective. "The python swallows rabbits, but never a porcupine."

The African hospitality was over, the gods had spoken. The message was clear---these unwanted visitors must either depart the land hurriedly and live, or stay behind and die slow and miserable deaths.

"Though these Oburonis were armed with cannons, but as the saying goes, "a dog that gnaws bones cannot gnaw stones," they became extremely vulnerable because they had no defense against this disease," Zotor explained, also alluding to the curse he'd put on them.

In the land, all over this unhappy land, in the forests and across the savanna grassland, the mosquitoes buzzed.

FOUR

T HE NEWS THAT THE KING'S half-brother had betrayed his own brother by selling out to the Oburoni traders sent a shock wave throughout the kingdom. This was a time when the kingdom was at a crossroad in its battle against the enemy. This came at a time when the king had finally got what it would take to defeat the enemy. Now his own brother tried to sabotage his plans. So he wanted his brother to face the wheels of justice, but he had to struggle with the fact that the accused was his own blood brother, and so should he temper justice with mercy?

"If I let the obrafuo execute my brother, I would get many people in the kingdom talking about what a heartless king I am," he told the elders. "If I can punish him without executing him, I will take that road."

"But this old warrior had committed treason against his own motherland, and he must face his crime like a true warrior," Mankrado told the king.

When the platoon leader, who thought the whole story was a hoax or some kind of dreamy nightmare, went to bring him to the king's palace for justice, the accused Batuka, his long time friend from their age regiment days, got the shock of his life. He'd once "eaten fire with" Batuka to protect each other in the rain, in the storm, but mainly in gunfire on the battlefield, so he didn't believe that this same friend who had fought for the kingdom alongside him would commit treason against the same state. He also didn't believe that he was trying to take his own life with a rusty gun that he had not used for years because he couldn't deal with the shame.

"Batuka, what are you thinking? You don't have to kill yourself," Fayati, the platoon leader, pleaded with his old friend, Batuka. It flashed through his mind how he had once saved Batuka's life by shooting an Oburoni trader a split second before he plunged a deadly knife into his heart, after he'd pinned him down. Batuka saw what his friend did and got up and shook his hand and vowed to return the favor. He promised to save his life one day. "Whatever it is, I have saved your life once and I will save it again, but that is if you put down the gun and allow me to help you."

"Fayati, my life is over. We once ate fire to stay alive, but that was long ago. That was when we were young soldiers in our youthful years," he told Fayati. "My only regret in life is that I never got the chance to return this favor to you as I promised."

"Well, we still have time, but if you kill yourself, you will never get the chance to return the favor. But if you stay alive; perhaps, you would save my life one of these days. Who knows what the future holds?" He moved toward him fearlessly and as he approached him closer and closer, Batuka lowered his gun and willingly gave it to him. "I couldn't believe my eyes. This whole thing is like a horrible nightmare for me. Why did it have to come to this, Batuka?"

"Well, it took many things over many years to do what I have done. I couldn't live with the humiliation anymore. So I just decided to take the frustration on my brother." He shook his sweaty hand firmly and hugged him warmly. He made him sit down on a small stool, so his old friend could exhale and get rid of the anxiety, anger and frustration that had built inside him. "I don't want to continue living with this kind of pain anymore. I have reached the end of my journey."

But what made Batuka to turn against the very motherland they'd both sworn to defend with their very lives, the land he Batuka had nearly lost his life defending were many and complicated,

"You wanted to be crowned the next king, but the kingmakers passed you over for your half brother, a younger person, I think that wound, that bitter disappointment never healed. It is still there and has festered all these years," he told Batuka frankly. "But that is not enough to turn you against your own brother, your motherland and against everything that you've fought for all your life."

"Well, I know. I am wrong. I have tried to make peace with my brother, but it has not been easy. Some people still call me names today because I have failed in my bid to sit on the golden stool." He paused and swallowed some lumps, sighing heavily. "Well, I really didn't give out any secrets; I just went to get some rum and guns. That was all I did."

"Are you sure that was all you did?"

"You know I don't lie and I am not about to start now," he opened up to his childhood friend.

"You shouldn't have gone up to the castle. You knew the king has issued a decree that no one from the kingdom should go to the castle, but you have defied him and went there, against your own brother's decree."

"I have visited this Oburoni man regularly. I have been friends with Captain Thompson for the last seven years and he supplies me with all the rum and gun that I need," he told his friend

"But he is the enemy, and at this critical time in our fight with these traders, don't you think it was wrong to go to him for anything?" Fayati asked him.

He asked his friend to get up and they both walked to the king's palace, the rest of the platoon members were fifty yards behind both men. It was a solemn and dignified walk to the place, but Batuka had a tough time keeping his head up for the five minute walk, because of the deep shame he felt.

For fifteen years, King Zendo had ignored his half-brother's loose talk, his insults and now his conspiracies against not only him, but also the state. But by violating the decree not to divulge the secret weapon to the enemy, he knew his brother had committed the mother of all crimes---a crime punishable by death or banishment from the kingdom.

"Do you know what got into your brother to commit this horrible crime?" Mankrado asked the king rubbing his eyes, anxious and worried. "He really hates everything about you. How could he continue to nurse this old grudge?"

"My brother is like "a bag of porcupine" for me to carry. I can't carry him comfortably and I can't get rid of him either. I have showered him with gifts, and with every position in the kingdom, including a position on the Council of Elders, but he'd turned them down. Instead, he'd made trouble for me at every opportunity that he gets. He is okay in my face, but behind my back he wishes me evil. But he is still family---my half-brother. But he is also someone trying to unseat me from the golden stool."

"Well, Batuka loves to go hunting, to spend time making friends with the enemy on his hunting trips," Mankrado told the king. "His Oburoni friends have given him many weapons and lots of rum, so the visit was not unusual. He only violated the decree not to contact the enemy."

"He has not attended any of the meetings of the Council of Elders. Instead, he spends most of his time organizing people to get rid of me as the king. Whenever I hear about his plots against me, I simply chuckle and laugh at him," the king told Mankrado.

"Didn't you ask his mother to warn him not to work against his own blood brother, let alone against the kingdom?" Mankrado asked the king quite frustrated. "What a tragic man, he'd turned into."

"Well, sometimes, my heart goes out to him," the king admitted, solemn and unhappy. "He'd drunk so much political honey, so much Oburoni rum that he'd simply lost his mind, and, obviously he'd also vacated his sense of right and wrong."

"He is an old warrior. But he'd crossed the river of conscience and ended on the side of the enemy, and that is no mean crime," Mankrado told the king frankly.

"He is intoxicated with the idea of becoming the king one day, and this jealousy has destroyed his mind completely. When he'd tried to spill the blood of his own brother to reach his goal, he'd gone too far."

"He is not only bitter, but a man without shame," Abrewa said. "And he is also a bigger fool than we all thought. How could he do these things after all these many years?"

"Well, you remember Batuka asked to make peace with me and I agreed and tried to make peace with him?" the king asked Abrewa,

"Well, I remember that very well," she said to the king. I also remember how the entire kingdom came together to celebrate this day of peace-making between you two blood brothers. How can I forget the seven rams and seven roosters he'd brought to the high priest for sacrifices to the gods?"

"I remember that he asked me for forgiveness for trying "to split our blood" and I gave him my word that I have forgiven him," the king told her. "But my brother is like a chameleon. He changes color daily. And with each color comes another evil plot."

"Well that was fifteen years ago. Though you accepted and embraced him warmly, Batuka has forgotten about the peace and is still focused on the kingmakers passing over him and went for his younger brother and this shame has never left him. He is just not a very angry person, but also a dangerous one," Mankrado revealed to the king.

"I realize that now. Why should he not accept me, his own brother, as the king and enjoy the fruits of the kingdom with me?" the king asked his mother.

"Well, he is blaming the wrong person. He should be blaming his own "kra" for his misfortunes and not you," the king's mother explained. The king rose to his feet and headed for the balcony. "He has become a drunken mouse that is so drunk that he decided to sleep in the cat's bed just to get even with the kingmakers. He has refused to support almost everything I have tried to do in the kingdom and if anything goes wrong in the kingdom, is he not the first to lead a protest against me? It is so hard for him to forget the taste of political honey, once he got a little taste of it, he could never forget it."

"Well, the soldiers caught him going secretly to the Cape Coast Castle to the enemy camp to divulge the secret weapon to his friends," Mankrado explained to the king once more. "And as the saying goes, when chickens fight they never poke the other in the eye, but Batuka has poked his own blood brother in the eye, betraying his own motherland. He must, therefore, suffer the maximum penalty for his treason---death or banishment."

"Well, this is also a family matter . . . though this time he has obviously crossed the river of mercy," the king complained, "He went too far this time when he betrayed the land of our fathers and his own motherland."

"The "palm-branch does not open its mouth without any cause" as the elders say, "and so if this is just sibling rivalry or even the act of someone with a disturbed mind, it has become pure evil, and we have to get to the bottom of it," Abrewa blurted out angrily. She sat down for the elders to debate his fate.

"He is such a big headache to his brother," Mankrado told Abrewa.

"What is it going to take to drum it into his ears that he would never be a king in this kingdom because of his hot temper, his ruthlessness and his complete lack of compassion," Abrewa asked the elders.

"All this happened nearly twenty years ago. Apparently time has not healed his wounds. Why does he continue to nurse this grudge against you and the kingmakers over all these years?" the queen mother told the elders.

"He is not only a very wicked man, he is also very sick in the head," the king told him. "Maybe he is blinded with power or too preoccupied with getting power to think right."

"Well, I know for sure that he wants you to leave behind a wretched legacy," Mankrado told him. "He is thinking that if he couldn't be the king, you should not be a great one."

"Well, it is not your fault. He was supposed to get behind you to celebrate your good fortune, to share in the limelight, to support you and to even cushion you when you take a fall," Abrewa told the king who was nodding repeatedly. "But now he is too selfish and too evil to be a true brother to you."

"That is true, you are right," the king said.

"But he prefers to dig holes under you rather than work to support his brother. He does not want you to become the legend in the land that your "kra" had positioned you to become. But the gods have exposed his true colors and have shamed him."

"Well, at one time, acting on the advice of the governor, Batuka even tried to kill me to seize the throne. He wanted to allow the governor free access to the trade routes as a payback," the queen mother told the elders. "But he quickly found out that killing his own brother would not endear him to the kingmakers, so he decided against shedding his blood; instead, he decided to betray him, violating his sacred oath to the ancestors."

Whatever it was, the chilly Harmattan winds sent cold shivers down everybody's spine and the glow of the setting sun did not prick Batuka's conscience when he sat down with Major Thompson that night. There were dozens of crows flying along the beach competing for the steady flow of flies from the rotten palm trees in the infamous Coconut Grove. He still did not realize on which side of the river he ought to be rowing his boat, or where to make his bed.

Major Thompson, his long-time Oburoni backer and friend, however, did not think much about what he told him. He told him nothing of essence, and so the man simply dismissed the conversation as being immaterial and a total waste of time.

If Batuka expected Major Thompson to tell the governor to go after his brother the king and the elders because they had juju pots to use against them, Batuka was very much frustrated. After Major Thompson heard all his stories about the juju weapon, he simply laughed it off because he did not believe in juju anyway, let alone thought anyone using this as a plot against them.

As for the king, he missed the good old days of brotherhood when they were growing up, especially those days when the ancestors used to create art and craft products.

The king's mind was on the one-week Oyster Festival, because this was the time when the king had to display pomp and splendor. All the subordinate chiefs were expected to bring their courts to pay homage to him. The king's leadership was supposed to be evident during this festival more than at any other time of the year. It was also the time for his subjects to bring their annual tributes to the golden stool. Now he had to wonder what this dark cloud of treason over a member of the royal family would do to his authority.

All the paramount and divisional chiefs showcased their courts. That included queen mothers, war captains and other important traditional sub-leaders who worked under them. They were to display their wealth, their gold and magnificent clothing. The paramount chiefs with gold mines in their lands must give generously to the king. And these chiefs competed to see who would give his majesty the largest gold nugget as they brought these big gifts to greet the king and pay homage to him. The king valued the gold more than those leaders who brought only cows, goats and sheep.

The king was very supportive of those chiefs that the Oburoni had looted, raided, decimated and plunged into deeper economic chaos during that year. He knew about the catastrophe that had befallen them and so he once more extended his sympathies to them. They were his subjects and also his allies and his extended family members.

When the people of Abum, the most recent victims got up to pay homage to the king, the flutes sounded louder and the talking drums vibrated filling the arena with a much louder pulsating rhythm, which made everyone's hair stand up. You could hear the women shouting in their high pitched voices and the children rushing to the arena to see the newest heroes in the land.

It was sad to see everyone from Abum in the traditional dark adinkra mourning cloth. They were still deeply buried in mourning, though their king tried to put on a brave face on their recent tragedy. The new chief, Saka Ledo Dompre, the one who'd replaced Apentem, the one Don Pedro and his raiders killed, got the loudest cheer from the audience when he shook hands and embraced the king. The war captain allowed this king extra five minutes so he and his people could acknowledge the outpour of grief and goodwill from the spectators.

The asafo soldiers who'd surrounded the new chief did their best, but it was obvious many of them were new to their roles. But the women dancers did not disappoint at all because many people, including the king himself, stretched his neck to the breaking point to watch them do the Adowa dance. When Ekua Mensah, the beauty queen of Abum, turned her vibrating posterior in the king's direction, the spectators roared with laughter. And when she did the complicated "triple Adowa jump dance move," the audience shouted with joy. They broke into spontaneous applause when Ekua's eyes met the king's eyes, and the king flashed the V sign of approval and gave her a captivating and inviting smile. The queen mother saw it and whispered something into the king's ears and they both laughed with the king nodding a few times.

Whatever enjoyment they had that year, the Oyster Festival never reached the crescendo it used to reach when the king first took office. That was some two decades ago. For one thing, the Oburonis had become much more powerful than ever before, and with the steady flow of new weapons, they'd inflicted more death and starvation on the people than ever before. Also, life had become much more insecure, and much more dangerous that many of the inhabitants were reluctant to attend the festival. They didn't want to leave their children behind for the one-week festival because they feared the Oburoni slave traders might go behind their back to round up their youths and haul them away to the land of no return.

The children enjoyed the festival much more than the grown ups, the men and women. Though the event was the ideal time for those who were looking for spouses, searching from among hundreds of thousands that had gathered at the grand durbar, it was also a hectic time to find the right person. The women, however, dressed up in their best attires with huge, sophisticated head gears, beads and golden trinkets to match, if they could afford to do so. Some even opted to braid their hair in all sorts of styles; some even looked like bamboo leaves or rows of banana on a tree. Others made their hair to look like rows of tiger nuts neatly arranged on top of their heads.

The older women put the younger ones who had completed the initiation rites that year in front for the men to see and admire. In fact, they led the pack in the dancing in every traditional area. And many of them did not disappoint as they swayed their firm bodies from side to side, jumped up or bent down on their dances to attract potential mates. These were the youngest of the women. Most of them had just been officially declared grown women three months before this festival. No doubt they'd very firm and shapely bodies, impressive chests and were at their best---they had beautiful smiles and shapely bodies.

Mankrado, who had other ideas beside the festival, was present in his war regalia. He was looking handsome, but also fearsome in his best war attire. The irony was that his wife was watching him like a hawk to see which of the women he would go after. It took the second day for his eyes to finally lock in on a nice-looking middle-aged woman. Her shape was still fine, and she had a shining ebony dark complexion. The woman already had four children and had been divorced for more than seven years. His wife told him to stay away from her because the previous owner would not have sent such a nice looking hen back to the market for no apparent reason. She told Mankrado that this woman was either "fighting with other hens or was eating her own eggs," so he must move on and forget about bringing her home to become a member of their family. The woman, however, was flattered that the king's right hand person, the next most powerful man in the kingdom, found her attractive and she was worth some attention.

For the first time in ten years the king got up and danced at the grand durbar. He did so on the last day of the one-week festival. He'd not danced in a long time, because he did not want to be dancing when the enemy was still abducting and killing his subjects like flies. But that year, he decided to display dancing moves, which were so impressive that the women started shouting at the top of their voices. Some of them poured powder on his arm and showered him with praises. Other women burst into tears as they recalled the memories of their departed husbands and sons.

"Your majesty, you are a living example of the saying that when a tortoise brings forth, the offspring does not resemble a snail," Abrewa remarked to the king in a flirtatious tone, teasing him, though she was just actually trying to embarrass the king. "You dance just like your grandfather and your late father both combined, but you dance even better than both of them. And if I wasn't ninety and too young for you, I would have suggested that you send a big dowry to my people for my hand in marriage."

The elders roared with laughter.

"I will send your people one hundred cows for your hand," the king said and he stopped to laugh with the old lady, holding her hand. "You are worth all the cows a man can afford."

"I am flattered because that is the highest dowry amount anyone has ever offered for any lady in the land," Abrewa told him.

"That's true, my dear, you are worth every one of those cows," the king said, looking excited.

She expected the king to smile and laugh, but most importantly, she wanted to boost the king's morale after the bad news she'd heard about his brother's treason. She hated the way Batuka had stabbed his own blood brother in back, and tried to sabotage the secret weapon, the way he'd betrayed the ancestors.

The king decided to wait till after the memories of the Oyster Festival faded before he sentenced his brother. He didn't want to increase the anxiety of his nieces and nephews, and the shock they felt when he charged their father, his own brother, with treason.

"A diver never knows what goes on behind him," Mankrado told the asafo soldiers who spied on Batuka. "He thought he could hide his treason, but as we say, the fruit always falls under the tree. So he finally got caught inside his own trap."

The king, however, tried everything in his power to get Batuka to understand that though he was not the king, as the saying goes "when one man kills an elephant, everybody in the village can eat some of the meat," so he should get behind him and enjoy some of the fruits of his good fortune.

But Batuka was too proud to get behind his brother.

King Zendo sighed deeply when he told an audience, "Batuka was never satisfied with anything. Only the ancestors know how much I have tried to help him to work out his problems, to clean up his foolishness that has grown like kudzu plant. He must face the consequences of his treason like a warrior."

"The king could banish his brother for seven years to live in shame each day, or he could order his execution. But executing him would be too kind for him," Abrewa, the old lady, declared. "He must live each day with this shame and continue to mull over his foolishness."

FIVE

As the African saying goes "if you are running for your life, you must never run in a lazy manner." So the messengers never looked back when they took to their heels to tell the governor the bad news from the king.

The war captain asked the town crier to beat the drums for an emergency meeting. "We need to prepare for an immediate attack from the governor and his trading partners, because the king has asked for war, a battle which would affect everyone in the kingdom," he declared.

"Does it mean we might be going to war even before the secret weapon is ready for use," the queen mother agonized. "Why the king couldn't wait for another week for the rains to end before he provoked the governor into another war surprises me."

The governor said that he was "the most stubborn leader" he'd ever met in the land, but the king took this as a compliment and not an insult. The feeling was mutual. He had very little respect for the governor, so though he had next to no weapons in stock, he would have no choice but to go to war if the governor decided he wanted to go to war. From the look of things, the secret weapon made the king even bolder and much more defiant. But, somehow, from what the queen mother got out of Captain Wyndham, he was convinced that the governor would not attack his kingdom during the rainy season, but would wait till the dry season when it was safer for his soldiers to travel in the rain forest.

So the king waited with his soldiers for the rains to end so he could teach the governor a lesson in traditional medicine and humility. He knew, with time, the secret weapon would silent the governor's booming cannons and quiet down their deadly Danish rifles, something the king and his people had wanted to do for a very long time.

"The last time you sent the seven pieces of rocks to the governor, we lost a lot of people when he invaded the kingdom. So are you ready for another war? You know we don't have the weapons to fight another war with these Oburonis?" the queen mother expressed with grief.

"This means another war, I know," he told her. "The seven pieces of rock should make that very clear to everybody, including the governor. My hope is that the gods will wipe the flies off us just as they'd done for all animals without tails, though that protection is not promised at all times."

"What if the gods fall asleep on us once again as they did in the past?" she asked the king as he sat down next to her drinking his palm-wine.

"Hopefully this would be the last major battle between us anyway, if the gods agree. We have placed ourselves in the hands of the ancestors from now onwards, and we are more certain than ever before that they will intervene on our behalf," Mankrado said.

"You know Batuka, the traitor, had given the secret weapon to the Oburoni enemy, but we are not sure how much he'd told them. So you can't be so sure that this is the last war," she told the war captain. "I can't stand blood fighting blood, but I hate the traitors hidden among us even more. Whatever rum and guns his Oburoni friends had given him for this betrayal, it would continue to haunt his conscience for the rest of his life."

"Because he'd betrayed his own brother, nobody cares if Batuka dies today or lives," Abrewa, the old lady, declared in an angry voice filled with resentment and pain. "He knows that no one points to his father's house with his left hand, but Batuka has done that too." Although she wasn't the type that could wish anyone dead, she felt Batuka must definitely die because he'd betrayed his people.

"I have the same feeling about him," the queen mother said.

"If he dies, we would drag his body through the streets and like his friends the Oburoni traders, set it on fire in the Coconut Grove," Abrewa mumbled. "He cannot be buried with honors in any part of the kingdom."

"He has put his brother in a very difficult dilemma," the queen mother lamented. If he executes his brother people would cry foul and if he banishes him, they would still cry preferential treatment."

"The gods know how many times his brother had tried to get him to let go of his anger and hatred," Mankrado declared. "Now he'd gone too far."

"Well, let us talk about the governor who wants to give us some guns so the king could reopen the trade routes for a few more months," the queen mother told the war captain, quietly and with some hesitation. "But from the look of things, it appears the king thinks we no longer need these weapons. He is counting on the secret weapon to solve all our problems. What if this new weapon does not work?"

"Oh well, you know the king. Just as he'd done over the years, I know he is still not ready to accept guns to reopen the trade routes, not for the Oburoni traders," Mankrado told the queen mother. "He will not sell his conscience for any number of guns. So, go back and tell Captain Wyndham that the king has refused his request and the trade routes would remain closed for good."

"Though I hate to admit it, your words are like music to my ears," the queen mother said, humming a song and moving her body from side to side to the rhythm in a dancing mode.

"You realize we never stopped trusting you," Mankrado told her.

"Now that all of you are wrong, you owe me an apology." She clapped her hands for a minute and laughed out loudly, placing her hands on her broad hips, excitedly. She wanted everyone to show her respect and affirm her innocence. "Listen, I am a queen inside and outside, and from head to toe, but you have no idea how much you have hurt my pride."

"She is definitely the best looking of all the old hens here," Abrewa reminded Mankrado jokingly. And some of the elders who were listening to the funny drama burst out laughing. "She looks good, but everyone is afraid of her because she is such a strong-minded lady. She is a handful for any man to handle."

"She is the only woman who has managed to force the Oburoni traders to obey her demands," Zotor said avoiding her eyes. "Her face shines like gold and her personality sparkles like diamonds, so she gets a lot from these aliens. But I hate her close ties with the missionaries and the way she's helped them plant their religion in the land. Maybe, they like her because of her beauty and special charm."

"Whether she wanted Danish rifles, slave muskets or kegs of gunpowder, she easily gets them," Mankrado told Zotor and the elders. "Without her help, I wonder where this kingdom would be today."

"We might all have ended in their stinking boats and taken to the land beyond the blue ocean," Abrewa told them, using her sharp sense of humor. "But I am too old for them to take as a slave."

"But some of the women hate her connection with the Oburoni traders," Mankrado told them. "They are simply jealous of her."

Mankrado and the queen mother had a good laugh together, but the king grimaced because he did not like what he was hearing from the queen mother. Something deep inside the queen mother triggered the king's suspicions. Then, a confrontation that had been brewing for months erupted openly between the king and the queen mother. And Mankrado, who had been working with both of them, was caught in the middle---the king was the most powerful. So should he follow the tide or ride against it?

"Tell me, during your romantic meetings with Captain Wyndham, has it ever crossed your mind to tell him about this secret weapon?" the king asked the queen mother inquiring as Abrewa, the high priest and three other elders leaned over closer to hear every word of the heated conversation between the two.

"How could these two leaders rule in one kingdom?" Zotor said sarcastically. "They are both hard-headed individuals, but the queen mother has exceeded her shoes. She must start listening to the king and not fighting a war of words with him."

"I brought into the kingdom a lot of guns and gunpowder, but the king simply sat down and drank his palm-wine," she told the elders in front of the king. "How does he expect to defeat the enemy?"

"You must not talk to your king that way, young lady," the linguist, the king's spokesperson, said half jokingly, but he was very serious. "Another rude remark like that and you would have to bring seven rams and seven roosters with seven bottles of Kantamanto gin."

"What is wrong with you these men? Listen to this woman's heart and not to her words, then you will find what you are trying to get out of her," Abrewa told the king and the elders quietly. She was very much frustrated and so she decided to hum a song and chew her kola nut.

"She could never betray her motherland to the Oburoni traders, not for all the weapons in the world," Mankrado told the king. "I will speak on her behalf. I firmly believe that the queen mother has been genuine, sincere, devoted and truthful to the state all these years." The queen mother was very happy. She was happy that at least someone believed in her innocence and did not see her as a traitor.

"You mean you have never betrayed us to your missionary lover, Captain Wyndham?" the high priest asked her pointedly. His anger went beyond the queen mother's activities to the battle between the two religions—the new one that the Oburonis had brought and the deities they had before the beginning of time itself. "He seems to have your heart and maybe he even contaminated your mind and soul with his shameful beliefs."

"Well, since you have declared before the old lady, Abrewa, that you have never stepped to the edge of the cliff and tried to convert," the king told her quietly in hidden words what he felt in his heart. "I take your words to be the truth. But I would not hesitate to banish you or even ask for your head in the future, if we find out that you have revealed the secret weapon to the enemy. It does not matter who you are, or how valuable you have been to the kingdom, if you betray your motherland, if you stab your own people in the back, you must suffer the punishment."

"Oh, I know. And I know how far to go to get what I want from these Oburoni locusts. I only do what I had to do to get the weapons we so badly need for the Asafo soldiers."

"Can you tell them what you use to outsmart these traders," Abrewa asked her laughing. "You seem to be so talented in misleading them."

"Well, I use my smiles, my beauty and my charm. And if those don't work, I sway my broad hips and then I do the vibrating dance to divert them," she said softly, looking at the two leaders with laughter in her voice. "They are wicked traders, but some of them are bored, anxious and ready for interesting adventure, so my charm always worked on them like magic every time. It is yet to fail to deliver the weapons that we need."

"Anyway, you are part of the royal family, but I am always afraid that one day they might seize and keep you in the dungeon as a slave," the king mumbled to her, blinking repeatedly. "But I pray that you remain lucky. Having been betrayed by my own blood brother, can you understand why I distrust everybody around me and that includes even you?"

"Yes, I do understand, your majesty," she told the king politely, thinking about the seriousness of what his brother had done. "I don't understand why he bent so low to do what he did, but I hate to be in your shoes when it comes to this."

The queen mother became a center of gossip among her fellow women. The woman who criticized her most was her own cousin Ayeko, who had been talking about how loose she was, since she was sleeping with the Oburoni enemy. She was the one who painted this image of her, an image that gave her a very uncomfortable feeling when she showed her face among the women she was supposed to be leading.

When a song which ridiculed her good name was sang in the public square, she nearly shed tears because it distressed her and lowered her morale. She didn't know whether she should explode in anger or keep her cool. She even considered running into exile in the nearby kingdom and leaving the Bakano kingdom altogether. The songs labeled her a traitor and even a common prostitute, two charges that nearly forced her to end her life, had she not seen her aged grandmother in her dreams the night before.

The fact that she once belonged to and served Dente did not save her reputation. She knew that the god of gods could easily clear her name, but why it chose not to do so at the time baffled her.

The high priest, who hated the new religion that the Oburonis had brought into the land, hated her for going to the castle to foster good relations with the Oburonis. He had already warned her not to get involved with the alien religion. He even threatened to take away her "kosinor" amulets, the status of being someone that was once married to Dente.

She lived a life that had been tainted from her youth. The men feared to get involved with her because she'd once been married to Dente, so they refused to risk the wrath of the supreme god of the land and avoided her hand in marriage. The custom rendered her and the other women who had been married to Dente before sacred women of the gods. They could only be married to strangers from faraway lands, but if any man from the kingdom got married to any of these women, he would have earned the anger of this powerful god on his head.

"Have they lost their minds?" Abrewa asked the women who were dragging the queen mother's name in mud. "How can the daughter of the paramount chief of Abum become a traitor to her own motherland? I believed in your innocence from the very beginning. You worked hard behind the scenes to make sure that we won't lose everything and become slaves to the Oburoni locusts. You are such a brave soul and I want you to know that we are so proud of you. You are nothing but a great pride to the royal family and to this kingdom."

The queen mother became relieved. At least the old lady believed in her. And so, though it was difficult for her, she quickly forgave her enemies. As a result, she regained the respect of many women who were the very people that had ridiculed her in songs and on several occasions. This ordeal rather made her a stronger leader, and the women began to view her as a true leader. They thought she might even be a possible successor to the conscience of the land---the old lady, Abrewa herself.

"What if this weapon becomes the biggest failure in the history of the kingdom?" the queen mother asked the king one day. The king simply walked away, but she saw the concern on his face. "You better be right or we would be marched out of our own land into slavery."

When another attempt on the life of the king missed him narrowly and the bullet hit a large baobab tree next door, the elders became very much concerned about the king's safety. This latest attempt on the king life came from the son of a man the king had banished five years earlier. He shot at the king, but the king later wrestled him to the ground, overpowered and personally subdued him. This dramatic incident made the king the bravest legend in the land.

Though the elders advised the king to be strong, they also told him not to make himself look like a butcher whose sense of justice knew no boundaries. Was he going to go down in history as the king who could not spare even his own blood brother from the death penalty? Worst of all, some of the elders wanted him to sell his brother to the same Oburoni traders that he'd befriended to teach him a bitter lesson. The king thought that was the most humiliating of all the punishments for Batuka, but he gave it a thought.

The more the king tried not to think about this moral dilemma, the more he descended into a drunken stupor. He got up and left when Batuka's children confronted him once again the next morning and demanded that he released their father, his own brother so he could come home. "You cannot execute a member of your bloodline, no matter how bad your brother has behaved," Anani, Batuka's oldest son told his uncle. "If you execute your own brother, remember the gods would desert you and the evil that would befall you and the kingdom would be huge." But when the king did not release their father, they sat on the floor and continued sobbing torrential tears hoping the king would change his mind, but he remained firm.

"You can't banish, or send your own brother away from your nephews and nieces," Togonor told his uncle after looking at the documents the king had shown them. "But he is not the only one who had friends among the Oburoni people. What about the queen mother who has an Oburoni lover?" They waited in the hall of the king's palace and continued to cry tears of sorrow hoping that the king would have pity on them and release their father. But the king had to consult with the elders before he made his final decision to release their father.

"Ask Mambo to come here immediately," he told Togonor.

"Make beds for my nephews and nieces in the guest rooms, feed them well and let them spend the night here if they want to," he told his wife. She escorted the children, who ranged from seven to nineteen, to the kitchen to feed them. She asked them to sleep in the guestroom, but the children were in no mood to sleep that night. They wanted their father back, and not comfortable sleeping beds.

Throughout the night, King Zendo debated whether execution, banishment or outright freedom would be the best punishment for his half-brother. Execution might taint the king's image, making him look like a brutal butcher. Shedding his brother's blood might also put a curse on the royal family, which might haunt him later.

The king, who had been quite happy about the secret weapon, remained excited about the future of the kingdom, but this decision was over his head like a baobab tree that made his life very unpleasant. Whenever he saw his nieces and nephews walking with their heads down, some were crying their eyes out, it troubled his conscience. He had no clear path to follow, so he called on the gods to guide his steps to make the right decision.

"Maybe the elders would solve this difficult case," Mankrado told the priest. "Or we should leave it completely to "the Abrewa, the old lady" the one with the final word on this difficult case, a first of its kind in many years?"

"Kings are supposed to be wise and tough at the same time," Zotor told the king during a turbulent session in the palace. "It is time for you to rise and shine, or falter and fall. Whichever decision you make, you must live with it, but as a king, your subjects would judge you and continue to either support or oppose you."

"Either way, you know it won't be that simple," he told him.

"We can only wish the king lots of wisdom to make the right decision," Zotor whispered as Mankrado started to jog with the soldiers as they headed toward the fifth river landing.

The king's servants finally rounded up the seven roosters and rams they'd been chasing in the park all morning. They brought these animals and the seven bottles of "akpeteshie" moonshine to the Shrine of Dente as gifts to the gods. These were sacrifices for past misdeeds against Dente and libation for future favors. Zotor received these gifts happily on behalf of the gods and proceeded to offer them as gifts to the ancestors.

"These sacrifices came from the heart, so make sure you tell the gods that," the linguist told Zotor, the high priest. "Tell them that their subjects have given them the best they have in the land, and they expect nothing in return except good news, peace, but death to the enemy."

"Well, I hope the gods are open to your wishes," Zotor told the linguist and the elders. "We don't have time for any more tragedy so we would no longer leave anything that must be done undone. We need the gods completely behind us; they must be on our side."

"Don't blame our misfortunes on the fact that women have secretly poured libation to the gods," so the queen mother asked the priests to bring seven gourds of fresh, unfermented palm wine for the women to drink, instead of these women just sitting down watching the men do all the drinking, and hurling insults at some of them later.

There was a deafening silence in the palace hall later on.

"So do you want women to go to the battlefront during the next battle?" Mankrado asked the queen mother sarcastically as he took his seat next to the king. He was suspicious of some of these women who were asking him to let them go to the battlefront to fight alongside the men.

"Are you saying we don't have the courage to fight?" she asked pointedly. "Of course we don't want nursing mothers to go to war, but there are several women who are brave enough to go to war, women who would fight, kill, bleed and even die for their motherland."

"If I send even a single woman to war, the people would make songs about me making me look like a thoughtless war captain who had sent women to war to die," Mankrado said in a mirthful voice. He shook his head from side to side. "The women must just support and nurse the wounded soldiers when they return from war, some of these warriors get seriously wounded. Well, I would prefer to become a slave in the land of no return rather than see my mother, my sisters or even my wife go to war," Mankrado protested against what the women had suggested to him.

"You are just too stubborn to see the wisdom in what I am trying to tell you," the queen mother told him.

"Well, what do we tell the ancestors when we finally join them some day? Do we tell them that under our watch we have allowed our mothers, daughters and wives to fight and die in war because the men have become too weak, too soft or too lazy to fight our battles?"

"What is wrong with the ancestors hearing about women helping to defend the land, a small change in our traditions?"

"Well, that would not happen under my watch. This can happen under another war captain's watch, but as for me, I will keep the faith until I pass the torch to the next war captain."

Ayeko dreamed about going to get foodstuff from her farm, because the sight of her starving children growing leaner and leaner everyday broke her heart. When she heard their stomachs growling repeatedly, it gave her no other choice but go to the farm to get some yams to feed her children. "Mama, we are hungry. What are we going to eat tonight?" Mamfio, the youngest child, asked her mother, though very faintly but politely. And after a while her mother became tired of hearing this same bleak voice asking the same question over and over again.

"The children are hungry," she told her husband. "I hate to see them dizzy, and desperate. Ofosu and Sikawa fainted yesterday because of hunger."

"Why should the Oburoni enemy tempt her to such a limit? Why wouldn't they allow the women to get some yams to feed their children without abducting and enslaving them?" her husband asked.

Trying to contain her anger and frustration at the same time, Mama Ayeko held her head in both hands and chuckled loudly. "I don't want to go to the farm because the slave traders would come from behind the bushes and put their "kunyowu" chains of death on me and haul me away to the land of no return. But I can't sit here either and watch my children starve and reduce to skeletons. They are just slowly starving to death."

"Well we want you here as a mother. Your presence alone will satisfy us more than any yam fufu on our table," Mamifio told her mother with tears running down her cheek. But when the tears started to run down her mother's face, she regretted that she had even said what she said to her. "I don't want you to start crying again, Mama."

"You know after the king, your father is the next richest man in the kingdom. And as your mother, I work very hard to grow the foodstuffs, so why do we have to sit here and watch our children starve to death as if we were birds with broken wings or lions with broken legs?" Ayeko blurted out loudly, letting out a volcano of anger that had been building inside her for months. "We have plenty to feed you, but it is only too risky to go to the farm to get the foodstuff to feed you."

There was a long pause. Ayeko was wondering whether she was doing the right thing, whether she was being a good mother. But with the hungry look on her children's faces, she knew she had to do something.

The children would later on remember their mother's serious dilemma. They would never forget the conflict she felt inside her soul, her dilemma to stay at home and do the right thing, and her fateful decision to venture out to get some yams from the barn to feed them.

These were the memories that would stay with them for the rest of their lives. They would never forget her devotion, her goal to be the best mother ever.

"Maybe the men must accompany the women once more this week to the farm, because the children are starving in my house and in many other houses," Ayeko suggested, and several other women placed their hands on their hips and supported her suggestion. "The remaining corn flour I saved had finally run out. The meat had run out or had spoiled. The children had lost a lot of body fat, many of them had been reduced to walking skeletons, and I am tired of hearing their stomachs growl day and night."

"And the same holds true for other families too," Mamifio told her mother, though she did not want her to do anything stupid, to take a fatal step that would deprive them of her love, separating her from her children forever.

Though Ayeko remembered the saying that what went into the belly yesterday is not in the mouth today, she went inside the kitchen hurriedly and put a small pot on the fire and added the last corn dough left to the banku dough inside the pot. She whipped it up quickly to a boil and made one more meal for the children. As for the adults, they went to the nearby gardens to eat some mango fruits. She was very sad and sighed repeatedly as she placed the last food they had left on the small mahogany table and invited her seven children to the meal.

"If your father does not go hunting, there would be nothing to eat from now onwards," she mumbled angrily. "This is what the "Oburoni locusts had done to us."

Her family was a well-to-do family. And she remembered the rows of corn inside their ten acre farm and the big yams, which were still resting in the hot belly of the earth on three farms because it was dangerous to go to these farms to harvest them.

The town crier had announced that the Oburoni human lifters had been seen in the area searching for human cargo like hawks. This made everyone worried. So, the elders warned the farmers to stay at home with their children until the soldiers announce that the danger had passed.

"Give these traders a taste of their own wickedness, we beg you Dente. Please, don't let them get away with the murders they'd committed in our land. And for all your sons and daughters they'd stolen, send them into their graves without mercy," she knelt down and pleaded with the gods. She was seated next to the high table, poured a calabash of palm-wine on the ground to the ancestors, and pointed her right hand toward the shrine of Dente, lamenting and pleading with the gods. "Dente, please don't let us perish, you must hear our cry."

Her mother felt her agony and held her against her warm body to soothe her pain. She gently patted her hair to comfort her and spoke to her soul softly. "Even if it takes hundreds of years, these "sansabomsa" Oburonis will answer for the crimes they'd committed against us. They must know that "if a pregnant woman falls, the child in the stomach will avenge her, so if not right now, these traders will definitely answer for these crimes in the near future."

Her father Grimpo Gator took his gun and stormed out of the house angrily. He went to attend the meeting under the mahogany trees. When he heard people blaming the gods for abandoning them, he got up and told the king that "If the owner of a hunting dog is not strong, his dogs never catch any prey. So the Oburoni problem had gotten worse since he, King Zendo had become the king of the kingdom. We have lost more youths than ever before. They'd simply vanished, and there had been more bloodshed in the kingdom, and more fear and insecurity in the land than during any previous times," Grimpo said, putting responsibility for all these problems in the kingdom solidly on the king's head.

"This is what happens to a kingdom when the head is alive and you give the crown to a knee to wear," Azevedo, Batuka's friend said in support of his friend. "We must do something before we lose our way of life completely. We must stop our sons and daughters from vanishing into the deep hole of history."

"If you disrespect the king one more time, he would impose a fine of seven rams and seven bottles of Kantamanto gin on you, so watch what you say to the king from now onwards," the linguist told Azevedo sharply, gesturing with his hand toward his face.

"Your majesty, whether you like it or not," Grimpo said defiantly to the king. "We have decided to send armed guards to help our wives to fetch some foodstuffs from our farms to feed our children. We don't want to watch any more of our children fainting from hunger. Hunger has arrived in every household in the kingdom, except maybe your palace."

"You are exaggerating the fact," the linguist told him.

"We don't care how you look at it, many brave men are ready to take these women to their farms to get some food for the children," Azevedo said, standing up to the elders and laughing at the king through his nose disrespectfully.

The linguist rose up, straightened the cloth around his shoulders and told the rebels that since two kings do not rule in one kingdom, they were virtually on their own if they violated the curfew the king had imposed and he ventured out to the forest to hunt, and to get some yams for their children.

The women waited restlessly under a tree. They were dressed in their farm clothes, and they had machetes in their baskets and gourds of water ready to go to their farms. They were torn between loyalty to the king and feeding their children as mothers. So they were ready to defy the king and the elders.

"I have heard your complaints but I want you to know that I have spent many sleepless nights thinking about all the hungry children in the land," the king told them and paused for a minute. "This problem has occupied my mind for many nights. But I can assure you that it would not be too long when these Oburoni pests flee our land."

"Listen carefully to what the king has just told you. The saying goes that if a blind man says he is going to stone you that means he already has his foot on a stone," Mankrado told them as he tried to give them a hint about the secret weapon and how the king would finally prevail against these traders.

"The king had said the same thing on several occasions," Azevedo shouted trying to disrespect the king, but the linguist asked him to withdraw his words and apologize to the stool or face a heavy fine.

Mankrado, the war captain, roared in anger, screaming like an angry lion. "Silence, silence, let the king speak, and you must give the king the respect he deserves." The warriors began to plead their case and tempers flared up. Some of the men, whose wives had put pressure on them to get some food for their children, broke away from the meeting in anger and decided to take matters into their own hands.

Pongo, the elder statesman, appealed to the farmers for patience and compassion. "You must give us the chance to serve you. The king has told you that the days of our suffering, the days of watching our youths starve or disappear from the land in the millions would soon be over. The African proverb says, "He who sits still does not eat," but we have to exercise patience. The ear is not basket, so those who have ears to hear what the soldiers are saying, let them hear."

"Well, there are rumors that the "white locusts" have entered the Zangba Forest last week," Mankrado told Grimpo and his group quietly. "We have to wait them out for a few more days before we go after them. We don't want to lose any more innocent people."

"I can't wait any longer. I am tired of hearing my children's stomachs growl night and day. Have you ever listened to your children's stomach growl or listen to the little infants crying in the middle of the night asking for something to eat?" Grimpo asked him.

"I know about hunger pain. I see hunger everyday, and I can't stand it any longer either, but we have to still be patient for a few more weeks."

"Don't worry, Grimpo," the king's linguist told him with a bright smile, expecting better things in the future. "The days of hunger would soon be behind us, if nobody leaks the plot to the "white locusts" by betraying the gods."

"Though this is very dangerous, we the warriors of the Dome Nyafa clan have decided to take our wives to Zangba to get some yams to feed our hungry children," he told the linguist to inform the king. "We heard what the king said, but we can no longer sit idle and look at the hungry faces of our children."

The linguist whispered into the king's ears something urgent as he broke a piece of red kola nut into two halves. The king grimaced with discomfort as if what the linguist had told him had hurt his ears. But he remembered vividly what his grandfather once told him. "When my subjects anger me, I don't squeeze my face, I simply squeeze my bottom," the grandfather once enlightened him. So he squeezed his behind, as his grandfather told him, and kept his composure, refusing to lose his dignity.

"Tell them that the road they are trying to take is not what the ancestors want us to travel on. And if they are not careful, they might end up as slaves crammed into Oburoni slave boats of horror. And when that happens, they should not blame the king, they should blame themselves."

"How many guns do you have?" the linguist asked, because the king still wanted to extend some help to the group. But they were too angry to listen to any suggestions from the king and the elders.

"We have twenty-one guns and ammunition for three rounds," Grimpo finally told the linguist rudely. "But we won't be gone for long so that should be enough, and if they are not enough, let the ancestors have our souls." Because they knew the land so well, Grimpo was very confident that they would survive any attack from the traders. But the Oburoni raiders had more firepower than they did, so the elders knew they could land themselves in the middle of a thunderstorm of bullets, in a lot of trouble.

Grimpo ignored the king's request to take additional armed men for complete safety and shook his head when the war captain suggested fifty more warriors. Hours later, he would find out that he should have listened to the king and the war captain.

Ayeko had a basket on top of her head and was ready to go, followed by twelve other women who called themselves the Amazon Female Hustlers. They'd strapped Danish rifles to their waists marching toward the farm like male Asafo soldiers. They were famous for breaking the large beads they wore around their waists to use in their guns as bullets whenever there was shortage of bullets during any war. Also, when the men hesitate to fight the enemy, they threatened to take matters into their own hands and fight the enemy. These women stood on the road to the Zangba forest ready to go to their farms. Most of them were anxious and scared, but few of them cared less.

Naturally they knew they were risking their lives so their children could eat. This was a natural thing for any mother worth her salt to do. So, their children lined up the road, several of them had torrential tears rolling down their cheeks like raindrops as they came to wish their mothers good luck and goodbye, just in case it turned that is the last time they ever see their mothers and fathers again---the final separation.

These women and the warriors thought it would be a safe trip to the farm as they disappeared sweating, quietly, into the blistering heat. The silent air inside the woods was the only thing that threatened the peace since they were sure that Dente would protect them on the way and bring them back to their children safely.

"Danger does not announce itself when it comes to a place," Abrewa said, because as an old lady, she was very uneasy about this trip. "Why can't they listen to the king, after all, he is our leader."

Obviously, it didn't matter to the Oburoni locusts how many rusty guns this party brought with them. It also didn't matter how many men or warriors were in the group on the trip. They'd made a fatal decision to challenge their fate. They'd defied the king, defied the gods when they violated the king's decree that forbade anybody from going to the Zangba forest to farm.

As destiny had it, the "white locusts" were waiting for the group on the outskirts of the town. They hid themselves inside the thick forest, behind the tall elephant grasses with the latest guns and waited patiently like spiders for their prey to enter their hidden webs. The raiders emerged from the bushes like leopards and attacked the group after they'd crossed the river outside the edge of the forest. It was so sudden that none of these veteran soldiers in the group fired even a single shot at the attackers. The sudden outburst of repeating rifle fire shocked them. And against everything inside their soul, they all froze with fear. When two of the Oburoni tried to tie up Grimpo's hands, he managed to free himself, being a very powerful warrior. He fatally stabbed two of the traders with his hunting knife. But though he'd overpowered the two attackers and killed them, another Oburoni shot Grimpo through the heart and he died cursing the Oburoni traders with his last breath. "Your days in our land are numbered, you would die slow, painful deaths very soon, mark my---," he told them before he stopped breathing.

The sun disappeared behind the dark clouds and night fell rather quickly that evening as the whole town waited on these brave souls to return from the farm with plenty of food to feed their children. When it was past many people's bedtime and the owls started hooting repeatedly, at that point several people suspected that the worst had happened to these brave parents. The children started to scream softly and the people started to gather under the trees near the king's palace expecting for a miracle from the gods, unprepared to hear the tragic news.

When the search party sent its first messenger to the king, the elders started whispering among themselves. When the old lady clasped the top of her head with both hands and smoked her stinking "bibitama" inside her bamboo pipe, sending the smoke everywhere, the women almost knew the news was bad.

The sad beats from the talking drums, sounds that reached every corner of the kingdom and broke the hearts of those who were still clinging on to hope that their loved ones might return home alive, confirmed every one's suspicion. They realized what the painful reality meant---the disappearance or death of these brave parents. They would never return to the kingdom again. Another dreadful blow had landed on this unhappy kingdom. This group went to get some food from their farms to feed their hungry children and the Oburonis made sure that did not happen.

"If only they'd listened to the king and the elders, they would have been with us right now, alive and well," the queen mother said with a heavy heart, but she dared not go too far in her criticism, to add insult to the hurt of the family members of the victims, so she tried to keep the rest of her comments under her breath.

"But who can blame these people for trying to feed their hungry children?" Abrewa asked the queen mother. "Maybe it is because you have never been a mother, and have never given birth to any child."

"You don't have to insult me everyday for being childless," she told her angrily. "It was never my fault that I didn't have any children. It was the fault of the high priest and Dente, the god of gods."

"This is not the time for personal insults. Let us think about the terrible loss we have suffered, these are people very dear to all of us, so these very painful losses, indeed," the king declared. "We need to be there like mahogany trees for their children and for their family members. They must lean on us in these hard times."

The children of the victims wished the whole thing was a bad dream from which they would finally wake up and be told that it was all lies. The younger ones wanted it to be a vivid dream and not the reality, because they knew this was never supposed to be that way, not the normal for a family. This was going to haunt them forever, especially for those children that had lost both parents.

"Danger does not wear a red headgear when it is on the way to the kingdom," the queen mother remarked, "but in this particular case they wouldn't say that they didn't see the signs of danger on the horizon."

"The king warned them not to step into the forest because the "white locusts" had been spotted," the linguist reminded the gathering.

"The signs of danger were everywhere, but they'd decided to still tempt nature," Zotor said. A superstitious man, Zotor poured water on the ground to calm things down.

"You are right, they needn't have to leave us," the queen mother mumbled, keeping her tone sad. "Now several children are motherless and fatherless---they lack the necessary support---the latest orphans in the large number of orphans in this land."

That night, under the moonlight, the king rose to his feet and stood solidly on the balcony of his palace, clad in his "batakari kese" battle uniform. He was ready to comfort the family members of the victims. Though he looked calm, his heart was very sad. He was very disappointed and angry that the enemy had inflicted another painful tragedy on his kingdom, perhaps the last one.

The war captain narrated the "sane agbo" that the rescue party had brought to the king telling them about how many got kidnapped and how many had been killed. Then the king personally wanted to go after these bloodthirsty Oburoni killers, so he could punish them himself and finish them off immediately.

"They defied your decree, your majesty," Zotor reminded the king.

"It didn't matter whether they'd defied my orders; these were loyal subjects whose only mistake was that they tried to feed their children, defying incredible odds to get to their farms to get some foodstuff to feed their starving children," he told the gathering. "If I had not been the king, I definitely would have been among these parents who put their lives on the line to make sure that their children did not die of hunger and starvation." He got a round of applause from the audience, though the news plunged every one into deep mourning.

This was the kind of sad drama that dominated the coast and the forest regions for many centuries. The warriors had to chase the slave caravans, which were made up of the Oburoni master traders and a few local traitors as they marched hundreds of innocent victims, took their latest cargo of captives to the Atlantic Coast. The search party had lost sight of them a dozen times, but the colony of vultures and pack of hyenas that trailed them gave their long trail away to the rescuers.

Over the years, these human tragedies became the harsh realities of life for the African people inside their own continent. Indeed, these tragedies were harder on the youths and the children who saw so much horror that only the setting sun hid these hideous sights from them, but they knew that the night was even no comfort, it held another round of painful agony in the darkness.

King Zendo was a king who loved to do things that will bring progress to his kingdom and make his subjects happy. He pondered every idea carefully, accepted or rejected several ones, endorsed or disapproved of suggestions from his subjects. For two decades, he'd received dozens of suggestions about the best way to rid the land of these loathsome vermin, the Oburoni enemy---to smash the locusts headlong, the position of the hawks in his council---trade slaves for more powerful weapons so they could feed lobster to lobsters, and force them to let go of their chokehold on the lives of his people.

The most powerful force that drove him out of bed each morning, ready to fight these "white locusts" was the fact that they'd killed his grandfather, his father, and had done havoc to his kingdom for centuries. But, most importantly, he resented the inroads these human pests had made into the kingdom when it came to religion and their lofty beliefs when they were brutalizing and hauling his people away as slaves. He hated that these locusts had made connections with some people in the kingdom by bribing them with gifts, which were usually rum, guns or other luxury goods such as broadcloth, beads and trinkets.

The king decided that it was time to end the carnage. And like his father and grandfather before him, he even decided to risk his life to search for and drive these aliens into the mouth of the ocean, even if it meant every soldier in the land dying for that goal. "The time has come to drive these unwanted pests out of the continent of Africa once and for all," he told the elders.

It was unusual for the king to question the will of the gods. "How could the gods preside over all these chaos and bloodshed and watch the torrential tears of their children for centuries without striking down their enemy?" he asked angrily. "Why did all our invocation against the evil traders, our pleas to the gods to rid this land of these greedy locusts in our mist not yield any positive results for all these years?"

The gods have not forgotten them, he hoped.

He still believed in the ancestors. He knew that the continent, no doubt, is a continent of diversity, of gold and of diamonds. It is also the oldest of all the continents, a land of kings and queens, and it has a history filled with legends, of excellent storytellers that were called griots. These griot usually told of civilizations as old as time itself and always remembered the dynasty of legendary kings and queens whose courage and wisdom no ruler would ever be able to match anywhere in the world. "We are the first, the beginning of time itself," the griots loved to say to the children. And these children cherished their heritage, all the history and the ancient wisdom he gave them.

These old storytellers had long memories that dated back to before men became men and women held the world together. They made the children sat at their feet to listen to their tales of valor, to dote on stories about the life and death struggles of their ancestors, the death struggles, the bloodshed, the abductions, but he also spoke vividly of tales of survival, of resilience and of a proud and fearless people.

When he talked about the ancient times, the griot loved to tell the children about the time before the "white locusts" stumbled upon their land, they claimed. But they rather invaded the land---destroying the golden era of innocence, disturbing the peace and freedom. They tell of how people went from village to village to attend funerals, to make merry at weddings, to celebrate family marriages, initiations and "outdooring ceremonies" of newly born children. They visited people who lived in neighboring villages without fearing that the Oburonis would abduct them. Of how they mingled with relatives and sometimes even broke bread and made merry with total strangers. They talked about how they danced and poured libation to the gods, remembering the ancestors.

The griot also talked about the "gbolo women"---the official dancers at many of these events that the kings organized in the land---entertainers of the crowds at these events, whether it was a happy or sad occasion. At these festivals, these free-spirited women danced seductively to get the attention of the men, to catch those men that were looking for wives. They wanted these men so they could make more children to replace those youths that the Oburonis slave traders had hauled away in chains.

The kingdom had suffered too many losses and left several widows, and the need for more children to replace the lost youths became a grave matter of survival. The king needed more men to carry guns and more women to continue to be the backbone of the families---nurturing, molding and shaping the children's character. Thus, the king promoted multiple unions among the men and women. This was an old age practice, nothing he invented, a way to replenish the population and get more gun-carrying youths to defend the kingdom against an enemy that had a voracious thirst for blood money.

The king and the old lady were glad when some of these "gbolo" women received marriage proposals after dazzling the men with their dancing abilities---vibrating posteriors, and some swayed their bodies in dizzying fashions---making enticing sexy moves.

The drummers and the lead singers, who displayed their talents publicly, had a special advantage over other men when it came to wooing these women. Their singing and dancing won the hearts of these women quicker than the men who just prided themselves on their family history or fighting abilities.

The king did not impose this lifestyle on the people. It came out of the needs of the times. Society actually encouraged widowed women to get attached to other families so their new husbands could feed, cloth and shelter them. So these widows searched the faces of eligible men, made faces at them at gatherings, to see if any of them needed a wife, or additional companionship, or were capable of taking care of them and their orphans.

But this was not an easy practice. Some of the women could not live with the idea that a man could love more than one woman at the same time or treat all his wives equally or fairly. The joke was that the old hens, particularly the divorced women, had to dance harder to find another husband or to find another man to marry them and take care of their children.

The griot usually told a story about how the old men and women warned the youth about buying old hens---divorcees---women that their husbands have returned to the market. They warned the youth that a divorced hen was not always a good hen. Either that old hen was pecking at other hens or eating its own eggs. So the buyer of an old hen on the market must always be cautious. In essence, they were saying that though these women might look extremely high-quality women, their husbands did not send them to the market for no reason. They were either trouble makers, "going to town" or were eating their own eggs---they had serious character defects.

The Oburoni missionaries condemned all the things that the African people cherished. They told the Africans to throw away everything traditional since they had no value for them. So the more the leaders fought to preserve what was left of their ancient ways of life, the harder these missionaries worked to destroy everything they found in their trail.

The king whose heart was as strong as an ebony tree was not deterred. "When it comes to our traditions, we are swimming upstream, rowing our boats against the tide of the Volta River," the king said. He arranged the gold necklaces in neater rows around his neck, placing the bigger ones on his right side and smaller ones on the left. He placed the diamond plated ones next to his heart, feeling very proud but hopeful that the future might become brighter. "Very soon, everything would be the way our ancestors had left it behind. Why should our children continue to starve when we have so much food in our farms and so much gold in the kingdom? Is it because we allow these unwanted visitors to prevent us from doing what our ancestors had done for centuries?"

Zotor the priest sneezed very loudly and Abrewa looked at him sharply. "Ask the gods to take their anger on the enemy, and it is time for you to tell them to start killing these intruders and leave our youths alone."

"The gods have no choice but to save this land," he said.

There was danger everywhere, tragedy in the forests and death in the bush pathways. A group of women, who'd traveled to a wedding in the neighboring village, attended their sister's wedding disappeared into a cluster of morning dew of tears. Don Pedro was the person responsible for seizing them. The search party found their beads, headgear, clothing items or even strands of braided hair. These were the only signs these victims had left for their loved ones.

The greediest of locusts had descended on the land, and they'd built their palace-like castles along the coast, though they'd stolen the lands upon which these castles stood. From behind these strongholds, they came out to gather slaves, snatching and trading them for the blood money.

Don Pedro was a heartless and thoughtless trader whose interest in the trade was as high as Mountain Afadjato, one of the tallest mountains along the African Slave Coast region. He had just returned from a bloody raid, his hands were still dripping with the blood of many innocent infants and their aged grandparents. As he sat in the courtyard to enjoy his favorite pastime----drinking rum and eating antelope khebab, he said a quick prayer to his creator. Then when he saw a slave captive running across the compound in the courtyard trying to escape, he reached for his gun and shot the poor captive through the heart. No one rushed to the side of the dying slave, to try to save him except Captain Wyndham, the kind-hearted missionary who risked his life to save the victim. But it was too late, so the victim bled to death an hour later.

Don Pedro, after drinking heavily that night, went into the dungeons to get some female slaves for the night. The servants closed their eyes and pretended not to see or hear these female slaves who were being assaulted because the traders threatened to kill them if they said anything. They had to block their ears not to hear their pitiful screams to be set free and their agonizing groans.

Don Pedro loved to beat any female slave that resisted his advances with his big fists. And some of these women died from these beatings, some became unconscious and when they woke up the next morning, they found themselves upstairs in Don Pedro's bed, still bleeding and barely clinging to life.

"Don Pedro was the most notorious slave trader that ever stepped on the African continent, looking at all of them over the generations," griot Bokorvi said. "He was mean-spirited, numb in conscience and horrible by nature. He started brawls with the missionaries and shot some these preachers point blank. Sometimes, it took dozens of soldiers in the castle to subdue him during his drunken brawls."

"He is such an evil man, I wish I can get my hands on him and cut off his balls and put them into his bloody mouth," the king told the war captain.

"This man had sent more Africans slaves to the land of no return than any other slave trader and I hate him for doing that to our people," the war captain said.

Don Pedro grew up poor in Lisbon. His parents were homeless, and so he grew up with very little or no discipline. This gave him the perfect disposition to be a dishonest slave trader unsympathetic, conscienceless but hardworking. He'd amassed a lot of fortune in seven voyages, which made him one of the richest slave traders. After he became wealthy, he decided to continue the trade anyway because of his love of the adventure, especially his addiction to the free rum and his pastime of drunken brawls.

He had a total of twelve children, seven males and five females that were scattered across the African Slave Coast. He forced himself on a lot of the slave and free women by beating many of them badly if they refused his advances. So the king wanted his soldiers to bring him to his palace alive, so he could get justice for these women. He was clearly that greediest of monsters that lurked behind the tall elephant grasses frequently looking for African youths to snatch, shackle and haul away as cargo.

When Don Pedro arrived to raid a village in his kingdom, though the king was not to go to war, he put on his battle gear and led platoons from seven villages and went after him. Fortunately for Don Pedro, he got so drunk that night that he did not go on that particular raid. The king's soldiers did not capture him alive or killed him because they could not find him, and so this narrow escape solidified his image as the most notorious slave trader along the so-called African Slave Coast.

Though he got lucky that time, the king knew he would finally catch him unprepared and make this monster pay for all of his crimes against his subjects. He got away from the king's justice, but could he escape the wrath of the gods?

"The price the king had put on his head stayed in place for seven years," the war captain told the soldiers. "Anyone who kills this monster would receive a large pot of gold from the king and seven new brides from the queen mother." After hauling away millions of youths and killing many millions more, Don Pedro became the most wanted person in the land.

"The women brigade has sent a party into the forest to look for Don Pedro," Ayeko, a sister of the queen mother said. "He needs to face the wives and mothers whose hearts he'd broken and did so without any remorse. We need to skin him alive or beat him to death."

"The king has offered a lot of money for his head," the war captain told the soldiers. "It was meant to get the soldiers to ambush and capture this monster or just kill him,"

"I will give them more gold if the soldiers bring him to my palace alive," the king assured Mankrado in a passionate tone. "I certainly want to confront him face to face, or strangle him using my bare hands whenever we catch him."

The search for Don Pedro became furious all across the land. Anytime Don Pedro stepped out of the castle, half a dozen search parties followed his every step looking for him. They wanted the chance to capture him alive to collect the money---the pot of gold---a huge price for the task.

The king's brother told Don Pedro that he was a valuable target for the king and his soldiers. There were several soldiers following him everywhere he went, but he was not intimidated. He continued to drink during these raids, but he did his drinking mostly at night, when he sat in the castle courtyard raising his glasses and emptying bottles of rum. He knew that the king wanted him dead and followed his movements like a hawk, so Don Pedro always traveled with armed colleagues. Many Asafo soldiers had tried to lure him into the deepest part of the forests, so they could capture him, but he always escaped these traps using the latest guns. One day he and his friend were trapped in a bamboo grove, they had to shoot their way out,

"We cornered this monster near the river in the bamboo grove," the war captain told the king. "But he killed seven of our best soldiers and retreated to the castle quickly."

"Well, this monster is living on borrowed time, I have no doubt in my mind," the king told the soldiers as he stood on the balcony in his palace counting the dead for that week. "No matter how long it takes, we would eventually get this greedy bastard and make him pay for his horrible crimes against our land."

SIX

M AMA MAMBO WAS THE SPIRITUAL mother of King Zendo. And she also served as the Abrewa, the conscience of the kingdom. Everyone honored and respected her as the matriarch of the kingdom. She was filled with wisdom and gave regular advice to those who asked for it, but her loyalty, devotion and services were mainly to the king and the elders on the king's council. She was eighty-five years old and was like a second mother to the king, because she was a woman who had a lot of patience and loved to think things through very carefully. Anytime the king could not decide a tough case, he secretly turned it over to her to get her advice.

The king, in return, treated her like a goddess. According to the kingmakers, the king owed his crown and stool to this small-framed Abrewa lady. When every other member refused to look at King Zendo's dynamism and purposefulness, Mama Mambo was the one who insisted that of the twenty contenders he had the best temperament and attributes needed in a king. And she insisted that his half brother, Batuka, the reckless veteran warrior, was the wrong person for the golden stool. She was the one who pointed out Batuka's impatience, vindictiveness and his anger to the kingmakers---she highlighted his tendency to explode into anger like a volcano. And it turned out later that she was absolutely right about him.

His subjects thought that the king placed Abrewa even above his own mother, though his mother held a special place in his heart, a place that nobody could ever take. He was never shy to admit this whenever the other women teased him about it.

Like the Harmattan, Mama Mambo dominated the land. The weather dried the leaves across the land, forcing the brown and yellow leaves to fall on the ground, piling up into huge heaps after the heat had killed them.

She was the "abrewa," who gave the final verdict in every capital case that the king tried in the kingdom. Mama Mambo was lenient when leniency was needed, but she was also as ruthless as her deceased husband Mankrado Dodomba when need be. She had very little patience with murderers because she believed that only cowards took the lives of other members of their clan. Instead, she told them to take their anger on the Oburoni enemy. It was her favorite saying that the forest only makes noise when a big wind blows through it, so if you commit a horrible crime, you must be ready for the dance of horror.

King Zendo took Mama Mambo's advice to present a unified front against the enemy. In order to forge this grand alliance, the king allowed her to travel on several goodwill missions to durbars, festivals and funerals to foster solidarity among the groups in the kingdom. He sent her to yam festivals, oyster celebrations and even to many annual solidarity durbars. She represented the king in several traditional areas and carried the goodwill of the king to these leaders.

The king valued her role so much that whenever Mama Mambo made the trip, he always tripled the security guards to protect her. Even the soldiers sometimes carried her in hammocks anytime she was too tired to walk. In return, she told these soldiers interesting Ananse stories along the route and these stories kept them laughing all the way.

King Zendo refused to worry about the six month deadline that Don Pedro, the notorious slave dealer, had given him and the elders to get a quota of five hundred slaves ready. The deadline was just seven days away, but he was in no hurry to get the five hundred slaves for the traders. Unlike in the past, this time around, he cared less about not coming up with the quota. He refused to go to war against his neighbors, the Efutus, with whom he and his folks had plenty of blood ties. So he didn't want to take their warriors as prisoners of war to give to the Oburonis. Why should he satisfy the needs of "these pack of hyenas?" He asked the elders. He and the elders were locked in their stubbornness like bamboos in a thick grove when they decided not to honor the quota. Starting from the day he came to the golden stool, he made the decision not to exchange any slaves for guns or give in to the demands of the slave traders to go to war against his neighbors to take them as prisoners of war. This made him the most adamant, the most hard-headed, if not the most difficult king that the Oburoni slave traders ever dealt with in the former Gold Coast---renamed Ghana.

In the past, whenever the quota deadline arrived, his wives had to stay away from him; because they saw their usually amiable king and husband transform himself into a worried and visibly angry human being. But this time around, they were surprised that he'd not gotten up in the middle of the night to pace the floor like a caged leopard. He'd not scolded any of the children or threatened to divorce any of his wives. They also noticed, surprisingly of course, that he was glad to see dawn burst into the morning tropical sun, which was blazing like a fireball with palm oil inside it. He used to be worried because he didn't want the Oburoni traders to come to his doorstep to seize him, the elders and the members of his household and sell them into slavery. This time around, he never ignored the breakfast his wife had cooked for him.

He, however, continued to see visions of his father and grandfather in his dreams telling him what to do. They both asked him to go all out to stop the "white locusts" from destroying every crop in the land and from ruining everything they'd worked for during their lifetime. His father told him that it was far better for him to die fighting these alien locusts in the land than to sit by like a weakling and let them take over the kingdom, underhandedly destroying the mind and soul of the inhabitants.

But the Abrewa lady thought King Zendo had taken the war to the enemy quite well, and his soldiers had stopped many raids when they'd ambushed, captured or killed the enemy. But because the slave dealers had brought bigger guns, more rifles and cannons that shattered people's eardrums, they had the upper hand in these wars at all times. They saw the priest put the names of many more victims on the Wall of Shame. But he closed the trade routes for years, longer than any other leader ever did. And he'd slowed down the slave caravans which ran through the kingdom, bringing them to a screeching halt.

Those who said his stubbornness for not trading slaves for guns weakened the kingdom, he called traitors and sell-outs. And he yearned for the day he could run such sellouts out of the kingdom or send them to the Fifth River Landing, where they would be punished severely.

As the griot pointed out in the proverb that says that a man must call his small porridge a big porridge, King Zendo refused to call his achievements big successes. His critics held the fact that he did not lead his soldiers into pitch battles against the Oburonis very often a weakness. He refused to do this because he didn't want his soldiers to become sitting targets for the Oburonis. And secondly, that was the way the slave traders killed his father and grandfather.

"Nothing in this fight is guaranteed," his grandfather told him in his dream, speaking in a shaky, venerable voice. "The kingdom you have inherited is like a bag of porcupine. It brings a lot of headaches, deadly pricks and plenty of worries, but it would also bring you joy and satisfaction a few times. You must remember that anytime the waves from the ocean bang against the shoreline, it is the spirits of the ancestors asking you to avenge their untimely deaths, to send them to the eternal rest they so badly needed." He paused for a minute and then continued pouring his long buried thoughts out. "Don't forget to seek atonement on our behalf for what we'd suffered at the hands of these uninvited Oburoni traders. You are the only one who can make these trespassers and human thieves pay for the past."

He usually mumbled something back in a dreamy state of mind, "We hear your wishes and we would never let you down." That charge was what he wanted to hear from the ancestors anyway, because he was eager to force these "wild locusts" out of his beloved motherland anyway.

"We have given you the new weapon to defeat the enemy once and for all. Soon, the enemy would become helpless, prostrate at your feet and you must crush them. When you should begin to crush them, we would tell you later, but it would be very soon. In the end, you and your subjects would be victorious---the enemy would die like flies, and the rest would flee like squirrels---cowards with shame written on their foreheads."

"Well, your father and grandfather died in war," Zotor the high priest said. "So their spirits are restless, because you have not performed the proper custom so their souls could enter the land of the ancestors. You have not arranged for us to pick up their souls and placed them inside "lubu," the small black pot that a close relative must carry on top of the head, escorting the spirit of the dead from the place of death to its final resting place. Since these rites have not been done for your father and grandfather, their souls are still restless. They will continue roaming around you demanding this rite from you."

Very perceptive, and the king nodded repeatedly as he reviewed what had happened to his forebears in the past. "My father and grandfather had died years ago; in fact, decades ago. But if this rite of passage is what is standing between them and eternal rest, then I have to perform these rites as soon as possible." He got up, smiled, slowly straightening up his adinkra cloth around his shoulders, breathing heavily, maybe because he was feeling ashamed or anxious. He'd been mourning the latest victims that the Oburoni slave raiders had killed and many of them were his close friends and relatives.

"Well, you are fortunate your father and grandfather had not put a curse on you and on your children for not performing this rite of passage for them," Zotor told the king. "It means even from their graves, they still want you to succeed as king. They know you are a good-natured and a very capable human being and a great king by your nature and deeds."

"You are right," the king told him embarrassed by the compliment. "If they had been angry with me, they would not have given me the "secret weapon" to destroy these cold-hearted enemies."

"Their anger against the Oburoni pests is stronger, more than what they felt toward you for not performing the "tsibu carrying" ritual to free their souls," Zotor explained to the king. "But since the ancestors can't wait in this half-way state forever, you must free them within days."

The saddest side of the chaos in the kingdom was that the cloth weaving industry, for which the kingdom had made a name for itself, had begun to stall, if it had not yet come to a total standstill. The weavers have been bereaved and the youths could not go to work, so the business plummeted and dwindled to a trickle.

Zotor pointed at the several skulls of the Oburoni victims on the walls of victory. Several of these Oburoni traders had fallen unsuspectingly into traps that the soldiers had made for them. The soldiers usually hid in ambush and waited anxiously to hack the slave raiders to death. They either captured or killed those that fell into these traps and shot those who tried to flee.

A month after the annual Oyster Festival, Pangobo, the announcer, blew his animal horn early in the morning and summoned all adult-gun carrying-males to the meeting ground, which was next to the king's palace. The drummers beat their drums to send emergency messages with these talking drums to the people, summoning every adult male who had been initiated, men who were capable of carrying guns to race to the assembly ground with their weapons for an important duty.

Mankrado, the war chief, spoke on behalf of the king and told the warriors that seven traitors who had been caught helping the Oburoni enemy had escaped into the hills and the king needed to bring them back into custody. He revealed to them that someone had secretly untied their hands and feet in the middle of the night, and that was how they managed to escape into the woods.

"Why don't we sell these cowards to the same enemy that they tried to help against their own?" Zotor the high priest suggested earnestly. He sat next to the moonshine "akpeteshie" drinks intended for libation to the gods to seek their help for the task at hand.

"Listen to what the high priest had asked of the king?" Elder Landonu remarked with horror. "I want to execute these traitors for the gods, instead of selling them off to their Oburoni friends for weapons."

"Well, they have no conscience, these traders would buy their former allies and haul them out of the land and make them bats without homes," Abrewa told the elders. "I want to see the look on their faces when their friends put the "kunyowu" shackles on their feet to make slaves out of them."

"Well, they're still our blood brothers, though they'd turned against us," Zotor said. "Maybe the gods would touch them one day."

"Blame the devil for polluting their hearts and minds," Mankrado, the war chief said as he stood on the bamboo balcony that early morning, his soul on fire though he was soaking himself in the warmth of the Atlantic Ocean breeze.

The king frowned, very angry that the man that was his greatest nightmare had escaped. "You must recapture Amenyo even if that means going into the forest personally to look for him," the king declared angrily. "He is a very troubled individual who needs a hard lesson. I will send him to the Fifth River Landing where the soldiers would bury his body, with his head sticking out for the birds to devour. I will starve him to death slowly."

"If I had my way, he would die working with hard labor inside the royal plantations for the rest of his natural life," Mama Mambo suggested.

That did not satisfy the king's desire for revenge.

"You have a harsh punishment in mind for this young man," the queen mother mumbled laughing. "But don't forget to punish Zabena your wife too. I know you still love her, but she betrayed your love and confidence, your majesty. And she ceased to be an angel from the moment she slept with this man, even a younger man."

"Please spare me the embarrassment," the king told her, scratching his head. He'd been trying very hard to forget the pain and the humiliation Zabena had caused him. "Do you have to keep reminding me about how she went behind my back and humiliated me in my own kingdom by sleeping with a younger man?"

"Well, maybe you are a poor hunter, because your hunting dogs have gone astray...you must shoot better, perform better and maybe even push harder?" she teased the king. It is a disgrace for the king when his wife "went to town" to seek conjugal ecstasy.

The king reluctantly nodded his head in agreement, still boiling with anger. He rose up and walked out to the front of the palace to decide the punishment for the young man. And then he thought about what he should do with his wife, someone he'd loved so dearly, who had gone "outside the house" and humiliated him." He had a seven year old son by Zabena, so he realized that family matters must be handled with extra caution because they could become complicated and unleash shame on one's head.

Abrewa sat uneasily after she'd shrugged her body in disagreement. She could not help but laugh at the king's dilemma. "All these old men who have been marrying these young girls without thinking about the age difference must learn a lesson from the king's dilemma."

"When a sixty-five year old man has a twenty-nine year old wife, he couldn't build a good enough fence around her to keep the thieves from plucking some of her beautiful flowers," Elder Landonu laughed, teasing the king, shaking his head in disbelief.

"Leave the king alone, he is under enough pressure," Mankrado told Elder Landonu.

"You all agree with me that he planted too many delicious fruits by the roadside, which the men could not resist in his absence," Elder Landonu hammered home again blaming the king.

The king hated him because he had a devastating sense of humor. "Are you saying that the king might look young, but his bones have been cracking at the joints," the queen mother also added for a laugh.

"The king had been a strong warrior in the past, but every general slows down with time," Mankrado said as a joke. "He had his great days of youth and vigor, but as an elder statesman, he cannot do in bed some of the things the youthful ones can do."

"Oh well, hold your tongue, there are children within earshot of this conversation," the old lady warned. She hated the idea that the elders were gossiping about the king.

"Why did the young man penetrate the fence the king had made around his garden?" Elder Landonu teased, whispering. "How much damage did he do to the royal family, to the king's flowers?"

"Who cares about reputation, anyway?" Mankrado asked.

The linguist gave him and the queen mother a stern look and then warned them, though he acted as if this was not a serious matter. The king had already divorced and sent Zabena, his youngest wife who had gone outside their marriage, back to her family in Yamoranza, a village five miles from his palace. Though the king wanted his dowry of twenty cows back from her family, he simply kept his son and forgave her the dowry. It was because this would prolong the divorce process, so he decided to forget about the twenty cows so he could return her to her village within three days.

The irony was that the king still loved Zabena very dearly, but the love was not enough to forgive her the adultery. "Sometimes, beauty is not everything; character also matters," the king told Abrewa. "The pawpaw might appear delicious from the outside, but it could be rotten inside, and it can make you sick inside your heart and stomach."

"If I were in your shoes, I would have ordered the soldiers to cut off this young idiot's vital parts, so he won't be able to sleep with another person's wife again," an elder statesman suggested jokingly, and he got everybody roaring with laughter again. "Show him where power lies and take away his man power."

"Oh, you want the king to take his gun from him and send him out of the house. You want him to lose his ability to fire his gun, if you understand what I mean," the queen mother said with quiet sarcasm, laughing. "The way he embarrassed you ---that was very disgraceful and insulting. It was as if he did this to purposely show disrespect to your majesty."

The king nodded, but he wanted him back in custody to face his anger. "He deserves more than that," the king retorted quickly. "He was being too bold when he decided to eat Zabena's delicious red pawpaw."

"I suggest we castrate him," Mankrado said as he placed his rifle on the ground. He was obviously trying to show toughness to make his point.

"Well, if he can't use his gun responsibly, then he does not need to own it," the queen mother suggested again jokingly. "You must take his manpower away and change him from a man into a woman."

"In the land of the ancestors, changing a man into a woman would be a curse that would follow that person into the underworld of the ancestors with everlasting torment and a pain," Zotor the high priest said.

Amenyo was a friend of Batuka and was one of his supporters in his bid to be king. So he decided to disrupt the king's family as an act of retaliation on behalf of his friend. Was that the reason he tried to destroy what was dearest to the king's heart? Or was he trying to fulfill all the base passions deeply buried inside him?

SEVEN

T HE KING WAS RESTLESS AND his heart and soul were screaming with
rage.

He loved the rainy because it brought new life to the land. The
crops grew with vigor and the thick dust that covered the land usually
disappeared for a while. But that year, the king couldn't wait for the
rains to end and for the dust to return soon enough.

He wanted to use the secret weapon against the blood-shedding
enemy aliens. The soldiers became impatient as they waited anxiously
for the ground to dry so they could move the pots from the lagoon area
to the slave castles ready for use against the persistent nightmare that
clouded the land.

But before he started the final drive to eliminate the enemy, the king
asked the high priest to pour another libation, to ask for the blessing of
the ancestors before getting on with wiping out the enemy.

The king, he'd been unable to sleep very well that whole month
and woke up at dawn each morning fearful that the Oburoni enemy
would go to the lagoon, discover the plot and destroy the only realistic
hope they had of defeating the Oburoni enemy. He was afraid that he
might not get the chance to drive them into the Atlantic Ocean, his
greatest wish in life.

"We need to make the final trip to the lagoon before our secret vengeance on the aliens begins," the king told the war captain, gesturing with his hand earnestly.

The war captain had visited the lagoon every day to make sure that his troops were getting the "little soldiers" ready for the final assault on the enemy. The pots were hidden from the enemy and the mosquitoes were multiplying inside them with speed. He'd kept all intruders away from the lagoon area to insure the utmost of secrecy for this mother of all weapons to go in use, he thought.

"This new weapon----whoever thought about using these insects as a weapon must be a gifted thinker? When we bring the mosquitoes out in the hot weather, even just a few of them, would turn the world of these invaders upside down. It would be like a death sentence...a curse to them. It would make a drastic difference in whether they lived or died.

The king secretly sold the idea to every leader who'd heard about the plot, so the king quickly swore them to secrecy. They knew they would no longer rely on the generosity of a few Oburoni missionaries. Or exchange prisoners of war for weapons to fight the enemy. They knew that these "little soldiers" from the lakes, lagoons and rivers would free them from the chokehold of these alien traders, which was much more practicable and realistic.

"We have a long memory of all the pain and suffering that we'd suffered over many centuries, and how they'd killed hope and ended the promise of a future for our children," Mankrado, the war captain said. "Since we celebrate the god of music with much more devotion and fanfare, I feel the gods have decided to return us to the lost era of innocence, to the good, old quiet times of peace and progress."

"This god has stood for sweet melodies, vibrant and rhythmic drums and harmonious songs, and pleasurable sounds from flutes," the queen mother said as she started to display her latest dancing steps herself. "You ought to have a heart of stone not to be moved by the titillating sounds from the xylophone, the bongo, the zither and the banjo. The talking drums, the "dongdong" and the "fontomfrom" drums have remained pure excitement for the people, though some years were so filled with sorrow that we never got the chance to sing and dance."

"But what have these gods done about the Oburoni locusts?" Elder Landonu asked laughing. "So far, the king has done next to nothing and the gods have also not made any aggressive moves on their behalf."

Meanwhile, instead of being calm and pleasantly breezy, the Atlantic Ocean was boisterous and angry. It kept banging itself with fury against the pristine shoreline and then retreating like a rejected lover back into its inner soul. For a whole week, the waves rose higher and reached up to forty feet in the air, banging the shoreline with its notorious thunder blasts as it tried to conceal plots that had been conceived in faraway places, needs brought from beyond the reach of the foamy, pregnant ocean. The elders wondered if these aliens ever gave any thought to the fate of the inhabitants, not just the immediate repercussions of their raids and thievery, but also the long term impact of inadequacy and weariness.

"Who sent these fiery waves inland" Zotor the high priest asked. He placed some food by the roadside for the ancestors, an ancient belief that the ancestors still actively participate in human activities. "Who says our gods are dead?"

After all the suspense in the air, the festival for the god of music finally ended. And it was much more solemn that year because the elders knew that they would soon release the "little soldiers of fortune" to go to work on the enemy, to stop these traders in their tracks once and for all.

As custom demanded, the fishermen could not go fishing till the god of music received its sacrifices of seven ram, seven roosters, seven gourds of palm-wine, seven Kantamanto whiskey and seven gallons of "akpeteshie" moonshine. The fishermen were wondering if the catch for that year was going to be more plentiful than the year before. They hated it when the high priest ordered them to wait patiently until he'd appeased the gods before they started setting out to sea to begin the fishing season.

The high priest was very vigilant; he made sure that the fisherman did not go fishing before this annual ritual, which was dedicated to Dente and the infamous god of music. The seven fishermen he caught violating this decree the year before were barred from fishing that year and he asked them to bring gifts to appease the gods or risked death whenever they went to sea. And the rams, roosters and drinks they brought to the shrine for defiling the gods were given to the ancestors and priests.

Centuries in the past, long ago, these gods didn't settle for only rams and roosters, with the head priest smearing the blood on the effigy of the god of music, carved out of a big stone and kept in the inner room of the castle. These gods used to demand human blood---the blood of virgins---the ultimate sacrifice, they thought.

"I hope the gods understand that we can't continue to wreak havoc on our young virgins just to quench their thirst for human blood," Abrewa told the queen mother. "We are tired, just give them some sea water to drink and let these gods choke to death on the salt."

"The gods are everywhere, so do not speak evil of them," the high priest said. And then he rang a small bell to invoke the gods before he poured the "akpeteshie" on the ground for the ancestors. You could smell the alcohol on the ground as the spirits of the ancestors soaked it all inside.

"Well, so far they've not complained, they have decided to settle for the blood of rams, roosters and cows," the queen mother said, agreeing with the old lady. "This was an old, foolish practice that was born out of lack of knowledge. Because, though this was good for the gods, it was an atrocity against all the young adult women in the land."

"So do you think our ancestors had made the gods so angry that they would abandon their offspring completely?" Mankrado asked. "I suspect they might get tired of us, but they might never desert us."

Zotor sighed and nodded repeatedly. "We should be able to calm them down with libation and animal sacrifices," Zotor told him.

The priests got rid of the virgin sacrifice and they'd settled for a sacrifice that was much more humane and tolerable. This ancient practice forced the young girls to give up their virginity at very early ages to avoid becoming the sacrificial victims of these thirsty gods.

The celebration at the shrine of the god of music had not always been a happy occasion for everyone. It was also a time to remember all the years that the Oburonis had lured those who lived along the coast to the shrine, which was deeply buried inside the Cape Coast Castle, fed them good food, gave them barrels of rum, gourds of palm-wine and cheap akpeteshie moonshine. Hundreds of these invited guests ate and drank until they could no longer consume any more. Some of those who overcame their fears and left their anger behind and came to the shrine to drink all the rum they could consume, ate all the fresh fishes they could eat, baked or fried, had the surprise of their lives. Their hearts would have fluttered if some one had told them that they'd eaten their last meal on African soil.

Soon, they were confronted with the mother of all nightmares.

The music became sweeter with every drink, the rhythm of the drums became much more vibrant, and the food was much more delicious, it was then that the enemy went to work. Those who became too drunk to leave, and those who passed out in front of the god of music, ended inside the secret boats that the traders had placed next to the castle floor. They did not know that they were no longer in the castle, on African soil. They found out hours later, when they finally woke up from their drunken stupors that they'd been tricked. They were twenty miles out to sea, out of sight of the land; because, they were miles into the journey to the land of no return.

They couldn't see through the generosity of these alien locusts, the fatal smiles on their faces, or the constant hooting of the owl or the whispering of the bats near the shrine. Was this the fate of these victims, or was this a misfortune they'd inflicted on themselves?

"A bed, no matter how rough and hard, does not get a sleeping person into trouble," the wise Abrewa told the victims. "They should have stayed at home, drank their akpeteshie and slept on their hard beds instead of falling for the meals these aliens had fabricated as generosity to lure these victims into danger."

These victims charged at the boat owners, rocking the boat from side to side as they tried to deal with their predicament, their self-inflicted tragedy. Agony and pain and tears, fetid with the finality of their journey, the cutting edge of loneliness and the departure from the familiar, became their only option, their only choices. You could hear them fighting to overturn the boat, to reverse their fate. You could feel their bitterness, their desperation and the deep internal agony within their souls. But they did not resign to their fate easily.

The sunrise was no comfort to these victims. Neither was the gentle breeze from the ocean. In fact, as the boat of shame moved slowly away from the African continent nothing could describe the regret, the anger and the disappointment on their faces. They realized how they'd fallen for this clever trap that these Oburoni locusts had used for many years. Some were too sea sick to even fight back. They were more concerned about stopping their sea sickness---the vomiting and the nausea that had plagued them.

Those they'd left behind, mothers, fathers, siblings and cousins also became extremely angry, but they blamed the ancestors for allowing the "Oburoni locusts" from beyond the ocean to force another batch of their sons and daughters out of the motherland, abducting them from the bosom of Mama Africa using this clever but cheap trick.

Maybe the bad weather was a punishment from the gods. For weeks and months, these traders were unable to move a single soul out of the land. The slaves simply pined away in the dungeons of despair, miserable and grief-stricken. They'd been crammed in the dungeons beneath the courtyard like schools of herring. But Mother Nature many times stood in the way and blocked the ravenous greed of these Oburoni with bad stormy weather, but this only lasted for a while. They had to wait for calmer weather to resume their horrible trade and continue their war with the African gods.

During the bad weather, these Oburoni traders overwhelmed the servants serving them at the castle, because many of these traders and sailors became restless, angry and bored. The level of drinking among them increased. Those who brought their ships back from sea joined the slave raiders in the nightly orgies of drinking, womanizing and dancing. And since they had a lot of time on their hand to fool around, to play and to plot more evil against the African people, they made the best of their misfortune. Many of them preyed, prayed and made love during the long wait for better weather.

The level of violence against the servants also increased. Notorious traders like Don Pedro once slapped a servant for not bringing him the right mixture of rum and juice, and he did that to these servants a dozen times each day. He sometimes even touched the female servants on the buttocks and watched them squirmed or screamed. Why should these aliens treat the African servants as if they were next to lower animals?

These traders celebrated being alive in different ways. Some of them even locked themselves in warm embraces making love openly in the courtyard. These servants were not surprised because they'd seen these Oburoni aliens doing worse things to the slaves underground inside the dungeons before.

The Oburoni women who usually wore hats, short pants and bare tops in the dry season, which were too revealing for the servants, but high fashion for the Oburoni visitors, competed with the male sailors and traders gulping down gallons of rum and whiskey. The so-called missionaries were not to be outdone. They also took leave of their books and indulged themselves eating, drinking and courting at these fun-sessions. They didn't wait for their own happiness after death beyond the blue sky as they'd taught the chiefs and their people. They enjoyed their heavenly bliss right on earth at the slave castle.

The servants who knew of the king's plot still worked in silence, but they couldn't wait for the day of vengeance to come to pass---they'd been briefed about the secret plot---a final move to bring the traders to their knees, to make them beg for mercy from those they'd abused all these years. They would flee the land when they start to die in throngs.

"Why did these traders invade our land with such unashamed disregard for human life? They'd desecrated our sense of security and turned our way of life utterly upside down," the queen mother told Abrewa at a meeting with the women that evening. "These are people who have no conscience and know no shame."

"One of the priests told them that it was the gods that had placed this curse on the land, that was why they were suffering, disappearing and dying in such large numbers," she told her softly. "Why the gods did such an evil thing to their own, nobody could ever explain."

As the sorrow and resentment mounted in the land, the women became very dissatisfied with the Asafo soldiers. Many of them had lost confidence in the ability of these soldiers to defend and protect them from the enemy. A lot of them had also given up on ever finding their lost loved ones, people who had been missing for years. The number of mothers who died of broken heart and those who simply threw themselves into harm's way out of despair climbed higher, and it kept mounting until it reached millions, a staggering number.

"I believe these "Oburoni locusts intend to wipe us all out," the old lady said slowly, trying to walk toward the door. Her heart sunk with pain considering all she had seen over the years. In spite of her gloomy views, something deep inside her revealed a sense of hope in the long run. Something kept telling her that her people would prevail over the enemy, and it would even happen in her lifetime.

King Zendo became the king of the Bakano kingdom at the age of twenty-seven. He grew up as a young man who had fought in his father's army. But at the age of twenty-seven, when the Oburonis suddenly killed his father in a fierce battle at the River of Blood, he took over as the next king of this magnificent and ancient kingdom.

The king was the ideal person to sit on the stool during years of furor, the era that roared with danger, mainly from the threat that the Oburoni slave traders posed.

The king and the elders turned to the ancestors once again. Zotor remembered the Amanie Oracle that said that the gods would finally defeat the invaders with a secret weapon and turn the Slave Coast into the "white mans' nightmare".

"Then we would know freedom again and be safe once more in our own land," the queen mother said smiling. She sat down with a big bowl of soup, breaking the bones of grass cutter meat shamelessly.

"Only the gods know how we would celebrate, if we succeed in getting rid of these blood-sucking pests, people who'd brought so much pain and suffering into our land," Abrewa, the old lady, said as she separated the corn from the husks. "They'd stabbed us in the heart and killed our spirits for far too long."

Whatever was in the air was pregnant with evil and couldn't be anything good, because the land was filled with strange and mysterious happenings. There was fear, there was death, and there was suspense. And all the torrential tears everywhere in the land were signs of sorrow and desperation.

There was no sweetness in this once pleasant land.

"If we fight together as one army with one destiny, we would prevail against these locusts," King Zendo told the Akwamus, the Kepis and the Ewes. He wanted a large, unified coalition against the enemy, an army that spoke with one voice and had one goal in mind---defeat the enemy and send them back home.

And so the king smiled and drank more because he'd finally found something to end the constant bloodshed from the Oburoni slave traders, to end the exodus of the youths. He would stop the river of blood that left nothing but chaos, devastation and trails of crimson bloody tears all across the land.

But the queen mother and the leader of the Amazon Female Brigade became sad, discouraged and anxious. She had been very worried about the wives and mothers across the land. The women thought about taking matters into their own hands; of course, over the king's objections. Abrewa, the conscience of the land, had to calm these women down. She knew that if a thousand soldiers fall, another one thousand would rise up to take their place, so she called on the women to exercise some patience and give the soldiers another chance.

And when the king announced the secret weapon to the elders, Abrewa knew for the first time that the ancestors had not forgotten them, but they'd only been bidding for time to finish off their uninvited enemy. She knew that no matter how long, the day would come when the pregnant woman would finally deliver the baby, when the gods would deliver them.

The Oburoni were such fun-loving folks that as soon as the rainy season was over, and the weather became warm, they felt completely safe to come out of their rooms bare-chested, to step outside to enjoy the tropical breeze. They also assumed that the warm weather had driven all the mosquitoes off the land and for a good while. But what they did not know at the time was that the king had a big surprise for them. They'd forgotten that the hunchback does not sleep on his back. So it was with the king, who never stopped wracking his brain for a solution to the dilemma.

Meanwhile, the queen mother asked three women, who had been known to have loose lips, and gossiped a lot on their way to and from the riverside, to keep their mouths closed, or risked being banished from the kingdom or even sacrificed to Dente, the god of gods. And those with ties to the Oburoni enemy he asked to stay away from them for three months or risk banishment or worse.

All the solders that knew about the lagoon plot, people who bred the "little soldiers," had been sworn to secrecy. The king asked them to "eat fire," not to talk about this project to anyone. They were asked especially not to contact the Oburoni enemy. Children were even forbidden to go near the lagoon, let alone to go fishing in the area.

"Since the Oburonis arrived secretly at night, they must meet their end secretly at night," Zotor the high priest declared before the elders as he went into medicine to get the gods on their side.

"Those who do evil must die evil deaths." The king told the queen mother and a jubilant gathering that cheered him wildly; apparently the news about the secret weapon had gone around more than the members of the king's council were willing to admit.

So, as soon as darkness descended on the land, the soldiers asked dozens of women to balance "the pots of death" on top of their heads and make their way quietly past the coconut plantations to the slave castle. Then they were asked to sit these pots next to the Oburoni slave castles. Then the soldiers released the mosquitoes to make their way to these castles under the cover of darkness to do their damage.

To the Oburonis, these castles were palaces of pleasure and strongholds of safety. They were places to drink and party as if everyday was their last day on earth. They were places they warehoused their "African cargo" ready for shipment to the land of no return—the New World. But they were also places that they hid so the anger of the African people could not reach them. So from here they managed to escape the thirst for vengeance of the victimized African people.

On the other hand, to the African inhabitants, these castles had been nothing but torture palaces for their inhabitants. Every time they'd looked at these castles, which had been nothing but eyesore to them all along, they remembered the pain and degradation these traders had imposed on them and on their ancestors. They symbolized the pain, the sorrow, the starvation, the insecurity that the Oburoni had brought in their saddlebags and filthy boats of greed.

Because of all these suffering, before the soldiers released this secret weapon, the priest asked the ancestors during a libation for their help and cooperation.

The king loved every part of that ritual.

He realized that libation to the gods ahead of the day of vengeance was a very smart idea. So the high priest "fo aha de anyi" before the era of vengeance began. After the high priest drank the akpeteshie, the king ordered the soldiers to open the first pot of death and let the mosquitoes fly freely into these fantastic-looking castles.

The enemy was caught unprepared when the first ones started buzzing in their ears. Some of them were in total denial when the mosquitoes continued to bite them because they knew that the rainy season was over. So when they exposed their bodies to enjoy the sweet ocean breeze, they'd left themselves vulnerable to the disease.

They didn't think mosquitoes could buzz in their ears during the dry season, or bite and infect them with malaria. It was their fault when they chose to walk around half-naked, assuming that the mosquitoes would not rear their ugly heads during the dry season. And this was good for the king and his soldiers because they took advantage of this fact.

Given the way a few of the missionaries had conducted their activities in the land, the king tried to spare some of them from the wrath of the mosquitoes. Though he did not intend to kill all of them, the "little soldiers" had no way of knowing which of them was a good missionary and which of them were slave dealers, so they took their vengeance on all of them, at random. According to the king, "It is better to kill all the missionaries than to let one guilty slave trader escape the long jaws of the gods of vengeance."

The king was obviously happy that Dente had started to smile on him and his people. When he heard the anger of the gods in a series of thunderbolts, lightening strikes and heavy storms he was humbled. When a sudden tornado ripped through the kingdom, destroying houses ten miles away from the Cape Coast Castle, he knew this was a sign from the angry gods. But instead of fighting the Oburoni with their impotent guns and seeing more death befall the people, the gods sent in a swarm of mosquitoes.

Wrong thing to do, the Africans knew. Craving for fun again at the expense of the African people, the Oburonis walked around half naked basking in the tropical sunshine. They loved to take advantage of the warm weather, but this time the mosquitoes were there to attack them and they did so with such vengeance that many of them later regretted this mistake.

The warm weather soothed their bodies and delighted their souls, but this led many of the Oburoni traders to their doom. The mosquitoes simply infected these traders with the malaria parasites, sending their lives downhill, shortly thereafter. The servants knew these aliens could have avoided the mosquitoes if they'd stayed indoors or worn proper clothing, and not reveling around half-naked in the warmth like crocodiles.

The Amazon women, who had been very angry with the men for years, suddenly became very excited about the plot. They carried the pots on top of their heads willingly and released these armies of mosquitoes next to the slave castles. Then they watched them go to work on the Oburoni enemy, buzzing, biting and infecting. And they slapped them off as these insects quietly bit them on their faces, on their arms, and on their legs and on their backs. With every bite, these insects infected these Oburoni invaders with the deadly parasite of death, since there was no known cure for the disease.

"They relied so heavily on their cannons, now let them use their heavy guns against these tiny mosquitoes," Mankrado teased them as he smiled broadly and pointed his finger at the slave castle. He liked the way the women had placed the pots very close to the castle walls and opened them just as the sun reluctantly disappeared behind the amber sky. "They will be at the mercy of these insects every night and for weeks to come."

"You sound very happy and satisfied," Abrewa said quickly about the war captain.

The mosquitoes, which flew in small platoons, infected the traders at an alarming rate. Almost every trader who had gone out during the night in those weeks had caught the disease, especially those who sat up in the courtyard drinking gallons of rum and whiskey late at night under the darkness of the coconut trees.

Suddenly, the majestic castle, the most fortified of all strongholds in the land, was no longer the safest place for these hyenas to hide. It was also no longer a palace of pure joy and pleasure, nor was it any longer the house of sexual pleasure. For these adventure-seeking Oburoni people, this once paradise of a palace had turned into a castle of chills and fever, comas and death. And it was soon transformed into the abode of slow and painful death.

The women, the Asafo soldiers and the king, watched from the distance as these mosquitoes attacked and bit these Oburoni traders savagely and infected them, one after the other. How these insects descended on them with a volcano-like anger that had been simmering for centuries, surprised the king and the elders.

Without any weapons of mass destruction, these little soldiers had fatally infected many, if not most of the enemy. After they'd been infected, it took only a few hours for them to become feverish, chilly and very weak. And some of them eventually slipped into coma and many never woke up from this sad, dreadful state.

The Oburoni traders who had used their big cannon guns repeatedly to stop any African resistance to the infamous slave trade, ironically, had no armor against these tiny mosquitoes. This was much more deadly for them, because they'd no immunity against the malaria parasites that the mosquitoes had unleashed on them. They thought the dry weather meant that it was completely safe to come out, but they'd underestimated the anger of the gods, the patience of the ancestors and the wisdom of the African leaders.

When more than one hundred missionaries, administrators and slave traders contracted the disease within one week and many had lost their lives in less than fourteen days, the governor realized he had a disaster of great proportions on his hand. He quickly informed his supporters, backers and hundreds of investors back home, supporters that included royal families all over Europe, about the horrible setback in the notorious business.

When the sponsors got the bad news, the governments back home struggled frantically to find a cure for the disease, but no one at that time knew any cure for this deadly disease. They knew it was incurable and potentially a death sentence.

These Oburoni traders were vulnerable, and so bewildered that they refused to seek local help. Whether a government official or a missionary, rich or poor, they were all convinced that the worse thing that could happen to them, was to die and be buried in the bosom of Africa. And some of them fainted when they realized that the mosquitoes had bitten them and later learned that they had the disease. The parasites usually attacked their immune system, making them very sick shortly thereafter. They sweated profusely, and many of them quickly became dehydrated, feverish, and chilly and then grew weaker and weaker by the hour. Then they became bedridden in the infirmary after five to seven days.

To the king and his subjects, each sick Oburoni trader, official or missionary meant a slave trader that could no longer continue to catch and haul away their innocent youths to the land of no return. One moment they were trading the flesh and blood of slaves and then the next they breathed their last and headed to the cemetery in the notorious Coconut Grove.

These uninvited Oburonis traders, who had descended on the land like packs of hyenas, could no longer pursue the greed in their hearts, nor realize their fatal dreams of wealth. Many had to forgo their zest for adventure, this irresistible passion that dominated their lives, a force in their blood. They had to forget about their main goal---wealth from the flesh and blood of their African victims and head home.

"The Oburoni traders have been devastated. Many lay helpless on their beds like dried cocoyam leaves as they went into irreversible coma," Tobo informed the king who leaned back on his stool with his hands clasping the top of his head nodding. "We have rushed hundreds of them, sick, to the infirmary. Many were near death, and others had lingered in this malaria comma for days. Can you imagine what we felt when the death and devastation shifted from the slave dungeons to the Oburoni infirmary?"

The king waited for the queen mother to confirm the news. Then he sent some coffins to the governor as an act of provocation, or fabricated sympathy. But he waited for these uninvited aliens to die slow painful deaths."

EIGHT

THE WEATHER WAS HOT AND humid, causing many people to have heat strokes. It was the kind of heat in which people had to lift their feet quickly off the ground to prevent them from getting blisters at the bottom of their feet. The small children who ventured outside screamed in pain when they walked with their bare feet on the hot ground, over the cracks on the ground, some of which were as hot as burning charcoal.

There was a satisfied look on the king's face as he and the elders sat under the shade to celebrate the happy turn of affairs. The Harmattan was still at its best---the scorching rays of the sun, the chilly nights that required everyone to get under some sort of thick "akponi" cover or risk getting sick from the cold night weather.

For the whole week, the king ignored the quota of five hundred slave "cargo of blood" that Don Pedro wanted from him and the elders, the quota for that quarter. He knew that the traders would soon arrive on his doorstep like pests to demand it and if he failed to produce it, they would remove him from the golden stool. But, this time around he stuck to his policy not to wage war on his neighbors just to round up their youth, to seize the young adults that were filled with vigor and enthusiasm, and hand them over to the slave traders to haul away by the boatloads to the land of no return.

He knew the time had come for the gods to intervene.

"I have no doubt that the secret weapon would soon drive the enemy away," Mankrado told the high priest. "The avid appetite of greed that had taken hold of them, numbed their conscience and had refused to set them free must definitely come to an end."

"War captain," Zotor called for Mankrado, who had an angry look on his face. "I want Captain Wyndham, your Oburoni friend, to be one of those who should die from the malaria disease. Don't ask me, I have my reasons."

"I don't agree with you on that one. You know he is a friend of the kingdom. Have you forgotten all the weapons he'd given us over the years?" Mankrado barked at him, bowing his head and avoiding his eyes. "Give me one good reason why we should pay this man back with death."

"He'd helped us with guns and gunpowder in the past. But I am not talking about his weapons. Do you know he is promoting the new religion in the land and I hate him for confusing our people?" Zotor told Mankrado. He sat on an elephant mahogany stool, brooding deeply over whether the captain should die or live.

"You want Captain Wyndham to die?" Mankrado started to clean his rifle furiously because what Zotor had just demanded irritated him. "Why, do you want this man who had risked everything he had to help us on so many occasions to die like the wicked traders?"

"Because he has been promoting his religion of greed and love," Zotor told him. "He'd been spreading confusion among our people and he'd done a lot of damage to the minds of our people, perhaps even more damage than the cannons have done to the warriors."

The queen mother made her way to the palace and asked permission from the king and the elders to save Captain Wyndham, her Oburoni friend and secret lover. "He'd paid his dues, so we must spare him from the disease. We must give him the secret herbal mixture, the local antidote to the malaria disease so he could live."

"We don't want any one to give the herbal mixture to the enemy. We must guard this information with our very lives," the king gave her a very stern warning. "We must put business before our secret love sessions?"

"We don't want to watch our friend to die like the rest of the traders in a matter of days," the queen mother muttered. She had tears in her eyes and sincerity in her voice. "Captain Wyndham had risked his life to get us a lot of weapons through the backdoor. He did this because the Oburonis traders refused to sell any more weapons to us because they didn't like the fact that the king closed the trade routes and refused to exchange slaves for guns. I had to get some weapons for the soldiers for the kingdom so we could survive attacks from our neighbors."

"She is right. But for her resourcefulness, the kingdom would have been wiped off the face of the earth, sending everybody into slavery," the war captain explained.

The queen mother had never forgotten Captain Wyndham's generosity to the kingdom. She recalled how Don Pedro, the notorious slave dealer, had planned a raid inside our kingdom, but because the captain had forewarned the king, they were able to stop the raid and saved many youths from slavery. She also remembered the tons of guns and ammunition that he'd given to the king to fight his countrymen and women back. The captain's activities also led to the capture of several slave raiders, people who could no longer continue the notorious slave trade.

"Is it her love for the Oburoni captain, or what he'd done for the kingdom in the past, or his kind-hearted nature that drives the relationship? Or is it her desire or search for romance that is pushing her to save the captain?" the linguist asked the elders, after bowing his head searching his mind.

The queen mother's strategy was simple. She prepared splendid African dishes for the Oburoni captain, fed him some mouth-watering banku and tilapia dishes with hot groundnut soup, a delicacy the captain could never resist. She then gave him some fresh, foamy calabashes of palm-wine, the only one of its kind dessert she mixed with bubbling brown sugar, pineapples and honey, a drink the captain strongly craved.

The queen mother usually entertained the captain in the château that he had helped her built on the other side of the Coconut Grove, a secret retreat, which was hidden from both the inhabitants and the other Oburoni traders. This was where the captain stored several kegs of rum, whiskey and hundreds of smuggled guns and gunpowder.

The queen mother always dressed up in flashy and colorful kente cloths and "mpaboa" golden sandals to match whenever they were together. She braided her hair in large strands, which she meshed neatly on top of her head like the true queen she was. Some of the inhabitants said that she was such a good-looking queen from a long line of queens. She wore her best dresses and dazzled them.

Anytime she went to meet the captain, she saw these Oburoni traders in their hammocks, sitting like royalty, forcing the servants to fan them for hours. Others dozed in the courtyard reclining in their lazy chairs, telling low humor jokes, eating bush meat and drinking rum.

The king summoned the elders and the war captain to the palace to celebrate the good news. The women brought them grass cutter meat and fufu that evening for a grand feast. An old lady tied seven beads representing the seven sub-divisions of the kingdom around the king's wrist. This was when Chief, Nana Obodum, was elevated to the rank of paramount chief. He had to take a new oath before the king and the elders.

"We don't want to be celebrating the misfortune of other human beings," the king told the elders. "But we must congratulate ourselves for meeting the Oburoni challenge headlong this time around, though we had experienced many defeats in the past. These traders had killed many of our leaders, including even my father and grandfather. But the ancestors have decided to give us a fighting chance against these traders, something we never had before."

The old lady, Abrewa, warned King Zendo not to celebrate the victory too soon. "You can't start drinking until the Oburonis have thrown their hands in the air and headed back home."

"Some of these white locusts are like cats, they have nine lives," The high priest, Zotor told the gathering, feeling cheerful and laughing hilariously after he'd finished a heavy meal of banku. "The ancestors had finally received our sacrifices and our libations, though the king had not done what he ought to have done for his father and grandfather. But they have finally decided to come to our rescue."

"Well, we need to thank them sincerely for telling us to use the mosquitoes as a weapon against the Oburoni enemy. Maybe they'd put the idea in Kondo, the medicine man's mind," Mankrado told them. "Or maybe the gods had nothing to do with putting the idea in his head. He just thought about it."

"I heard that there are many signs of the disease among the Oburoni. Some of them are sweating profusely, their eyes have become yellow in color and their urine was also yellow---signs of malaria. And several of the Oburonis have slipped into coma and some have died from the deadly disease already," the queen mother said laughing before she threw herself into her ebony lazy chair. "After all, they are human like us. They are in a state of shock, the king had given them such a vulgar surprise."

"The idea that this disease would save many young men and women from being taken away in chains into slavery has been a gift from the gods," the king stated and then he pumped his fist and flashed an infectious smile. "Shall we spare the lives of the missionaries or let them die as well since their people had no misgivings about taking the lives of innocent people---infants and aged men and women."

But the king and his soldiers could not separate the good Oburonis from the bad ones. For that reason, Captain Wyndham, the kind-hearted Oburoni that nobody wanted to become a victim, also came down with the deadly disease. This captain had treated the Africans with respect and kindness. Unlike Don Pedro and the rest of the slave traders, the elders, including the queen mother and the old lady, Abrewa, wanted this good-hearted man to live. Maybe he would drink the herbal mixture of lemon leaves, tree bark and creeping plants and live.

Even as the queen mother was trying to get permission from the king to give the captain the "ogeling ogeling mixture" her critics started to accuse her of divulging the closely guarded medicine to the enemy, of telling the captain and the rest of the Oburoni community. Word got out that she had a loose tongue and gave the closely guarded secret to them.

She heard an earful of idle gossip from other women. Ayeko had started in full force the latest effort to damage her reputation and get her banished from the kingdom, the rumor had it that it was her closest rival, Ayeko, who was behind the new verbal attack? Some of the women said that the high priest, the one who resented her because the captain had been promoting his alien religion in the land, was the one behind it. Or maybe the fact that she'd mobilized the Amazon women soldiers to fight in the place of the regular Asafo soldiers because they'd been very ineffective in their wars against the Oburoni slave traders triggered the backbiting. The weapons that she'd brought to the kingdom became something that irritated some of the men in the kingdom, so they resented her because it gave her too much power.

She had to deal with a very difficult decision she'd made long ago to build bridges into the enemy camp. While the others preferred that she shunned the Oburoni traders altogether the same way they did, she decided that it was better to build bridges with the good ones, those who opposed the slave trade and fought against their own countrymen in an effort to end the practice.

But to many of the women, she was a traitor. She had betrayed a kingdom that she swore to defend and protect. She had not only slept with the enemy, but she had probably committed treason. So the women wanted her removed from her ivory stool as the queen and then banished from the kingdom.

"There is really no reason for you to hate me. All I've done is to bring in the guns to save this kingdom," she sighed heavily and said out loud to her critics.

Though the king and the elders did not disclose her contributions to the general population openly, they hinted that everything that the queen mother did was with their permission. The leaders understood that she was getting the weapons that the kingdom so badly needed through the backdoor, using her charm, her beauty and her romantic fervor to outsmart many of these Oburoni gun dealers.

"She had been a strong fighter against the enemy, though she did not shoot a gun to kill anybody," Mankrado revealed, if you go beyond her connection to her Oburoni friend. "Do you know that she risked her life to help us? She could have been executed or sold into slavery if the enemy had known that she was an undercover agent for the king? But, fortunately for her, they didn't find out her true identity or the double role she played."

The queen mother and Captain Wyndham discussed his options if and when he gets the disease. It was surprising that they didn't discuss weapons---guns and gunpowder---the essential commodities that she always wanted from the captain. Suddenly, the malaria disease had replaced guns and ammunition as the most important topic in the kingdom.

The captain became terrified. He'd been shaken to the core because he didn't want to die, he told the queen mother. He said that he wanted to live so he could keep helping the African people.

Two weeks later he came down with the malaria disease. He panicked and was in low spirits for three days. His mind was filled with nothing but images of death and burial to the point that he nearly suffered a nervous breakdown. He vowed to fight the disease as hard as he could. And in addition, unlike the other Oburonis, he sought the help of his African friends. And with several mental pictures of his guns and ammunition to them, they were more than willing to pay back his loyalty to them for over many years.

As his time was becoming critical and as an act of harmony with the people or defiance of the disease, the captain summoned the queen mother to their secret rendezvous for one more good time, though he was too weak to be his old fun-loving self. He wanted some final images to carry with him to wherever he was going,

Then the queen mother and two of the elders went directly to visit the captain. His eyes were fixed on the queen mother as if she was a pearl that he would surely miss.

"You know I am dying from the disease," he told the queen mother as she wiped the sweat from his face. He was dehydrated, his voice was weak and he had a worried look on his face. This was a nightmare for him because his body, his head and his joints ached badly as if he'd had fallen from a cliff and tumbled downhill for minutes.

"We would not let you die," the queen mother assured him, holding his right hand firmly. She used the back of her left hand to feel his face, to check his temperature, which was very high. When she realized how feverish he was, she felt very sad, making her voice shaky. So she washed his face with cold water. But she could not wipe away the mixture of regret, sadness and raw anger that filled him.

"He'd helped us on so many occasions, so he needs help from us now."

Though their eyes were teary, they both were glad to meet again. She felt sorry that they had to meet under such unpleasant circumstances. She held him by the torso with all her energy to stop him from falling. When he tried to rise to his feet, he then staggered again.

"Captain, you have to do everything we ask of you in order to beat this malaria disease," she told the captain, wiping the sweat from his face with a soft, white calico cloth. "Though your chances of beating this disease are not very good, you stand a good chance of beating it if you drink the herbal mixture. As of now, your days with us are numbered."

"Just tell me what I need to do to live, my queen, and I will do it," the Captain whispered gently, though he was excited as he held her lively hands staring into her big eyes once again. "Perhaps my good deeds to you and the king in the past would help me live."

"We better be quick with whatever we want to do. It appears you don't have much time left before you slip into coma, and, sad to admit that many people have never recovered from this coma stage."

Another elder, Gokah, who made the trip with her and carried the herbal mixture, whispered something into the queen mother's ears.

"Why are you wasting time, why are you even hesitating? You know he needs to drink the herbal mixture immediately; because he has very little time left," Elder Gokah warned the queen mother. "For all the help this Oburoni captain had given us, we would never be able to pay him back for his help, so the best we can do for him is to give him the herbal mixture right away; maybe we can save his life."

There was a short pause and the captain closed his eyes for a few minutes. He was tired and he was becoming weaker and weaker by the hour. She took a small pot of the herbal mixture, opened the lid with a simple twist and poured a large dose of it in a calabash for the captain to gulp down. It didn't matter to them whether he was an Oburoni, an alien European with a lighter complexion; he was a human being with a great heart, kind, respectful, unselfish and loving. That was all that mattered. She stood over him as if he was his son or husband---because he was the closest man she ever had outside of Dente's circle of priests.

"Please drink this medicine. It will save your life," Elder Gokah added his voice, speaking through an interpreter telling him forcefully not to waste any more time but to drink it immediately.

"Thank you very much for your help," Captain Wyndham told them as he gulped down a mouthful. He shook their hands with whatever strength he had left inside his sick body. I am surprised you are all so concerned about my health---whether I live or die---considering the fact that I am an Oburoni man."

The two of them smiled broadly and shook their heads. "But you are an unselfish and good-natured Oburoni. To almost everybody in our kingdom, including even Zotor your main critic, you ceased to be an enemy years ago."

She caught him looking at her face again after she said that---eyeing her natural, beautiful face. She knew the captain could never resist her beauty. But death continued to stare him in a menacing way, and the reality of dying had begun to hit home. He didn't want to leave all that pleasure, all that natural beauty and all the passionate love between the two of them behind. She knew that he was much more in love with her than she was, that was if she ever truly loved him, talking about deep passions that were not manipulative or unselfish.

Meanwhile, there were rumors in the kingdom that the captain, the queen mother's boyfriend had contracted the deadly disease and had days to live. "He was getting weaker and weaker by the day," Ayeko told the women the unsettling news and many of them were somewhat in a state of disbelief. "She won't have him around anymore, from what I have heard, not for long. He would be gone within a week or two like the other slave traders."

"Well for what his countrymen and women had done to our people over the years, he deserves to die like the rest of them---slow and painful death---the curse of the ancestors to all of these aliens," Ametor told her fellow women. There was no doubt that she had strong hatred for the captain and the rest of the Oburoni aliens.

"Oh no, the captain is very different. He is a good man who'd done so much for us and so he must continue to supply us with the weapons that we need so badly to fight against the slave brokers," Abrewa said, her attention drifting to the thought of the possibility of the captain dying, and not looking at her critics before jumping to defend him.

Those who had friends among the Oburoni invaders were torn between helping their friends to beat the disease and letting them die as a retaliation for all the abductions and killings their countrymen and women had done on the miserable African continent, though the richest land on earth.

Then they remembered the king's warning to them not to give the mixture to any Oburoni alien. "If anyone gives information about the secret weapon or the "ogeli ogeli" herbal mixture, the person would be banished from the kingdom, or even executed for betraying his motherland," he'd warned the people on many occasions.

"But what are decrees if we cannot defy and break them?" the queen mother asked. "Well, when it comes to this Oburoni captain, I will break this decree; I wouldn't mind sticking my neck out for him."

Suddenly, the women started to consider the king an extraordinary ruler, a genius who might become a legend in the land. They loved the way he and the high priest came up with the idea of breeding the mosquitoes and using them against the enemy. It was obvious their soldiers were no match for the invaders, when it came to pitched battles. And so when the king decided to do something completely different, everyone applauded him for his creativity and effort, except Batuka and his band of traitors who still disagreed with this new move.

"Let us be very careful about what we do," the king cautioned. "Remember the saying that when you have not finished crossing a river, and you are still swimming in the river, you never insult the mouth of a crocodile, so let us not jubilate too soon. Let us not stand by and see our good weapons supplier die."

The king got up and straightened up his big adinkra cloth around his huge torso. Though he was publicly worried about the captain, he had a big smile on his face. He was a proud king who wanted to follow in the traditions of his father, a king that had conquered all his neighbors and had succeeded in creating a loose confederation of all the competing groups, something his grandfather failed to do. And he'd forced the rebellious clans to drop their demands for independence.

Instead, they paid their annual tributes to him regularly without any resistance or protests.

"We need to keep more youths from going into slavery. Their names must never go on the notorious Wall of Shame," he told the war captain, Mankrado. "If the secret weapon would work the way it is supposed to, we should be able to stop the slave trade soon and force these aliens to depart our land."

"Leave it in the hands of the gods," Zotor the high priest insisted, gesturing toward the sky with his right hand. "We can never know what the ancestors would do next. We must trust that their eyes are watching over us and be patient until the very end."

The high priest wondered which was harder for the women---watching their youths gunned down, or seeing them stolen, shackled and hauled away like cattle to the land of no return.

Abrewa told the priest. "Anytime I see blood flowing from these youths like river fountains, infants bleeding freely from their skulls or fractured ribs or broken limbs, I have to fight myself not to attack every Oburoni I see. It causes a sudden heart attack within my chest."

"Maybe the agony of our people have finally forced the ancestors to act on our behalf," Zotor told the elders, happy, suddenly sounding victorious and jubilant because it appeared they were in total control of these Oburoni enemy. "We know that the elephant has a short tail, but that is what it uses it to drive away all troublesome flies."

"The malaria deaths among the traders are acts of the gods. It is their final justice to them," Mankrado said, his happiness about the misfortune of the slave dealers visible to everyone. "Finally, these Slave Castle strongholds are no longer safe hideouts, or comfortable places of luxury where they'd lived to hide, drink, party and sell our people. They have become abodes of slow and painful death."

From behind these castles, the enemy now saw their dreams of wealth went up in flames. The good times of rum and assaults on the slave women were over. For these once fun-lovers and dreamers of wealth, life had become a struggle for survival everyday. The African shore had become a risky place where an epidemic killed these traders freely.

"But for the mosquitoes, more of our youths would have ended up on the other side of the Atlantic Ocean in shackles," the king told several chiefs, shaking his head in total disgust. "I much rather see them die like flies than see our youths killed or hauled away daily."

"You are right. Some of these youths might not be here today. They would have been taken away in clanking shackles as slave captives," the queen mother joked. She was still angry and saddened at the same time, but she was glad that the slave traders had met their match the same way that their youths disappeared in the forests and some killed in senseless orgies of blood.

Devastated and rattled after months of agony, the governor brought his fellow traders to an urgent meeting and gave them a disturbing advice that the way to avoid the disease was to forget about their dreams and return home immediately. Some of them listened to his advice and fled immediately, departing the African shores with their dreams of wealth unfulfilled. The joke was that they took to their heels like squirrels, returning home like cowards, though that kept them alive.

Nevertheless, some had the dilemma of the greed in their hearts and their love of life. Some were too attached to their dream of wealth to let it go. In the end, they chose greed over life, and so those that stuck to these wicked dreams, died lonely and miserable deaths at the hands of the mosquitoes. They died because they could not let go of their quest to become wealthy from selling the flesh and blood of African slaves, a passion deep-seated in their hearts.

For the king and his people, the whole thing was a time of vengeance.

Like any epidemic, the inhabitants were worried whether the disease would kill them too, but many of them had natural immunity against the disease. Those that came down with it drank the herbal mixture. They recovered from the disease within days.

The land became a place of doom for these traders, as the missionaries the administrators and the traders died in the hundreds everyday.

"Our women could finally walk again with the rhythms of freedom---peace, pride and confidence. They could now go to their farms to get some foodstuff to feed their children," the queen mother said.

"And the men could also go hunting game to feed their families," Mankrado smiled, his voice clearer and energetic again. "Well, but no matter how many of the Oburonis died, our men could never go back to sleeping at night without loaded guns next to their beds."

After centuries of agony, the long nightmare for the African people, the centuries of suffering, of seeing their children killed, of seeing their youths kidnapped, of watching them sold and hauled away to faraway places, all came to an end.

It took such a long time to get rid of the enemy. But they were surprised that it was the tiny mosquitoes that became the silent heroes in their long struggle for survival. They flew, buzzed, and attacked the slave traders. The bites became deadly to the enemy. So they infected and killed them in droves, ending their evil dreams of slavery. They sent many traders fleeing back home, but those who resisted and continued to follow their fatal dreams, stayed and died by the thousands, ending in early graves inside the notorious Coconut Grove.

NINE

THE ASAFO SOLDIERS, WHO WERE still celebrating their victory over the Oburonis, brought the seven Oburoni captives to the king's palace and forced them to sit on the rough "hliha" stones. The captives bowed their heads in shame while the executioners stood guard over them, breathing very hard down their ears like hungry lions. Some were frightened out of their god forsaken minds, especially when the executioners touched the backs of their heads with their long knives.

"Do these captives deserve to live?" the war captain asked some of the women.

"Not after all the pain and agony they'd caused us," Ayesha told him bluntly. "They must not live, not after stealing all my seven children."

The women wore red broadcloths; they were still mourning the dead and the departed. The very angry ones used the red broadcloths to beat these captives on top of their heads; an act they knew would desecrate these captives. These acts caused a loud laughter among the women, because these were acts of defilement, the ultimate humiliation to the men.

The elders and the clan heads sat down quietly. The king sat in the middle, with the senior paramount chief on the right and another paramount chief on the left. The king did not sit on his golden stool that day because the meeting was not for pomp and pageantry; it was a very special meeting that involved life and death decisions. So no one was smiling, because several of the women were still shedding silent tears, or shouting angrily at the captives and trying to assault them. Those women who'd especially lost their relatives prior to the meeting; this was an opportunity to settle scores with the enemy.

The king had to wait for the Asafo soldiers, who did not arrive at the meeting grounds on time. They were busy beating their war drums in front of the Shrine of Dente, which was five hundred yards from the meeting ground. They made their way very slowly, inch by inch, yard by yard acting war scenes, dancing and marching with pride. Those soldiers who had been recently bereaved tied red dyed cloths around their heads to honor their loved ones. The women also painted their faces and lips with red clay and spoke very little. Some broke into tears, because they were still deep in mourning for the loss of their sons and husbands, daughters and mothers from the past.

The seven official executioners of the king stood over the captives with their sharp machetes ready to do the king's bidding at a moment's notice. There was something strange about these Obrafuos, something that was mean-spirited and threatening about them. This was disturbing to every one present at the meeting including the elders.

The captives knew their fate was in the balance, but some did not show any fear. But when Isikana, who was the seventh Obruafuo, entered the square to take his place among his fellow executioners, the women burst out laughing loudly. This was because he had trouble controlling his wife the night before. His wife actually pushed him down and sat on top of him with her heavy, obese body. It took two of his friends to rescue him from under her. She told the other women that as an Obruafuo his husband was incapable of harming even a fly because he was a weakling. The insult was degrading to Isikana and this drew laughter from the audience, and so this made Isikana very angry, but he kept his composure in the presence of the king and the elders.

"Bring the captives to the center," the king ordered, looking stern and somber as silence descended on the square immediately. "We need to show them our brand of justice."

The obrafuo blew the horns of evil and the women remained silent. Dokuwa tried to kill the captives with her evil stare, but she ended up just chuckling and staring at them. Two women who had lost their children days before this meeting charged at the captives, but the war captain quickly restrained them, pulling them away. Seven other women tried to attack the captives, and two ended spitting into their faces.

The Oburoni captives sat in silence as they waited on the king and the elders to hear their fate. A few of them thought their roles as missionaries would save their lives. Some of the captives were not slave traders, but the war captain decided to kidnap and bring them to the king as slave traders anyway. He decided to kidnap these missionaries soon after the heir to the throne was kidnapped on his way from a hunting trip. The king wanted the Oburoni to tell him about the whereabouts of Botwe, the heir to the throne. But they simply looked at him and had no useful information for him.

When the chief executioner raised his long life to execute these Oburoni traders, the queen mother sprang to her feet to save those who were innocent missionaries. She said that they were members of the SPG, Society for the Propagation of the Gospel, the oldest missionary group in the then Gold Coast. She told the king that they represented the better side of the Oburonis, and many of them had converted several Africans, though the king hated the religion because he thought that it was forcing his subjects to look into two bottles with one eye.

The group had been in the kingdom for barely six months and had baptized more than seventy Africans. They were spreading the gospel faster than any other group before them had done. They, however, got several inhabitants torn between their traditional allegiance to the king and their new Oburoni religion that emphasized preparing for life somewhere beyond the blue sky, in a heaven after death.

"You realize, they are completely wrong when they tell you to work for better life somewhere after death, while they continue to loot our gold and haul our children away in the millions," Zotor the priest described the work of the missionaries. "That doesn't make any sense to anybody, does it?"

The queen mother recognized the bishop among the captives. He had condemned what his countrymen and women were doing to the African people, and he had even tried to stop the slave trade among his people by himself, though the powerful sponsors of the trade back in Europe, threatened his life if he did not cease his protest activities.

Ayesha, who had lost all her seven youths three years back, broke away from the group of women and charged at the captives once more. She kicked one of the captives in the face with her wooden shoes, slapped another one, before invoking a curse on all of them. She hated the evil fate they'd dealt to her children. The other women rushed to restrain her when she pulled out a hunting knife to kill one of these captives, but she narrowly missed stabbing him in the heart, though she stabbed his hand.

"Tell us where we can find Don Pedro," the king asked them sternly in an angry tone. Don Pedro was the most notorious slave trader that ever came to the continent. "The only way you can gain back your freedom is if you tell us where we can find Don Pedro so we can find out about where he'd sent Botwe, the heir to the golden stool."

"They must pay for their crimes one way or the other," Mankrado told the king, straightening the cloth around his shoulders and putting his amulets in order. "They deserve to die or be banished to the basement of woes."

"Can we proceed with the execution," the chief brafuo asked anxiously. The mere mention of Don Pedro's name made the brafuos angrier. The prospect of finally getting rid of this monster from the land was too sweet to pass up, that was if they could find him.

"Did Don Pedro elude your soldiers once again?" the linguist asked the war captain. "The scouts were positive that they had spotted the monster in the nearby woods. So how did he end up escaping from you?"

"Well, the soldiers wanted to take him alive so he could face the worst punishment they could think of, and the king did not want the soldiers to shoot him dead, so he was able to disappear into the woods once again," Mankrado told the king and the elders.

Don Pedro had left the group to drink water from a nearby river shortly before the asafo soldiers arrived for the round up. The thoughts of vengeance, which rose like dark rainy clouds in the sky, quickly disappeared that morning. The men gnashed their teeth and the women threw their "akaye" rattles on the ground in frustration and anger. Everyone was disappointed that the evil Oburoni trader, the monster without a heart, as the old lady called him, had slipped away from them once more.

"Maybe he does not deserve to die a quick death---even execution was not good enough for this man," the king told them. "Let him live to face the vengeance of our "little soldiers," a much slower and painful death for this monster."

"Just mark the king's words," Mankrado told her. "Don Pedro is living on borrowed time. You know that a guest can never outdo the host, so we will catch him sooner or later since somewhere, one day, his luck would run out."

"I think you are right, it is about time," the king told Mankrado. "Considering you'd lost him on six different occasions."

"Just remember, when a blind man says he will throw a stone at you, it means he already has his foot on a stone, so just watch what the future holds for this "sansabonsam" trader," the old lady said. "I cannot wait to see the brutal end of this evil man."

TEN

CATCHING DON PEDRO BECAME A very difficult task. He knew the land very well because he'd lived on the continent, on the so-called African Slave Coast, for nearly twenty years. The king had also asked the soldiers to bring him in alive to face traditional justice, and this complicated the hunt for his head, it slowed it down considerably. Six times the soldiers cornered him, but six times he managed to escape their dragnet. Mankrado the war captain nearly succeeded in catching him in the valley below the mountain, but he still managed to slip away like a clever squirrel. The joke among the soldiers was that he was as evasive as a he goat and as deadly as a cobra snake when in retreat. He'd earned the notoriety for being the slickest and the most vicious slave trader that ever came to the African continent.

He was the nightmare that every mother and child in the land feared. And the inhabitants treated him as if he was a wild white hippo. The mere mention of his name sent many youths into hiding. And many children went to bed with Don Pedro on their mind and woke up with thoughts about what this monster could do to them---he was the terror nobody ever loved.

The soldiers blockaded several bush paths, trade routes, and even dug deep holes in the forest in many places just to catch this

"Obroni Cobra." It was ironical that this was the nickname the soldiers gave Don Pedro because of the manner in which he struck deep into the hinterland and then left the scene like a lightening bolt, spitting venom of blood everywhere, taking slaves with him, especially women captives. But somehow, he always managed to get away before the asafo soldiers found out where he was.

Rumor had it that the high priest tied up Don Pedro's effigy in several banana leaves and buried his soul under a heavy "hliha" stone next to the Atakpla River, yards from the Shrine of Dente. He was hoping to kill off his spirit and leave his physical body much more vulnerable for the Asafo soldiers to capture. But it was shortly after this ritual that Don Pedro secretly raided the Bakano kingdom again and abducted Botwe, the heir to the golden stool. He took the seventeen year-old to the castle and then later on hauled him away in his Liberty Express boat to the land of no return.

That was one of his boldest actions in the land.

The abduction hit too close to the royal house for comfort. It made the king extremely angry and brought not only heartache to Botwe's mother and uncle. The number of black eyes this Oburoni trader had given the royal family were many. It became an embarrassment to the king and the elders. As the griot storytellers put it, after the gods saw these latest rounds of atrocities, and how Don Pedro had degraded the king, humiliated the elders, they decided to help them protect their children.

The servants watched the "Oburoni locusts" emerged from their castle hideouts without their umbrellas craving for the sunshine. They were yearning for the gentle Atlantic Ocean breeze. The men came out with their chests bare and the women secured their breasts in place with pieces of soft cloth. All of these women wore shorts, showing off their legs, which became paler because of the long hibernation during the rainy season. Dozens sat in their hammocks in the courtyard basking in the warmth of the sun. Many were smoking their pipes, some were gossiping and drinking as the ocean breeze caressed their delicate bodies while the sun drifted into darkness that evening.

The servants served them with all the rum, whiskey, wine and gin they wanted. A few adventurous ones preferred the foaming suds of fresh tropical palm-wine, maybe to soothe their troubled souls. The palm wine produced enough pulp to fill their hungry stomachs, which activated their libido. But many of them devoured the bush meat like carnivores and ate the fresh fishes that were caught directly from the ocean, prepared for them in a special way. The popular antelope khebab, large portions of wilder beast and roasted mutton were also delicacies that many of these aliens could not stay away from.

Ahmadu mocked them about their strong attachment to rum and whisky and other alcohol---fun times---addictions. "One thing these Oburoni people know better than us is how to enjoy their leisure," Ahmadu told the other servants. "They love to live their lives as if there will be no tomorrow for them."

"You know, Ahmadu, you are absolutely right," another servant, Ametor told him. "With the kind of work they do, raiding villages, capturing innocent victims, they could die at any moment."

"Well, do you know we are going to be busy serving them in the courtyard every night until they go into hiding again during the next rainy season," Tobo asked Ahmadu, his tone a mixture of anger and frustration. He was indifferent about their life expectancy. He paused and smiled broadly as if he'd heard some great news. "I doubt very much if they would survive what the king has in store for them."

"They are celebrating being alive, and this is something they have been doing at our expense all these years," Kwamiga growled from his throat. "They may have a very strong reason this year to be celebrating being alive."

"They're not really celebrating anything. They are just trying to drown their guilt in rum and whiskey, trying to ease their conscience with the bush meat. But no matter what they do, you can see their souls are still on fire. Good food and lots of drink cannot give them the inner peace that they'd been searching for. No matter how hard they tried, most of them could not make peace with their gods."

"They used to look down on the bush meat as crude, but after a few weeks, they'd become so addicted to it that they craved it just as they love the rum," Ahmadu told Kwamiga, shaking his head in disbelief. "Now we can't make enough of the antelope khebab for them. I usually look away when they start to devour it like lions tearing the flesh off zebras. Have you seen the way they lick their plates and roll their tongues in and out like chameleons hunting for insects?"

"It is amazing the amount of rum many of them consume each night," Kwamiga said. "Don Pedro can finish a barrel of rum each week, but sometimes, he finishes that barrel even sooner. Each night, this man drinks his sorrows away and soothes his conscience with the khebab. He is very rich, but he is living in a very troubled world, and has lots of pain. He is obviously a man with a lot of material wealth, but lacks inner peace---certainly true happiness."

"Whenever I run into him I go the other way, and that happens every time I see him," he grimaced as if his head was throbbing and he was in deep pain. "He has so much blood on his hands; maybe, that is why he tries to wash his tainted hands with the rum and whiskey each night."

"Well, you know when he gets drunk; that means trouble for the slave women inside the dungeons. When he is not engaged in drunken brawls with his fellow traders, he goes after the slave women downstairs, beating, dragging and molesting these innocent women. He takes his guilt on these poor, innocent women as if they could give him the inner peace that he craved so badly."

"I hope his fellow traders would kill him in the heat of one of these drunken brawls sooner or later, one of these days," he said with a passion, biting his lips angrily and repeatedly. "You may soon have your wish, because I heard the other traders plotting to stab him to death if he attacks them again or start another senseless brawl."

"That would mean the world to King Zendo. He would thank them very much. He'd wanted this man dead since the day he abducted and sold the heir to his golden stool into slavery."

"Do you think he would give them the pot of gold, the money he'd put on his head?" Ahmadu asked.

"Oh yes, he would do it. He hates this man so much," he said.

"The children all across the land would be free to roam the woods," Kwamiga told Ahmadu. "No more nightmares and bad dreams for thousands of children who went to sleep immediately their mothers mentioned Don Pedro's name."

The governor and his wife normally enjoyed their leisure in their private residence enjoying the evening breeze. But they sometimes watched the fanfare and the brawls in the courtyard from the governor's balcony. The governor's wife caught him several times watching the slave women in their dungeons, but she assumed that he would never stoop so low to bother them. But some of the ones he liked sometimes secretly ended up on the far side of his residence, and these usually were after his wife retired to bed. His extra activities usually took place without his wife's knowledge, but the servants and butlers knew about them and laughed at his two-facedness.

One night, Don Pedro had fooled everybody into thinking that he was still drinking, but he secretly left the castle and dashed into the nearby village with his friends to raid these villagers. Instead of being in the courtyard drinking and enjoying his fortunes, to the king's surprise, he went on another bloody raid.

"What forces drove this man on his endless raids? Was it because of the greed within him, an overpowering force inside him, or was it his secret addiction to bloodshed?" Kwamiga asked the other servants.

"He definitely has a devil living inside him that caused him to yearn for human blood and misery," Ahmadu said. "And he always heard a voice that asked him to spill blood, maybe this was an overwhelming voice he could never control."

"I don't understand why he decided to slip away from the courtyard with some of his evil friends and went on another rampage in the middle of the night," Mankrado told the soldiers angrily. "Which soldier failed to keep an eye on his movement? Whose fault was this?"

"Well, the man is as sleek as a cobra snake. First, he fooled us into thinking he went to sleep in his room upstairs after drinking gallons of rum at the big festival," Bangura, the platoon commander revealed, shaking his head in disbelief. "Instead, he slipped away through the backdoor with a dozen of his friends and the next thing we knew, they ended up in the nearby Abum village."

"So, Don Pedro went again into Abum to attack these innocent villagers. He managed to escape our dragnet once more," Mankrado told the king. "Yes, I am sorry he went on another bloody raid, spreading death in Sokode and Klefe villages, and killing over fifty innocent people that night."

"Well, how did he get so lucky again?" the king asked in a surprised tone. "How many did he have to kill and how many more would he have to abduct before he satisfies the unquenchable greed that burns like fire inside his soul?"

"He took fifty victims and killed another fifty last night. It was such a great surprise to our soldiers," Mankrado told the king with a lot of bitterness. "The demons inside him have broken free and attacked us once again."

"Don't worry, this blood-splattering vulture is living on borrowed time," the king said as he heaved another long sigh of disappointment. Once again his soldiers had been unable to catch this notorious trader, the deadliest of his enemies---the king cobra of all the slave traders---the nightmare of every ruler in the land.

"I agree with you. Hopefully, though he does not yet know this, he might be in his final days. This might be his last chance to hurt our youth, to create insecurity in this kingdom," Mankrado agreed with the linguist. "I can't wait for the day when he would be inside our grips, chains around his neck, shackles on his ankles, blood on his face, begging for mercy from the king like a hopeless slave victim."

"Sooner or later he will be where we had always wanted him to be---down on his luck, begging for his life," the linguist said smiling broadly. "We would hold the head of this lucky and sleek cobra, making it safe to handle or kill."

"Well, for all you do in these fateful days, just make sure that he is inside the castle when your men release "the little soldiers of vengeance" so they could carry out our brand of justice on him, which is retaliatory, secretive, but deadly; it is justice our own way," the king said and smiled for the first time in months as he expressed his determination to teach these notorious enemy traders the last lesson.

The queen mother went to visit Captain Wyndham in their secret rendezvous located on Cape Three Points. This was a journey she'd taken hundreds of times. But somehow as fate had it that day, the sentries on top of the lighthouse on the hill saw her through their binoculars and raised alarm. The breeze was still soothing and the grasses exuded fresh morning scent, because the servants had just cut the grass around the secret villa. Captain Wyndham had once assured her that nobody knew of their secret meeting place, so she had nothing to worry about. She didn't have to watch her back or take several routes to the secret place to avoid detection.

But that was over ten years ago and times had changed. The new lighthouse that had been built overlooking everywhere changed everything. One of the guards noticed movement around the castle. The captain was late that afternoon, so the queen mother simply made her way to the secret cabin and made herself at home, waiting for the love session.

She heard some movement and thought it was Captain Wyndham. This was the same movement she'd heard millions of times. She knew after that movement, the captain arrived and within minutes they got locked up in the warmest of embraces, followed by the most exhilarating encounters.

But before she could open the door that morning and let him inside, she heard boots and several steps on the cobblestones. "You are under arrest for spying for your king," one of the soldiers growled at her. "Captain Wyndham has also been placed under arrest for treason against his countrymen and women and we would soon send him back home to Liverpool, but the governor will deal with you personally."

Her stomach started churning, her head was throbbing and she suddenly became very dizzy. She wasn't sure if she was dreaming or if this was real. Curse words, angry outbursts and physical attack all came from her at the same time. Why they decided to arrest her before the secret plot unfolded baffled her. But she was very sure that she had too many friends among the Oburonis not to get someone to speak on her behalf to rescue her.

When she overcame the initial shock, she refused to answer any more of their questions. Her worst fears had become reality. Batuka and his friends had finally leaked out the information that her love for Captain Wyndham was not real. They had revealed that it was an opportunity for her to get her hands on some weapons and some valuable intelligence for the king's soldiers. They told the governor that she was to find out where the raiders were going to go in the hinterland for their bloody raids and when they were going to invade his kingdom.

"Tell the truth; otherwise, we have no choice but to send you into the dungeon to live among the slaves," the soldier told her in a serious tone, tightening the shackles around her feet until there was blood oozing down her ankles. The soldiers were surprised the way she bore the pain, how she refused to scream, refusing to beg frantically for her freedom. She was so silent and so composed till the soldiers realized that she was truly a queen mother.

"What do you intend to do with me next?" she finally broke her silence, still rattled, but pretending to be fearless. "I am not afraid, even if you want to kill me, you can do so."

"The governor would send you away with Captain Wyndham your so-called lover to his home next week," the soldier revealed to her. "Are you ready to go back home with him as his slave or his lover, or both? You don't have a choice anyway."

"If I get to see the Cap again?" she asked with exaggerated boldness. "That shouldn't be too bad for me, not really, I mean not at all."

"But that depends on the mood of the governor," the soldiers told her in a hostile voice as they escorted her from upstairs to the entrance of the female slave dungeon, hurling insults at her and calling her a whore in her face. "You are a whore and you deserve this treatment from us."

Fortunately for her, just before they removed her shackles and locked her in the dungeon, Major Wilson, the missionary partner of Captain Wyndham, emerged from his room to plead her case. "You can't lock her up in the dungeon---she is a Christian and a friend to many of us," he told the soldiers, almost panting for breath. "She has not only saved our lives dozens of times, but she has helped us tremendously in spreading the gospel among the heathen."

"You have to talk to the governor, we have our orders, but we will keep her in the Palaver Hall until you have talked to the governor, so we can get this resolved," the soldiers told Major Wilson and took her quietly to the infamous Palaver Hall, where the nightmare of many deals that sealed the fate of many slaves had been made over many years.

The queen mother simply sat on the chair and placed her shackled hands on the large mahogany table staring at the ceiling and also at the dried blood on her ankles. She thanked Major Wilson for saving her from going into slavery, the place the inhabitants called "the mother of all horrors."

When the servants finally brought her some water, she was very glad to see some African faces. But she was more concerned not about herself, but about the whereabouts of her friends Major Wilson and Captain Wyndham. "Make sure you give them the herbal mixture when the king's plot begins to unfold. They have just saved my life again, so don't forget to give it to them, even if the governor executes me," she insisted vehemently, before she even took a sip of the water.

"It is Batuka and his friends who told the governor that you have been working for the king and that you have been collecting information from the castle and sending it to the king," Binto, the head lady servant, told her. "Batuka is a man of shame who splits blood every chance that he gets."

She dashed forward to meet Captain Wyndham and Major Wilson and gave them both sentimental hugs, but because they did not find the key to unlock the chain around her neck, she just embraced them partially. "I am not sure what those traitors said about you, but I know that you both are good people, so when the right time comes, I will repay you for the hospitality you'd just shown me."

"We are not expecting anything in return for this," Captain Wyndham told her. "Your love alone is enough."

She placed her leg on the table and the two of them cut the shackles on them loose. The three of them went upstairs to the captain's room for a great celebration with drinks, food and hymns.

ELEVEN

IT WAS NOT AN EASY task for the king to leave his palace to take refuge in the old farm house at the bottom of the hills. He had to take his spiritual advisor, his wife and seven servants with him just to continue living like royalty until such time that he could return to his palace. He had to continue living a dignified life, because once a king he always had to live like a king. There was no term limit---a king or queen held the office for life, though only a few queens got the chance to ever rule the entire land.

The king could not leave his spiritual adviser, Bokornor, the one who poured libation to protect him from harm behind. He must accompany him to ward off all evil forces that his enemies might throw his way, and that included the governor. So the herbalist had to make the retreat with the king at all times.

When Fakpi, Batuka's spiritual leader, went against him from the very beginning of his reign, from the moment the kingmakers passed Batuka over and selected him as the next king of the kingdom, Bokornor began protecting the king. It was normal for him to hear his critics wish him evil or even try to hurt him spiritually, and some even attempted to assassinate him using knives or guns. Bokornor also protected him whenever these evil people placed voodoo items on his chair, or used spells to make him have a heart attack.

And it was rough to ward off all these forces from many people.

Bokornor, however, confronted these challenges. He foiled many, and when his subjects got to know all these later on, it increased support for the king and lowered the image of Batuka and his friends in the kingdom, making them much more unpopular than ever before.

The king proceeded to banish Batuka and his gang of seven rebels from the kingdom not only for their wicked plot, but because they'd committed treason when they betrayed their fatherland, when they sold out to the notorious Don Pedro, Major Thompson and his friends. Why they'd plotted with him to raid a nearby village, killing their own kinsmen and women, looting their gold, they had to explain these to the king. Why some members of the kingdom could betray their own for a dozen Danish rifles, seven kegs of gunpowder and seven bottles of rum only the ancestors knew.

Obviously, these "Oburoni locusts" knew about the sibling rivalry between Batuka and King Zendo and exploited it to their advantage. When Batuka and his rebel friends invoked the Oath of the Volta and threatened to remove the king from the stool, the high priest got very angry and went after these rebels with vengeance. Was that reason enough for these people to turn against the king and betray their own heritage?

The king sent his messengers to the kingdom of Benin--Oba of Benin---crossed to the eastern side to the Oyo Empire---the Alafin of Oyo, and crossed the Niger River to the roughest river in all the land---to the Congo River Basin. The king's messengers told these kings to use the "soldiers of vengeance" as a weapon to destroy the slave traders, but he asked these leaders to keep this a top secret, hidden from the Oburonis locusts. The king realized that if this weapon was not used all across the Slave Coast, the "Oburoni locusts" would simply move their operations from one kingdom to other kingdoms, which were safer places in the land where they would continue their horror of horrors against the inhabitants.

The messengers encountered several slave caravans along the journey but they were not surprised that the victims were overwhelmed with grief. There'd been obstacles on the way and the only way the king's messengers were able to reach their destination was because of what Captain Wyndham did. He had his Oburoni connections and with the help of the queen mother, he agreed to accompany the delegation to the other kingdoms along the sea coast.

Meanwhile, the rains suddenly ceased. The sun was up and warm and the nights had become dark and it was obviously pregnant with evil. There was no moon and the darkness was perfect for the king's plot to continue to unfold.

A woman was mourning her lost son, crying torrential tears. Her husband tried to comfort her, but she refused to stop crying. Her tears moved the king; he knew she'd a broken heart. He knew the women always mourned the loss of their husbands and sons for years.

But the king suddenly had high hopes of ending all the misery.

The darkness was ideal because as the saying goes, "those who travel at night return at night," and even before the messengers returned, the king decided to unleash his secret weapon against these unwanted Oburoni locusts, to drive them back home.

The high priest poured bottles of Kantamanto drinks into the lagoon for the ancestors. The seven bottles of gin were given to the ancestors, so Zotor could inform the ancestors about the king's journey of vengeance against the Oburoni enemy.

Mankrado led the way meandering his way on the edge of the lagoon with his torch held up high as he headed toward the pots. Unfortunately, when two soldiers tripped and fell into the murky lagoon and nearly drowned, the king came close to calling off the operation. He thought it was an evil omen of things to come. But the two soldiers swam quickly to the shore and lived to joke about this misfortune.

It was quite a mysterious scene in the night. With palm branch torches in hand, fifty soldiers, who looked like ghosts walking in a straight line on the edge of the lagoon, made their way behind the women, who carried these pots on top of their heads, and went to the slave castles in the area.

The women and the soldiers did not worry about getting infected, since every African had acquired a high level of immunity against the malaria disease over the years. It was the "Oburoni locusts" who had next to no immunity against this deadly disease that were at risk of dying from it.

The beauty of it, to the African people, was that the intended victims had no clue about what the king had in store for them, and what evil he had on his mind. They had no idea that he'd found a weapon much more lethal than their cannons, much more deadly than their Danish rifles. He'd already placed his secret weapon right on their doorsteps.

As the night gave way to dawn, the king's secret soldiers went to work on the enemy. Don Pedro and several merchants, who loved to sit outdoors enjoying the evening breeze, sat unsuspectingly drinking and dancing that night into the early morning hours. Many sat in their hammocks and others stretched in their lazy chairs, drinking rum and whisky heavily. Some of the women were gossiping and gazing at the mystery in the womb of the empty, semi-darkness in the sky, clueless about what the mosquitoes were doing to their legs.

The drummers made music for these Oburoni locusts, and at their request, the servants sang their favorite songs while the rum continued to flow like a fountain of joy. Many danced to the pulsating rhythm of the music.

Don Pedro had waited for two weeks for the stormy weather to end, and the waves, which had reached thirty feet high, did not subside for weeks. So the slave trade came to a grinding halt for a short period. Hundreds of sailors had to wait for more than sixty days before they could depart for the New World with their cargo.

From the grapevine came the news that the governor and the king had fallen out again. The king had decided to close the trade routes once again, and this time he'd closed them forever. He'd told the governor's messengers that no number of guns or kegs of gunpowder would make him change his mind to reopen the trade routes, or make him remove the guerilla soldiers he'd placed along the long meandering route, which crisscrossed the forests, traversed the savanna grasslands, climbed mountains, hundreds of miles to the Atlantic Coast.

Also, the seven pieces of rock he'd sent to the governor meant he didn't care if they went to war or not, his soldiers were ready to fight to death anyway. He tried the governor's patience, whether his soldiers wanted to go to war or wanted time to recover from the last battle, he did not care.

"There are several "avage" buzzing around the courtyard. The king has released his "little soldiers of vengeance" to go to work on the traders, he wants to give the ancestors the justice they had been waiting for," Chipolo told three other servants in the slave castle. "But we cannot start to celebrate victory yet, because we don't know if the king's plan will work."

"What do you mean it wouldn't work?" Ahmadu asked him sharply. "These Oburoni people are completely at the mercy of the king's "little soldiers" and so you are also completely clueless just like the Oburoni enemies."

"Well, from the way the traders were slapping their own ears last night; many of these traders would soon get "asra" and go to the infirmary. And without the "amatsi" herbal mixture to cure the disease, they would certainly die."

"We know some of them will die, but will enough of them die to force them to leave our shores?" Ametor asked in a concerned tone. "But if they decide to move somewhere else instead of going back home, what will the king do next?"

"They are supposed to become weaker and weaker, fall into a malaria coma and then die within a week or two from the disease," Titriku explained to Chipolo and Ametor and told them what the war captain had told the queen mother. "The Infirmary is going to fill up very quickly, if this works according to the way the king had designed this plot."

"They will regret that they'd taken off their shirts and tops in this warm weather," Ametor teased and started laughing as if she'd lost her mind. "I will be so happy when I no longer have to deal with Don Pedro, that beast of a man. Just looking at this man makes my heart sink with anger. Sometimes I feel like punching him in the mouth."

"Well, this will be really good for us. These traders will die in large numbers and instead of them abducting our youths---the little soldiers would turn out to be the greatest heroes in this fight for the soul of this land," Chipolo managed to say before Dalberto Gomez shouted his name, calling for some more khebab and another gallon of rum.

"His notorious friend, the King Cobra, did not go raiding another village that night," Titriku exclaimed as she rejoiced secretly over the presence of these two inside the castle when the soldiers released the secret weapon. The king's greatest wish---which was that these two traders must be present to receive their punishment by all means, to suffer the curse the gods had let loose on them."

"There he sits drunk as usual, dozing and snoring like a cow, unaware of what the king has in store for him and his band of raiders. I saw him slapping himself a few times last night, which means the "little soldiers" had entered his ears and had gone to work on him," Ametor revealed in a gleeful tone. She was clearly overjoyed over Don Pedro's misfortune. "I have seen some red marks on his chest, arms and feet. But he will know in three days if he has been infected with the disease or not."

"I hope he would slip into coma right now, instead of waiting for the usual fourteen days," Titriku joked. "Hopefully, this would be the case.

The king had forced the Oburonis' to have a date with destiny. He'd started to make them to face the wheels of justice. They could no longer feel safe inside the slave castles. He'd set in motion for them a slow and painful way to depart this life.

"Don Pedro is still asleep. He is snoring like a cow. Every now and then he wakes up to slap the mosquitoes away, but the "little soldiers" have already infected him, if I am not mistaken," Chipolo declared.

"If he is infected, that should be the best news for this land," Ametor said. "Maybe, he is on his deathbed. A few days from now, he probably will explain to the king where he'd sent Botwe, the heir to the kingdom and even show him how to bring him back before he goes on the long journey."

"The king and the elders are in no hurry for him to die. They really don't want him to die quickly. He has to pay for what he'd done to Prince Botwe----he must answer to the king," Chipolo explained, clearing his voice loudly, staring at Ametor and Titriku with a mixture of anger and sorrow, because he was a distant cousin of Prince Botwe, though many people didn't know this.

"It would not be a sweet victory for the king if Don Pedro is still out there raiding and killing people. He must face the justice from the gods soon."

"Just think about the number of innocent people, old men and women, children and even infants that they'd killed? How many children had become motherless and fatherless, the victims of these traders?" He asked and then pointed toward the Coconut Grove burial ground, which was a mile from the slave castle. "After Dente is through with them that would definitely be their final resting place."

Ametor blinked several times and laughed very loudly.

The king loved the blanket of darkness outside and knew the weather was suitable for his plot of vengeance to continue. When he'd received another messenger from the governor threatening him once more, a day after the operation began; he was in no mood to listen to any more threats or promises of gifts to reopen the trade routes. He sent him right back without even listening to whatever message he'd brought from the governor. "Just go back and tell him that the only way I will reopen the trade routes is if he goes to the beach and burns down the Atlantic Ocean," he told the messenger, who was very busy pleading with the king not to take his life for bearing such an insulting message from the governor.

The king, however, ripped apart his clothes, mutilated the hair on top of his head and sent another gift of seven pieces of rocks to the governor---the ultimate insult and a symbol of an open declaration of war.

The queen mother once again sneaked into the castle through the back door gate as usual with Captain Wyndham waiting for her under the stairs in front of the Portuguese Chapel. She wanted information about the impact of the secret weapon, after it had been in effect for seven days.

"Why is the courtyard so deserted?" she asked him, whispering under her breathe, trying to prevent the soldiers from hearing her question.

"Well, I don't know. Every one has fever, or nausea and they are sweating freely like herrings, some have body aches, vomiting and fever," he answered.

"They got what we call the "asra" disease from the mosquitoes," she told him.

"Well, we are doomed; more than three hundred people have fever, and are getting weak, with some having turned blue. Others are anxious because their world has been turned upside down because they have to go to the infirmary instead of going to work in the field."

The queen mother got close to him to feel her cheeks, worried that he probably had the malaria as well. His temperature was normal, so he did not have the disease at that point. "The saddest part of it all is that our doctors do not have the cure for this disease," he told the queen mother. "So, many of our people are going to die sooner or later."

She gave him a warm hug to wish him the best.

"We must give thanks to Dente, the god of gods, and to the other gods for giving us this brilliant idea," the high priest told the small gathering.

"This has made up for the many years of sacrifice and libations," Abrewa said calmly and in an excited voice. "I wish many of our departed leaders had been around to see the events of this day."

"The herbal medicine, though made from lemon leaves, tree bark and some creeping plants, has been the only known cure for the disease," the queen mother said.

"But who is worried about these slave traders dying?" the king asked fervently. "No one should be worried about them dying in masses. They have lived on borrowed time long enough."

"We need to start celebrating their death and departure, this is finally the intervention of the gods, our gift from them," Zotor declared.

"We are rejoicing over the misfortune of these Oburoni aliens because many of them would die soon, and the rest will flee the land so that our children and generations to come would live in peace and harmony once again."

The women who had gossiped about the secret weapon including those who mocked the king for relying too much on "his little soldiers" instead of asking the governor for forgiveness, started to change their mind about him and actually felt ashamed for putting him down. Fatimah, who'd insulted the queen mother behind her back, went to her directly and apologized for the foolish things she'd said to her in her face and behind her back.

The king sent the queen mother to brief the women about where he was leading them, but he warned her not to give away the details of the secret weapon. "Sometimes brute force of guns and cannons become useless against the power of the human brain. The brain could find ways that could make these big guns useless. "How good is your gun when you are too weak to fire them?" She asked the women in an emotional voice.

"They are of no use, they are useless," they shouted.

"This reminds me of the biggest enemy of the almighty elephant is the small fire ant. When the fire ant enters the elephant's ear and begins to bite inside its ear, this elephant hits its head against the trunk of a tree and continues to do so until it collapses and dies. The king wants me to tell you that he has listened to the ancestors, so the Oburoni would die in droves. And he will never lead you astray."

TWELVE

D ON PEDRO PRETENDED HE DIDN'T have the malaria, but he'd been unable to eat or drink for three days. He'd started growing weaker and weaker each day and sweating profusely, which were sure signs that he had the disease. Though he wished he was still as healthy as a hawk, swooshing from place to place and spreading his wings over the land, he had to face the bitter reality. He had a bout of nausea and then vomited publicly, so he must accept that he was very sick---he'd contracted malaria.

No matter how hard he tried to hide this disease, it got to a point he had to admit that his health was failing. He was feverish, thirsty, and unable to stand up without a cane. So he finally had to go to the infirmary for treatment---if the doctors could do anything for him.

The king had to try very hard to compose himself when he heard that Don Pedro came down with the disease. Though he didn't want to be seen celebrating another person's misfortune, but Don Pedro being the notorious killer and evil slave trader that ever lived, the king didn't mind openly celebrating his misfortune. He was glad that the man who had sent more victims across the Atlantic Ocean into slavery more than any person dead or alive, the man who had been rumored to have nine lives, had finally come down with the dreaded disease. More than likely, he was actually on his deathbed.

Suddenly the Oburoni traders, who had everything they needed, lots of money, slave boats and gold, could not use their wealth to prolong their own lives. "Money can buy every slave, lots of gold and any material thing, but it could never buy life for them," Zotor the priest pointed out.

Don Pedro, in spite of his tremendous wealth, knew he was dying. In the slave trade, he was like a tall mahogany tree, robust-looking, extraordinarily lucky during dozens of raids. As a merchant, whether his businesses were morally right or wrong, he was successful beyond his wildest of imaginations. But in spite of his riches, he'd become a desperate man who was pleading with nature to let him live just weeks longer---he was a dying man.

But would the gods buy him more time to continue his evil deeds? According to Captain Wyndham, the wealth Don Pedro had back home in Europe was larger than the wealth of several kings and queens. The Ewes described the worth of his wealth as "uncountable millions of millions." He had wealth in Whydah, Abeokuta and Port Harcourt, Senegambia, Tekrur that probably exceeded what all the other traders in the land put together owned.

Don Pedro owned over fourteen slave boats that he used to haul black cargo slaves and gold from Africa to the plantations on the other side of the blue Atlantic Ocean in the New World and then back to Lisbon. The Liberty Express, his favorite slave boat, traveled to the Gold Coast thrice a year to haul slaves to other parts of the world.

He was a clever person and he was aware that the hunchback does not sleep on his back, so he read the weather cycle very well. He knew the mosquitoes came out in the rainy season, but the dry weather was usually mosquito-free, so he and the other sailors knew when it was safe for them to come out, and to expose their bodies.

The king decided to use this knowledge against them, to destroy them once and for all. This was the only way to defeat and pay these slave traders back for their atrocities.

King Zendo, therefore, disrupted this natural cycle, disrupting the time when the mosquitoes came out by breeding these insects in the lagoons for all the seasons. Don Pedro and his gang of traders got confused and made the fatal mistake of coming out half-naked, faces, chests, arms and legs exposed. This was a critical mistake that would lead them to their doom.

Suddenly, the so-called less intelligent Africans were now not as stupid as Don Pedro and the other Oburonis had thought. The tide had begun to turn against the cannon-wielding Oburoni traders. Suddenly, their big guns were of no use and no longer a terrorizing weapon anymore. The castle stronghold and their big guns could no longer guarantee their safety. They could not avoid the mosquito bites and they were no longer safe in the land.

The reality was that the mosquitoes did a horrible job on Don Pedro's arms, chest and legs. His neck, face and feet had red marks all over them. Within twenty-four hours he began to feel feverish and chilly. When his urine and his pupils in his eyes became very yellow, he knew he had full blown malaria. He felt the chills and body aches, the nausea and vomiting. His body also began to sweat freely. This notorious and death-defying monster became as helpless as the slaves he'd always warehoused in the dungeons. Like these slaves, all he could do was to wait and see what fate had in store for him.

As the African saying goes, though a cobra strikes faster than the speed of light, whenever you hold its head, you have taken away its ability to strike at anything. King Zendo had used the secret weapon to hold down the poisonous head of Don Pedro---the slave trader who was known to many as "king cobra," he'd held down helplessly and those of the other Oburoni traders. They could not use their cannons against his people, because the disease had weakened them. Many of them were trying to survive rather than pursuing the path of wealth---the blood money from the slave trade.

The king was pleased with the panic among the Oburoni community. He could see the fear and frustration in their yellow-tinged eyes, and the regret on their pale, tired faces. Many wished they never stepped on African shores and bought and sold anybody.

Those Oburoni traders and missionaries that cared about their lives fled the continent quickly. They left the African shores hurriedly, many left on the next available boats, racing back home like fleeing cheetahs, or defeated warriors, broke, poor and low-spirited. On the other hand, the adventurers and the thrill-seekers, the headstrong elephants among them, stayed behind to continue pursuing their fatal dreams of wealth---the thirst for blood money.

The "little soldiers" did not have any mercy on them. Just as the Oburonis were relentless and ruthless during their slave raids, so the mosquitoes did attack them tirelessly? These insects buzzed repeatedly, bit them savagely and infected them with the malaria parasites stored inside their feeble feelers.

These Oburoni men and women, who descended on Africa from many countries in Europe, and some came down from American as well, had reached the crossroad in their crave for wealth. Their new mood contrasted sharply with the zeal and the bubbling sap of life that filled their eyes when they arrived on African soil. You could see the yearning, the craving and determination in them when they arrived. And you could also feel the intense passion to get rich---the raw greed---the voracious thirst for wealth written all over their faces.

The queen mother vividly remembered how the Oburoni came in with their hearts fired up like bamboo torches ready to make money from selling slaves. But she has seen how finally, this was surprising to her, the mosquitoes had destroyed their dreams. She was shocked by how these tiny insects decided to make these once callous slave traders vulnerable, powerless, crying, sobbing and cursing the day they'd stepped on African soil.

No one forced them to come to the continent to look for riches. The truth was that many of them were down on their luck back home and had no prospects back home of becoming anything or anybody, because many were not firstborns. They were second or third sons with nothing to inherit from their families. So they came to Africa because they wanted a second chance in life.

And then just like the chameleon in the forests, slowly but surely, the gods finally turned their anger against these traders, plaguing them with disease and gave the power back to the kings and their people. But this change came in a very dramatic manner, very quickly and drastically. "They have been weakened, so let us attack and defeat them," Mankrado told the king in a stern and angry voice. "The disease has shaken them up; their soldiers are too weak to use their cannons. Those who used to fire the cannons at defenseless and innocent victims have faded away very fast, headed into the sunset. The lucky ones are on their deathbeds with only a few days to live."

"These traders have started to die like houseflies. They'd finally met a secret weapon, which their cannons could not defeat," the king declared, laughing. The king mocked them when he said "a dog that gnaws bones can not gnaw an iron rod."

The new governor had probably learned his lesson because he tried to make peace with the king and the inhabitants. But it was too late. He'd realized that he had to deliver the bad news to the many investors and sponsors of the slave trade back home, people who wanted no other news but good news about the increase in the profits of this bloody slave trade.

King Zendo finally made good on his saying that two kings do not rule in one kingdom. So he forced the governor to be on the losing end. He closed the trade routes completely. He ordered the soldiers to shoot and kill any slave trader they'd seen with slave cargo. He also tore down many churches, which became leaderless because the preachers had all come down with the disease and died. Zotor the high priest cheered wildly with the turn of events. "The lost antelopes would finally come back home to the shrines of their ancestors," he mused, jubilant and satisfied.

The malaria disease suddenly made the slave trade a losing business.

The king was relaxed and jubilant as he watched the ugly tragic drama of death unfolded before his eyes. He knew that it was just a matter of time for the rest of the traders to die off. "How do they expect to continue the slave trade when there are no ships bringing supplies of rum and guns, calico or trinkets or cannons?" the king asked Captain Wyndham. "Their guns and rum created new power structures---elevating new kings and leaders and demoting some traditional ones. They got us fighting among ourselves, one group against the other, Fantes against Asantes, Gas against the Krobos, Ewes against the Akwamus, Wolofs against the Mandinkas, the Yorubas locked in a nasty civil war and the Fong against the Anechos. These guns created prisoners of war and many of the leaders exchanged them for more guns. The traders had destroyed everything we had before they came."

"Don't be too worried, your majesty, the rest of the traders would depart the land once the rest of the rum dries up and the wild parties cease, they would either flee the land or stay behind and die slow, agonizing deaths," Captain Wyndham told the king jokingly. "The wise ones would definitely flee for their lives."

The king became furious when he heard that the servants had kept a handful of these Oburoni alive by giving them the herbal mixture, but did this without their knowledge. In fact, these few survivors believed that it was an invisible force that had saved them.

These were the few lucky ones.

Instead of the king and his subjects being under pressure, it was the Oburoni traders who became desperate and anxious this time. These aliens became sick, destitute and defeated as they ran from the wrath of the ancestors, from the justice of the gods.

The king could not believe the drama of sorrow inside the slave castles and the chaos the disease had created among the aliens. He knew that the day of justice would come one day, but he didn't know that it would come so soon.

Don Pedro, Dalberto Gomez and hundreds of these traders were in a daze, scared because they were at the mercy of the dreaded disease. The governor tried to lift up their dwindling spirits by requesting additional doctors from back home, but many were too scared to venture into this treacherous continent. The remnant, many who had lost their friends and companions, but couldn't cope with their loss, simply gulped down more gallons of rum and whiskey to forget their sorrows as they waited for death themselves.

The resident doctor tried to treat those infected with the disease with sulfur, but he did not have much success. As these patients lay on their beds dying, they pondered their decision to come to the continent, their desire to become wealthy from the slave trade. From the look on their faces, many wondered if they'd made the wrong decision, wasted their lives, or if their fate had led them to their doom.

The moaning and groaning in the infirmary sounded like those from the slave dungeons below. The nausea, the excruciating headaches, the chilling fever were similar to the agony of the slaves down below the courtyard, and so were the endless cries from the dying missionaries and the traders. They knew this business was a dangerous one, but they did not know it would turn out to be a death warrant for the many Europeans and Americans that made the so-called "business trip" to the African continent.

"Do you think many would have preferred to stay back home and not come to our shores?" the queen mother asked Captain Wyndham. She felt sad, being a kind-hearted woman, to see so many of them die so quickly, but it was such a big relief to the inhabitants who wanted their country back.

"Well, many of them would not have made the trip at all," he told her bluntly. "If they had known about all the dangers, especially about this malaria disease, they would have stayed back in Europe and tried other ventures less contentious, enterprises that did not involve so much bloodshed, shame and guilt."

"Maybe they somehow regretted that they'd brought so much guilt on their conscience, and forced so much bloodshed and misery on the victims?" she asked.

The king and all the elders were saddened when Captain Wyndham's "asra" returned and his condition deteriorated. The king, who intended to use the disease to wipe out the bad kernels among the Oburoni, became disappointed when he heard that the captain, the only Oburoni he never wished any evil, was getting weaker, and he might die from the disease. The king, the elders, and the queen mother decided to help their long-time friend, some one who had been there for them for many years.

"You look a little better than yesterday, Cap. Wyndham," Chipolo said to his friend, nicknamed "the kind Oburoni." "We will make sure you don't leave us, trust me we know what to do to keep you alive."

"I hope you do," he said. "Who wants to die?"

"But you have to drink the mixture we are giving you," Chipolo told the captain.

"Why is my drinking water yellow-looking these few days?" he asked Chipolo quietly. "What have you added to the water?"

"Well, it is the herbal mixture in the drink," he replied.

"Don't you think you need my permission to heal me?" He asked jokingly, looking around to make sure that nobody heard what he'd said.

"Oh, I don't think you have a choice that is if you want to live. But do you want to live or die?" Chipolo whispered into the captain's ears, smiling in the mist of all the sorrow and death that surrounded the place. "If you value your life, then don't ask any more questions. Just drink what we give you."

"Oh well, I want to continue living. I really do, so I have to thank all of you for trying to save my life."

"You are not yet out of danger. The good news is that the king has sent you a special gift, just for you---a stronger herbal mixture---the queen mother brought it in yesterday. That is what would cure you of this deadly disease."

"Well, I pray that it works, because I intend to live and help the king and the elders for a few more years, just a little longer."

"Please, you can't tell the doctor about this. It must remain a top secret between us, the queen mother and all the servants."

"Oh well, I can keep a secret. I hope it really works to get me back on my feet once again."

"You will be back on your feet no later than seven days, trust me."

The king decided to honor the new governor's invitation to the infamous Cape Coast castle, especially when word reached him that Don Pedro had come down with the disease, and that the notorious trader was simply clinging on to life.

The king had been wrong all these years about Don Pedro being an invincible human being, a man with many lives. They never really got to know his weakest side---his frail health. His ability to shoot and kill his opponents the way no other Oburoni in the land could, did not matter now. He didn't need his guns any more, not when he could hardly walk on his own.

This was a man who had killed so many infants, sent many old men and women into their graves. But he was also finally dying. This was the man who could shoot his own mother if he had to do so, just to get the slaves he needed for his boat, the Liberty Express.

King Zendo had always wanted to meet Don Pedro face to face. Though a part of him wanted him dead, there was his other side that wanted to confront him face to face, to meet the man who had kidnapped his nephews and nieces and that included the heir to the golden stool.

So, when Don Pedro was dying inside the infirmary, the king decided to go and visit him. He'd set his differences with the new governor aside to attend to the unfinished business between him and the most notorious slave dealer that ever stepped on African shores, and profited from this evil trade---Don Pedro---the Oburoni every inhabitant in the land loved to hate. When children heard the name Don Pedro, they usually dropped everything they were doing and ran to their mothers or quickly took cover under their beds.

The end for this man whom the soldiers could never ambush and kill was finally near. The man who had been nicknamed "king cobra" finally walked into the last ambush when he staggered into the infirmary on his own feet, looking frail, weak and tired. The very talkative and arrogant trader was finally quiet and spoke only very few words. He quickly got into a bed in which someone died minutes before he got there. He gripped the edge of the bed, and then gritted his teeth and fell asleep minutes later. Just like he did whenever he got drunk in the courtyard, he started to snore like a cow, making a loud horrible sound that caused laughter among many of the nurses.

The greatest irony was that the infirmary was directly above the dungeons, the filthy place where Don Pedro had kept his eight hundred slaves. He was waiting for the boats and good weather to send them out of the continent on the endless journey to the land of no return. There was the notorious king cobra, lying in his own filth, clinging on to dear life, moaning, groaning and pleading for mercy just like some of his slaves in the dungeon below.

"Was this poetic justice, or the wrath of the gods?" Chipolo asked.

The servants watched Don Pedro as he tossed and turned restlessly from side to side all night and day. He was weak and in great pain. But as a last act of arrogance, he defied the doctor when he refused the sulfur treatment that the doctor had ordered for him.

The servants laughed at his arrogance even when he knew that he was staring death in the eyes. "Give me some water," he asked Chipolo, the same servant whose face he spat into when he brought him two instead of three jugs of rum. He was looking at the other side of the man he'd brought gallons of rum almost every night and for nearly twenty years. He once revealed to Chipolo that he drank so much because he had to drown his guilty conscience in gallons of rum each night in order to get the courage to wake up and go back to work the next day.

"What about a jug of rum for you, my lord?" Chipolo asked him, teasingly. "I can go to the store room and slip one jug past the sentries. Maybe where you are going, you might need some rum to help you on your journey."

He shook his head helplessly and bit into the soft pillow like a wounded hyena. When he finally looked into his eyes, he noticed that the notorious Don Pedro had tears in his eyes.

"No more rum for me," he mustered his strength and whispered to Chipolo. "Thank you anyway. My rum drinking days might be behind me soon. I will be a free man; my conscience would soon be at rest when I go home to meet my maker."

"Your journey is going to be very soon, my master. Good night," Chipolo told him.

"Still I have no regrets. I lived my life with the best I could do," he said and fell back asleep.

The servants led the king into the castle through the backdoor. He arrived secretly and came with seven elders and the queen mother, and three servants led them to the infirmary. The king said he didn't want to meet the new governor, he simply wanted to visit Captain Wyndham, a friend of the queen mother, the man who'd supplied them with so many guns over the years, but who had unfortunately come down with the dreaded disease as well.

"It is a shock to see you in your hospital bed," the king told Captain Wyndham in a tone filled with sadness. "We are asking the gods to save your life. You are a good-hearted man and you deserve to continue living. How can we continue our journey without your help?"

"I don't want to die, your majesty," he told the king quietly, whispering. "I thank you very much. The servants have given me the mixture and I am hoping that it will save my life to continue to help you and your subjects to defeat these evil traders who have so much greed on their mind."

"Have they given it to you?" the king asked, forcing a smile.

"Yes, Chipolo gave it to me seven times yesterday," he told the king.

"But do you believe this can save your life?" the queen mother asked him with tears streaming down her cheek. "This disease is not meant for someone like you; it is not for a good Oburoni like you. It is meant for the likes of "king cobra" lying in that corner over there."

"Thanks, anyway, for the compliment" he told them. "You told me you will never marry me regardless of how good I am. But I think that is too late now."

"Well, that is another matter altogether. But if you recover from this disease, who knows? We have brought you some freshly brewed mixture to get you back on your feet; hopefully, you can do so within a few days. But you must keep this a top secret from everybody, especially from the likes of Don Pedro and the governor."

"Well, you know that my lips are sealed. They have been sealed all these years."

The king liked what he heard from Captain Wyndham, and loved his attitude and so he shook his hand heartily. He asked the captain to point to Don Pedro's bed in the infirmary. He whispered something to the king, pointed to the far corner and then the king and the captain had a quick, subdued laugh.

"He is getting weaker and weaker by the day, he will definitely slip into coma hours from now and maybe he will be dead within three days," a servant nearby told the king and the elders.

The servants took the king to the notorious slave dealer who was barely clinging on to life. Contrary to his last wishes, the doctor placed him inside a tent filled with burning sulfur, the doctor's best medicine for the disease. The odor from the burning sulfur was obviously choking him and he seemed to lack fresh air in the tent. He only got to breathe fresh air if and when the doctor opened the tent to attend to him every two hours.

The king and his party stood there for a minute watching the man that stirred so much fear inside every child, panic inside every youth in the land, and hatred from every man and woman, struggling to breathe, panting for air and waiting to die.

"Finally, something has held down the head of the notorious king cobra," Mankrado said shaking his head in disbelief. "Can you imagine the mosquitoes doing what our soldiers could not do---they got justice for the dead---they'd defeated these blood-thirsty and shameless terrorists."

Through an interpreter, the king spoke to the notorious trader who refused to open his eyes even through a very bad cough. "Why all these evil, all the killings and why have you taken so may of our people into slavery?"

There was absolute silence. "We brought the mosquitoes into the castle to kill you for your crimes against our people," the king told him softly. "You will die a slow and horrible death."

Don Pedro was speechless, but he gestured with his hand to the servants for more water. Mankrado wanted the servants to deny him the water, but the king overruled him. After he drank a big gulp of water, he mastered his last energy to raise his upper body to look at the king and his party. "Everything was business from our end, and I still don't regret whatever I did." He told them and slumped back into the bed like a piece of mahogany log, closed his eyes and fell asleep again.

On their way out, the king, the queen mother and the elders heard many of the sick Oburonis moaning, groaning in pain and gasping for breath. Many of them looked around and took satisfaction in the fact that their end was not too far away. Many were feverish, thirsty, weak and dizzy as the malaria ran its course. The whole infirmary smelled badly, a bad odor of death filled the large hall. The breathing of the sick had become labored and uneven. The stench was suffocating whatever breath they had left in them. The odor of sulfur mixed with the stench from some of the dead saturated the infirmary from the floor all up to the ceiling. It smelled just like the same putrid odor from a mixture of urine, human excrement and sweat that lingered in the slave dungeons below. The groaning and moaning were the same, except the slaves below were pleading for their freedom and the chance to see their families again. And the Oburonis were asking for the chance to live, more time to live their lives back home.

At Don Pedro's request, the doctor took a pen knife to make some small incisions on his fingers. He asked the doctor to bleed him. The incisions were small, but he added some whiskey on pads and wiped the blood that oozed from these cuts.

The doctor's frustrated face revealed that he himself did not believe in what his patient had requested as a cure for the disease. Don Pedro was known for his toughness and so he was not to let a few incisions destroy his reputation for toughness. But he took it like a man and went back to sleep, but whether the procedure would bring back his rapidly disappearing life, they would soon find out.

If he had his way he would go chasing more slaves, even on his deathbed. He was not the only European who came for the slave trade, but when he closed his eyes, he would be the most remembered.

May the world never know this sort of brutality and greed again?

EPILOGUE

———·∞∘❊∘∞·———

T HE ABOMINABLE TRADE FINALLY ENDED centuries after it had started. It took more than malaria to end this trade, but thanks to the mosquitoes for reducing the so-called African Slave Coast into the "white man's grave." Otherwise, more victims would have been hauled out of the bosom of Mama Africa across the Atlantic Ocean to the land of no return. And many more would have died in the process of being enslaved or hauled away.

Forty million dead and forty million forcibly taken away had been too high a price to pay for the greed of other people. How can we forget the insecurity, the disruption in manufacturing and lifestyle?

The continent can never completely recover from this tragedy of historical proportions, but it is an old ancient land that is still holding its own. Children no longer walk around afraid of becoming victims to these "human lifters." The continent still have traditional rulers, though these traditional authorities in many areas, have been reduced to mere shadows of their former positions.

Though some of the traditional rulers are responsible to elected and officials that report to presidents, western-style heads of states, people still fight over these traditional institutions today. People still treasure some of what otherwise would have become token institutions. Hopefully, these ancient institutions, though they have become holdovers from the past in the modern political systems, would not die out any time soon. Hopefully our children's children over the generations would inherit some of these ancient legacies and pass them on to other succeeding generations.

Obviously, and this has been clearly documented, the continent has recovered from some of the effects of the population loss. Africa is heavily populated today and the population of some of these countries is more than one hundred million. But the damage and lost of skills we have not yet completely recovered, since the legendary and golden age "take off stage" in Africa's economic history has been lost forever.

Many people have been unable to overcome hunger and starvation in some areas. And though no one in his right mind can blame these problems solely on the past history of the slave trade, those European countries that had benefited from the sale of African human resources, those that had financed the Industrial Revolution in Europe with the proceeds from the slave trade, must assume the moral duty to help these struggling and suffering masses in Africa today.

The people of the continent, whether they are the victims of the trans-Saharan slave trade, or the East African "mfecane" to the Middle East, or the victims of the European trans-Atlantic trade, still suffer from the inferiority complex these aliens had imposed on them, a state of mind that comes from being once enslaved, whether by Europeans, Americans and the people of the Middle East.

The world has made a few strides in interracial matters; including electing and reelecting an African-American president, but we still have a long way to go. And Africa, a continent that had endured so much in its history, a continent that had helped so many other countries, the guilty parties must give back to the continent some of the human and material resources they'd taken from this ancient land.

The African people are still waiting for the descendants of the former slave trading Oburonis, the people whose ancestors had taken their people as slaves to show some gratitude for the past help these African slaves had given them.

They must make some form of atonement for the past---return some of the proceeds from the past injustices their ancestors had suffered. Until then, the angry gods of the continent would continue to unleash its vengeance on the people who had benefited from this notorious and brutal trade. Does the modern generation of this bloody past have any idea how the Africans bled, suffered and even died for several European countries to create the foundations of their economies, which are buoyant and bustling today? Do they have any idea about how the past still ligers around the continent today, devouring and sabotaging the present? They'd built their economic wonders using the proceeds from the sale of the flesh, blood and sweat of the African people. Though this trade ended long ago, they'd benefited tremendously from the fruits of this wicked trade that their ancestors conceived and masterminded---profiting from the sale of the flesh and blood of Mama Africa's sons and daughters.